DEADLY LITTLE SCANDALS

DEADLY LITTLE SCANDALS

JENNIFER LYNN BARNES

LITTLE, BROWN AND COMPANY
New York   Boston

Little, Brown and Company
Hachette Book Group
1290 Avenue of the Americas, New York, NY 10104
Visit us at LBYR.com

Originally published in hardcover and ebook by Freeform Books, an imprint of Disney Book Group, in November 2019
First Trade Paperback Edition: December 2020

Little, Brown and Company is a division of Hachette Book Group, Inc. The Little, Brown name and logo are trademarks of Hachette Book Group, Inc.

The publisher is not responsible for websites (or their content) that are not owned by the publisher.

The Library of Congress has cataloged the hardcover edition as follows:
Names: Barnes, Jennifer (Jennifer Lynn), author.
Title: Deadly little scandals : a Debutante novel / by Jennifer Lynn Barnes.
Description: First edition. | Los Angeles ; New York : Freeform Books, 2020. | Summary: While spending a summer at the family lake house, eighteen-year-old Sawyer finally learns the full truth about her complicated family.
Identifiers: LCCN 2018042050 | ISBN 9781368015172 (hardcover)
Subjects: | CYAC: Identity—Fiction. | Secrets—Fiction. | Mothers and daughters—Fiction. | Grandmothers—Fiction. | Family life—Southern States—Fiction. | Southern States—Fiction.
Classification: LCC PZ7.B26225 De 2020 | DDC [Fic]—dc23
LC record available at https://lccn.loc.gov/2018042050

ISBNs: 978-1-368-04634-3 (pbk.), 978-1-368-04433-2 (ebook)

Printed in the United States of America

LSC-C

1 2020

For Ti30.

LABOR DAY, 3:17 A.M.

"*S*awyer, are you there?"

"I'm here."

"I can't feel my feet. Or my hands. Or my elbows. Or my face. Or—"

"Sadie-Grace, just give me a second."

"Okay . . . Was that a second?"

"If I'm going to get us out of here, I need to think."

"I'm sorry! I want to stop talking! But I dance when I'm nervous, and right now, I can't dance, because I can't feel my feet. Or my hands. Or my elbows. Or—"

"*Everything is going to be fine.*"

"When I'm nervous and I can't dance, I babble. And, Sawyer? Being buried alive makes me *very* nervous."

FOURTEEN WEEKS (AND *THREE DAYS*) EARLIER

CHAPTER 1

"*H*as anyone seen William Faulkner's life vest?"

There was a point in my life when the question Aunt Olivia had just called down the stairs would have struck me as odd. Now it didn't even merit the slightest raise of my eyebrow. Of course the family's mammoth Bernese mountain dog was named William Faulkner, and of course she had her very own life vest. Hell, it was probably monogrammed.

The mamas of the Debutante set were very big on monogramming.

Really, the only thing surprising about Aunt Olivia's question was the fact that my aunt, who was type A in the extreme, did not already know where William Faulkner's life vest was.

"Remind me again why we're hiding in the pantry?" I asked Lily, who'd dragged me in here five minutes ago and hadn't spoken louder than a whisper since.

"It's Memorial Day weekend," Lily murmured in response. "Mama always gets a bit high-strung when we open the lake house up for the summer." Lily lowered her voice even further for dramatic effect. *"Even her lists have lists."*

I shot Lily a look intended to communicate something about pots and kettles.

"I have an entirely reasonable number of lists," Lily retorted in a whisper. "And I would have a lot fewer if you showed any inclination whatsoever to get ready for college yourself."

Lily Taft Easterling was just as type A as her mama, and both of them insisted on operating under the assumption that I was going to State with Lily in the fall. Matriculation at that fine institution was, I had been informed, a family tradition.

I couldn't help thinking that my specific branch of the family tree had our own traditions. *Deception, betrayal, no-bake cherry cheesecake . . .*

"Is it me, or did there use to be a lot more food in this pantry?" I asked Lily, to keep her from reading anything into my silence.

"Mama packs for the lake like a survivalist preparing for the end days," Lily said in a hushed voice. She fell silent at the sound of incoming footsteps, which stilled right outside our hiding place.

I held a breath, and a moment later, the pantry door flew inward.

"*Hasta la vista* . . . Lily!" Lily's younger brother, John David, punctuated that statement with a cackle and began pelting us with Nerf darts.

Ducking, I noted that our assailant was dressed in camo, had painted black stripes under his eyes, and was wearing an enormous life vest that I could only assume belonged to the dog.

"I try my level best to avoid fratricide," Lily said pleasantly. "*However.*" The *however* was meant to stand on its own as a threat, but I decided to lend a little specificity Lily's way.

"However . . ." I suggested, advancing on John David. "Noogies are more of a gray area?"

I caught John David in a headlock.

"You mess with the bull . . ." John David tried his best to wriggle his way out of my grasp. "You get the horns!"

"And *you* get a noogie!"

Lily stared at the pair of us like we'd just started mud-wrestling in the middle of Sunday brunch.

"What?" John David said innocently, before trying and failing to bite my armpit.

"You two are bad influences on each other," Lily declared. "I tell you, Sawyer, there are days when I'd swear he was your brother, not mine."

That was Lily's version of teasing, but still, I froze. Lily had no idea—*none*—what she'd just said.

No idea that it was half-true.

John David seized the moment and managed to wriggle out of my grasp. He was taking aim with his weapon when Aunt Olivia rounded the corner.

I'd swear he was your brother. Lily's words echoed in my head, but I forced myself to focus on the present—and the stormy look on Aunt Olivia's face. I stepped in between John David and my aunt and offered her what I hoped passed for a sedate smile.

"Aunt Olivia," I said calmly. "We found William Faulkner's life vest."

John David and I were summarily convicted of "inappropriately timed horseplay" and "wearing on my last nerve, I swear" and sentenced to loading the car. I wasn't about to complain about a much-needed distraction.

Months ago, I'd moved into my maternal grandmother's house after she'd offered me a devil of a deal: if I lived with her and participated in Debutante season, she'd pay for college. I'd agreed, but not because of the half-million-dollar trust now held in my name. I'd willingly become a part of this lavish, glittering world because I'd wanted, desperately, to know which scion of high society had knocked up my mom during *her* Debutante year.

And the answer to that question? The one Lily didn't know? *Her father. Aunt Olivia's husband, my uncle J.D.*

"Are you feeling okay, Sawyer? You're looking a little peaked, sweetheart." Aunt Olivia was holding a to-do list that appeared to have taken no fewer than eight Post-its to write. I was willing to bet that not a single item on that extensive list said *Find out husband slept with and impregnated my younger sister nineteen and a half years ago.*

Also probably not on her list? *Realize sister got pregnant on purpose as part of some idiotic, godforsaken teenage pregnancy pact.*

"I'm fine," I told Aunt Olivia, mentally adding that to the list of the lies I'd told—in words and by omission—in the past six weeks.

Under normal circumstances, Aunt Olivia probably would have tried to feed me for good measure, but she apparently had weightier things on her mind. "I forgot the backup avocados," she said suddenly. "I could run to the store real quick and—"

"Mama." Lily came to stand in front of Aunt Olivia. The two of them didn't look much alike, but when it came to manners and mannerisms, they could have been twins. "You don't need to go to the store. We'll have plenty of avocados. Everything is going to be fine."

Aunt Olivia gave Lily a look. "Fine is not the standard to which Taft women aspire."

Lily gently plucked the list from her mother's hands. "Everything will be *perfect*."

A third Taft female added her voice to the conversation. "I'm sure that it will." Even wearing her version of casual wear—linen capris—the great Lillian Taft knew how to make an entrance. "Sawyer, honey." My grandmother let her gaze settle on me. "I was hoping you might accompany me on a little errand this morning."

That was an order, not a request. I took inventory of all the rules and social niceties I'd flouted in the past twenty-four hours but was unsure what I'd done to merit Lillian wanting to talk to me alone.

"Should we wait for you, Mama?" Aunt Olivia asked, her eyes darting toward the clock.

Lillian dismissed the question with a wave of her hand. "You head on up to the lake, Olivia. Beat the traffic. Sawyer and I will be right on your heels."

CHAPTER 2

*M*y grandmother's errand took us to the cemetery. She carried with her a small floral arrangement— wildflowers. That caught my attention, because Lillian literally had a florist on speed dial. She also grew her own roses, yet the bouquet in her hands looked like it had been plucked from a field.

Lillian Taft was not, generally speaking, the low-cost DIY type.

She was uncharacteristically quiet as we walked a gravel path down a small hill. Set back from the other gravestones, in the space between two ancient oak trees, there was a small wrought-iron fence. Though the detail work was stunning, the fence was small, barely reaching my waist. The parcel of land inside was maybe twelve feet across and ten deep.

"Your grandfather picked this plot out himself. The man always thought he was immortal, so I can only assume he was planning on burying me here instead of the other way around." My grandmother let her hand rest on the wrought iron, then pushed the gate inward.

I hesitated before following her to stand near the tombstone inside: a small cement cross on a simple base. My eyes took in the dates first, then the name.

EDWARD ALCOTT TAFT.

"If we'd had a son," Lillian said softly, "he would have been named Edward. The *Alcott* was a matter of some debate between your grandfather and myself. Edward never wanted a junior, but there was something about the sound of his full name that I liked."

This wasn't what I'd been expecting when she'd whisked me away for a one-on-one.

"Your grandfather and I met on Memorial Day weekend. Did I ever tell you that?" In typical fashion, Lillian did not wait for a reply. "I'd snuck into a party where a girl of my provenance most certainly did not belong."

Unwittingly, my mind went to another high-society soiree where one of the attendees had not belonged. His name was Nick. We'd shared one dance—him in a T-shirt and me in a ball gown. Despite my best efforts to the contrary, the ghost of that dance had lingered.

"If anyone else had found me out, there might have been trouble," Lillian mused, continuing her own stroll down memory lane, "but your grandfather had a way about him. . . ."

The nostalgia in her voice allowed me to tuck the dance with Nick back into the corners of my mind and focus on the conversation at hand. Lillian almost never spoke about her early years. I'd gathered that she'd grown up dirt-poor and ambitious as hell, but that was about all I knew.

"You miss him," I said, my eyes on the tombstone and a lump in my throat, because she'd loved him. Because I'd never know the man buried here well enough to love or miss him, too.

"He would have liked you, Sawyer." Lillian Taft did not get misty-eyed. She was not one to allow her voice to quiver. "Oh, he would have pitched a fit when Ellie turned up pregnant, but the man would have gone to hell and back for his little girls. I've no doubt he would have done the same for you, once he came around."

Edward Alcott Taft had died when my mom was twelve and

Aunt Olivia was closing in on eighteen. I was fairly certain that if he *had* been alive during my mom's Deb year, she probably wouldn't have "turned up" pregnant in the first place. The fact that she had made a pregnancy pact with two of her friends didn't exactly scream "well-adjusted." But the fact that she'd chosen her own brother-in-law to knock her up?

That had *Daddy Issues* written all over it.

"Have you talked to her?" Lillian asked me. "Your mama?"

That put me on high alert. If Lillian had brought me here in hopes of inspiring a little family forgiveness, she was going to be sorely disappointed.

"If by *talk* you mean *steadfastly ignore*, then yes," I said flatly. "Otherwise, no."

My mom had lied to me. She'd let me believe that my father was former-senator, now-convict Sterling Ames. I'd believed the senator's kids were my half-siblings. They—and his wife—believed it still. The senator's son was Lily's boyfriend. Walker and Lily had just gotten back together. I couldn't tell him the truth without telling her.

And if I told Lily who my father was, what my mother and her beloved daddy had done . . . I'd lose her.

"I can't help but notice you've been awfully quiet these past six weeks, sweetheart." Lillian spoke gently, but I recognized a Southern inquisition when I heard one. "Not talking to your mama. Not talking to anyone, really, about things that matter."

I read between the lines of what she was saying. "Are we having this conversation because you want me to come clean to Lily and Aunt Olivia about the baby-daddy situation or because you want my word that I won't?"

Lillian Taft, grande dame of society, philanthropist, guardian of the family fortune and reputation, was not impressed with my choice of words. "I would consider it a great favor if you would refrain from using the term *baby daddy.*"

"You didn't answer my question," I said.

"It's not mine to answer." Lillian glanced down at her husband's grave. "My time to speak up was years ago. As much as I might regret my choice, I'm not about to take this one away from you now. This is your life, Sawyer. If you want to live it with your head in the sand, I'm not going to stop you."

When it came to the art of making her opinion known while explicitly declining to share an opinion, my grandmother was an artist.

After all these years, she was tired of secrets.

Like I'm not, I thought.

"The only fight Lily and I have ever had was because her daddy's name was on my list of *possible* fathers." I willed that to matter less than it did. "We made up because I 'discovered' my father was someone else and told her as much."

Lily worshipped her dad. Aunt Olivia was a perfectionist; Uncle J.D. was the one who told Lily, again and again, that she didn't have to be perfect to be loved.

"I think you underestimate your cousin," Lillian told me quietly.

I let myself say the words I was constantly trying not to think. "She's not just my cousin."

She was my sister.

"Don't you go feeling guilty," Lillian ordered. "This is your mama's mess, Sawyer. And mine. Lord knows I should have kicked J.D. to the curb years ago, the moment I suspected he would *dare*—" My grandmother cut herself off. After a moment, she bent to lay the wildflower bouquet at the base of the tombstone. When she straightened, she gathered herself up to her full height. "The point, Sawyer

Ann, is that this mess is not, in any way, shape, or form, yours."

"This mess isn't *mine*," I countered. "It's *me*."

I fully expected Lillian to take issue with that statement, but instead, she raised an eyebrow. "You are rather perpetually disheveled." She produced a hair clip seemingly out of nowhere and "suggested" that I make use of it. "You have such a *pretty* face," she added. "Lord knows why you're so intent on hiding it under those bangs."

She said *bangs* like a curse word. Before she could lament the fact that I'd had her hairdresser chop off a great deal of my hair, I preempted the complaint. "I needed a change."

I'd needed *something*. I'd spent years wondering who my father was. Now I was living under the same roof with the man, and neither one of us had acknowledged that fact. It would have been easier if I'd thought he was ignorant, but he knew I was his daughter. My mom had said as much, and on that, I was certain she was telling the truth.

The whole situation was a mess. My entire life, my mom had never once made me feel like a mistake, but somehow, discovering that she'd conceived me on purpose made me feel like one.

If my mom hadn't still been grieving her father's death . . .

If she hadn't felt like a stranger in her own family and desperately wanted someone or something to call her own . . .

If her "friend" Greer hadn't seen that vulnerability and sold her on a ridiculous, happy vision of becoming a teen mom . . .

Then I wouldn't exist.

"Sawyer." Lillian said my name gently. "Bangs are for blondes and toddlers, and you, my dear, are neither."

If she wanted to pretend that my hair was the real issue between us—and in this family—I was okay with that. For now.

"If you brought me here to check up on me," I told her, "I'm fine." I averted my gaze, and it landed on my grandfather's tombstone. "I'm a liar, but I'm fine."

I couldn't forgive my mom for deceiving me, but every day, I got up and let Aunt Olivia and Lily and John David go about life like normal. It was hard not to feel like the apple hadn't fallen far from the tree.

"Your mama was a daddy's girl, Sawyer." Lillian looked back at the tombstone. "Your aunt, too. Growing up the way they did, they never had to be fighters. But you? You've got a healthy dose of me in you, and where I come from, a person has to fight to survive."

That was the second time she'd referenced her origins. "Why did you bring me here?" I asked, unable to shake the feeling that nothing about this conversation—including the location—was an accident.

Lillian was quiet for a stretch, long enough that I wasn't sure she was going to reply. "You asked me weeks ago if I could find out what happened to your mama's friend Ana."

The breath stilled in my chest. *Ana, Ellie, and Greer,* I thought, forcing myself to keep breathing. *Three teenage girls, one pact.* Greer had lost her baby, and that meant that Ana's—if she'd had it—was the only other person on this planet with an origin story the exact same flavor of screwed-up as mine.

Her kid would be my age now, almost exactly.

"What did you find out?" I asked Lillian, my mouth dry.

"Ana was a quiet little thing. My recollection of her was fuzzy. She was new in town. I'd heard of her people but didn't know them. From what I've pieced together, she and her family picked up and moved back home around the time I found out about your mama's delicate condition."

By that time, I thought, *Ana was pregnant, too.*

"Where were they from?" I asked. "Where did they move back to?"

There was a long pause as my grandmother made an intense study of me. "Why do you want to find this woman?"

Lillian knew that Uncle J.D. was my father, but as far as I'd been able to tell, she had no knowledge of the pact. There was no real reason for me to keep it from her, but it wasn't the easiest thing in the world to come right out and say.

"Sawyer?" my grandmother prompted.

"Ana was pregnant, too," I said, clipping the words. "They planned it that way. I don't know if she had the baby, but if she did . . ."

Lillian weathered the blow I'd just dealt her. "If she had the baby, then what?"

I tried to find words, but they all seemed shallow and insufficient. How could I adequately explain that the same reason I'd wanted to find out who my father was, the same reason I'd longed to meet the family my mom despised, the reason I'd stayed here even after I'd discovered the truth—that was exactly why I wanted to know what happened to Ana's baby, too.

People who'd always had a family to count on and a place to belong couldn't truly understand the draw of that little whisper that said *There's someone like you.*

Someone who wouldn't hold my origins against me.

"I just want to know," I told Lillian, my voice low.

There was another silence, more measured than her last. Then she reached into her purse and handed me a newspaper, folded open to the business section.

I scanned the headlines but had no idea what I was supposed to be looking for.

"The article about the attempted corporate takeover," Lillian told me. "You'll notice that one of the companies is an international telecommunications conglomerate whose CEO is a man named Victor Gutierrez. The other company is owned by Davis Ames."

Davis was the Ames family patriarch, grandfather to Walker and Campbell, father to the man I'd once thought was *my* father—the man who really *was* the father of Ana's baby.

"Why are you showing me this?" I asked.

Lillian sighed. "Your mama's friend Ana? Her full name was Ana Sofía Gutierrez."

CHAPTER 3

A man who shared Ana's last name—*her father? brother? a more distant relation?*—had made a move against the Ames family's corporation.

Two hours of highway and back-road driving later, I was still mulling that over. As Lillian's Porsche SUV wound its way past a guard gate, a golf course, volleyball and tennis courts, and a pool, I couldn't help thinking that Davis Ames had once told me he'd *handled* the situation with the girl his son had impregnated. There was no telling exactly what that meant, but I had to wonder if business was just business for this Victor Gutierrez—or if it was personal.

Is this about Ana somehow? Revenge? For what, exactly? And why now?

"Here we are," Lillian declared, pulling into a circle drive. "Home, sweet lake home."

I had to compartmentalize. I couldn't be thinking about Ana or the pact or any of this around Lily and Aunt Olivia, not if I wanted to keep pretending that I was fine, and *we* were fine, and there was nothing for them to worry about or know. So instead, I focused on the sights at hand. When I'd heard the rest of the family refer to the "lake house," I'd pictured a cabin. Something small and rustic.

I really should have known better.

"This is your lake house." I fell back on stating the obvious as I stared up at an enormous stone residence. I stepped out of Lillian's Cayenne, and the front door to the home flew open.

"Sawyer." Lily was smiling. Not her polite, default smile, not her pained "you can't hurt me" smile—an honest-to-God, cheek-to-cheek grin. "You won't *believe*—"

Our grandmother stepped out of the car, and Lily cut herself off midsentence. "I hope traffic wasn't too horrible, Mim." That sounded more like the Lily I knew, but her dark brown eyes were still dancing. She waited a beat, then turned to me. "Come on. I'll show you our room."

Somehow, I doubted the energy I could hear buzzing in her voice was a reflection of her excitement at the idea of the two of us sharing a bedroom.

"What's going on?" I asked as we made our way to the front door and into the foyer.

Lily shushed me. Deciding that I didn't want to know what had gotten into her badly enough to be shushed twice, I focused on the house instead. The staircase winding its way upstairs I'd expected. The stairs going down I had not.

"Three stories?" I asked Lily. "Or is the basement just a basement?"

"It's just a basement." Lily paused. "With one bedroom. And a game room." She paused again, slightly embarrassed, because properly bred young ladies were always slightly embarrassed by the size of their vacation homes and the overall privilege to which they'd been born. "And a media room. A pool table. Ping-Pong . . ."

Deciding she'd said enough, Lily took to the stairs—the ones going up, not down. I followed, and together, we arrived at a small landing. Compared to the scale of the house, the second story was cozy: one bedroom with two twin beds, a bathroom, a closet. Aside from what I suspected was antique furniture, the room looked like it belonged in the cabin I'd imagined.

"I know it's a little small," Lily said softly, "but I've always loved it up here."

I walked over to the window and stared out at the lake below. "Who doesn't love a turret room?"

From this vantage point, it was obvious that the house had been built into the side of a hill. There was a steep drop-off, then the land sloped gently toward the rocky shore. The view of the water was breathtaking.

"Well?" Lily demanded.

"Well, what?" I asked, unable to tear my eyes away from the whitecapped waves as they broke and rolled slowly toward what appeared to be a private dock. Our cove was as big as I'd expected the entire lake to be, and from where I stood, I could see past the cove's entrance to the main body of Regal Lake.

The name didn't seem as ridiculous as it had on the drive up.

"Well . . ." Lily prompted primly. "Ask me again."

"Ask you what?" I played dumb. She'd shushed me. This was the price of shushing.

"Ask me what's going on." Lily came to stand beside me in the window and held up a long, flat box—too big for jewelry, but too narrow for almost anything else. "Ask me," she instructed, "what this is."

I took the box from her outstretched hand. It was matte black, with a card stuck to the middle. The card was made of a thick off-white paper—the kind I associated with wedding invitations—and a single word had been embossed on it in raised black cursive.

Lily's name.

I went to remove the top from the box, but Lily stopped me.

"Don't open mine." She nodded toward one of the beds. "Open yours."

A second box—this one bearing my name—sat near the pillow. I crossed the room, picked it up, and opened it. Nestled inside, I found a single elbow-length white glove. Pinned to the glove, there was another note, this one written on thinner paper in blood-red ink.

The Big Bang, 11 p.m., back room.

"Lily," I said calmly, "don't take this the wrong way, but is this an invitation to an orgy?"

"A what?" Lily Taft Easterling did not, as a rule, shriek, but this time, she came close.

"The Big Bang," I replied. "Doesn't exactly sound PG to me."

Lily glared at me. I grinned. Sometimes getting a rise out of her was just too easy. A pang came after a brief delay, and the grin froze on my face.

I could lose this. Lose her.

Putting those emotions on lockdown, I examined the contents of the box more closely. The pin holding the note to the glove was made of silver. Carved into the end, there was a small rose, and wrapped around the rose's stem, there was a snake.

"An orgy," I repeated, forcing a grin and trying to get the moment back. "With serpents."

Lily rolled her eyes. "When you're done repeating that word ad nauseam, I'd be happy to inform you that The Big Bang is a local establishment."

"A brothel?"

"They sell hot wings," Lily said defensively. "And beer. And . . . other beverages."

"So you're saying it's a bar." I'd grown up in a bar—almost literally. My mom and I had lived over The Holler until I was thirteen.

"Someone wants to meet the two of us in the back room of a bar at eleven p.m.?"

I was skeptical. The world Lily had grown up in—the world I'd reluctantly taken my place in this past year—was a place of charity galas and twin sets and pearls. A bar wasn't exactly the natural habitat of an Easterling *or* a Taft.

"Not just someone," Lily told me, removing the contents of her box and cradling it reverently in one hand. "The White Gloves."

LABOR DAY, 3:19 A.M.

"*A*re you *sure* that's how we ended up at the bottom of this hole, Sawyer?"

"Trust me. You were unconscious, but I held on just long enough to see the person responsible."

"Maybe it was an accident?"

"How do you accidentally drug someone, Sadie-Grace?"

"Accidentally . . . on purpose?"

FOURTEEN WEEKS
(AND *THREE DAYS*) EARLIER

CHAPTER 4

*L*ily refused to enlighten me as to who or what the White Gloves were until she could be certain that we wouldn't be overheard. At the lake, that apparently meant hitting the water. Within five minutes, the two of us were swimsuit-clad and Jet Ski–bound. We made our way down to the dock.

And Lily's father.

After more than a month of playing this game, seeing J.D. Easterling shouldn't have hit me so hard. I shouldn't have cared that he was in full-on Dad Mode, puttering around the dock and getting way too much pleasure out of power-washing everything in the near vicinity, including and especially the boats.

"How are my favorite girls doing?" he called out. "Making your escape already?"

Don't say a word, I told myself. *Don't think about it. Think about the White Gloves. Think about the snake and rose on that pin. Don't even look at him. Look at the boats.*

There were two of them, one a speedboat and one that Lily would have insisted wasn't a yacht.

"Sawyer's never ridden a Jet Ski." Beside me, Lily was talking.

"Think we could take out *Thing One* and *Thing Two* before the weekend traffic hits the water?"

I took a step toward the boats, telling myself that it was only natural that I would be curious, natural that I would focus on reading the name on the back of the larger boat, rather than joining the conversation between Lily and her father.

Our father.

"I have noticed, Daughter, that when you preface a statement with 'Sawyer has never . . .' you're usually up to something."

"You say that like it's a bad thing, Daddy."

The back-and-forth between them was so easy, so natural. There was no ignoring that.

"What say you, Niece?" J.D. turned toward me. "Ready to brave the ocean deep?"

This wasn't the ocean, and I wasn't his *niece*.

"I think I can handle it," I said, spotting the Jet Skis on the far side of the dock. I started toward them in hopes of ending this conversation before Lily caught on to the fact that something was off. I'd done a good job of avoiding her dad for the past few weeks. He'd been pulling late nights at work and had made more than one trip up here to check on the boats.

Think about that. Don't think about . . .

"Hate to tell you this, Lilypad, but *Thing One* is out of commission. Can you and Sawyer double up on *Thing Two*?"

"Not a problem," Lily responded.

He pressed a kiss to her temple. "That's my girl."

He didn't seem like the type to sleep with his wife's little sister. The type to sleep with someone our age when he was twenty-three. The type to call me Niece when he knew quite well that I was his daughter.

Don't think about it. Think about the White Gloves. Don't look at him.

"Earth to Sawyer." Lily was suddenly standing beside me. I hadn't even notice her approach. She held out a purple life vest.

I took it and slipped it on.

"Are you okay?" Lily asked.

I could feel Uncle J.D. looking at the two of us. Watching us.

"Right as rain," I said, turning back to the duo of Jet Skis. "Which one is *Thing Two?*"

CHAPTER 5

I'd known for a while that Lily had a deep-seated need for perfection. I hadn't realized that she also had a need for speed.

"Boat incoming!" I yelled in her ear, my voice nearly lost to the wind and the sound of the engine revving as Lily angled the Jet Ski into a major wave at forty-five degrees.

"I see it," she yelled back, her blond ponytail whipping in the wind—and at my face. "Hold on!"

My arms were wound around her waist, my fingers clutching the straps on her life vest. She cut across the main channel going full throttle, then hung a left past three massive coves. A small island, boasting a scattering of trees and the remains of a house, came into view. We barreled past it and into a long and narrow cove on the far side. Lily eased off the gas, letting her hands fall from the handlebars as we cruised slowly to a stop near the back of the cove. Compared to the main channel, the water here was like glass. The world was quiet—remarkably so, given how loudly I'd had to yell to be heard a minute earlier.

"Nice place," I told Lily, letting loose of her life jacket and shaking out my hands. "I especially like the way I can no longer see my life flashing before my eyes."

As was her style, Lily remained utterly unruffled. "I have no idea what you could possibly be implying."

For pretty much the first time since I'd met her, her hair looked unkempt—windblown and free.

Lily must have noticed the way I was looking at her, because she seemed compelled to offer an explanation. "The lake is my happy place. It always has been. Mama isn't a fan of the heat. Or the water. Or the bugs. But Daddy and John David and I have always loved it up here."

I couldn't afford to let that hurt. "I can see why," I said instead, letting my head fall back and taking in the wide expanse of sky above.

"That's King's Island." Lily gestured to the small blot of land we'd passed on the way in. "No one's lived there for years."

"King's Island," I repeated. "On Regal Lake." You would have thought that this was the Hamptons, not a man-made body of water in a region of the state known for its red dirt and surplus of deer. "Looks to me like this is a place where we won't be overheard."

"I'll tell you everything I know," Lily promised. "Just let me turn around so we can face each other. When I go left, you go right. We should be able to keep our balance if—"

Feeling wicked, I hooked an arm around her waist and leaned hard to the left, taking us both over the side and into the lake. Lily might have swallowed a bit of water. She definitely snorted in a most unladylike manner.

"Sawyer!" She began paddling toward the Jet Ski, which had floated several yards away when we'd gone in.

"What?" I said, feeling more like myself than I had in hours. "The sun is high, and the water feels good. Now talk."

"There's not that much to tell," Lily warned me. "Until I saw the boxes sitting on our beds, I wasn't one hundred percent certain the White Gloves actually existed."

"A suburban legend?" I quipped. Before Lily could offer a retort, I processed the rest of what she'd said. "Our invitations were inside the house when you arrived?"

"And all of the doors were locked."

Now she'd piqued my interest. "What exactly does the rumor mill say about the White Gloves?"

"That they're a secret society. That they recruit freshmen at State, U-of, and a handful of private colleges in a three-state region. Female-only, *very* exclusive."

In the world Lily had grown up in, *exclusive* meant *wealthy*. It meant old money, power, and status, having the luxury never to talk—or even *think*—about money at all.

"We should go tonight," Lily said. "Right?" She laid her arms on the back edge of the Jet Ski and rested her chin on her wrist. "I know where The Big Bang is. We could tell Mama we're sleeping over with Sadie-Grace. Lord knows Sadie-Grace's daddy won't know the difference."

"Who are you," I deadpanned, "and what have you done with Lily Taft Easterling?"

"I've done everything that's expected of me, Sawyer. My whole life, I've dotted *i*'s and crossed *t*'s. I followed the rules. I was everything I was supposed to be, right up until I started *Secrets*."

Everyone had their own way of coping with trauma. Mine involved a lot of compartmentalizing and a healthy amount of denial. Lily had coped with Walker dumping her last summer by creating a risqué photo blog where she wrote other people's secrets on her skin.

"You miss it," I commented. "*Secrets on My Skin.*"

I waited for her to tell me that I was wrong, but instead, she righted herself in the water. "Walker."

What about him? I twisted my torso, allowing my fingertips to skim the surface of the water as I turned in the direction of her gaze. About a hundred yards away, a Jet Ski passed King's Island and began to slow. I had no idea how Lily had recognized its driver from this distance, but I didn't doubt her claim.

Lily Easterling had impeccable instincts about two and only two things: proper etiquette and Walker Ames.

"Did you tell him we were here?" I asked.

"I haven't talked to him all day." Lily avoided my gaze. "But Walker and Campbell are the reason I know this place. Their house is on the point opposite King's Island, just two coves away."

I didn't have the chance to ask Lily if there was a reason she and Walker hadn't talked, before he glided into earshot and cut the engine. He slowed his forward momentum by holding his legs out to the sides, allowing his feet to drag in the water.

"Salutations, ladies." Walker took off his life vest, hung it over the handlebars of his Jet Ski, and dove into the water. He emerged seconds later, right between me and Lily. Moisture beaded on his chest as he shook the water from his hair, splashing us both.

I would never have made a move on Walker, and he only had eyes for Lily regardless, but now that I knew that he *wasn't* my brother, I didn't try quite so hard not to enjoy the view. Then, slowly but surely, my mind turned to thinking about another chest.

Other arms.

Nick had very nice arms.

"As I live and breathe," Walker quipped, drawing me back to the present. "Sawyer Taft and Lily Easterling. What are the chances of meeting the two of you here?"

Better than the chances of my path ever crossing Nick's again. I hadn't seen or heard from him since the night of my debutante ball. Not that I'd expected to. Not that I even really *wanted* to.

"Is that your way of saying you were hoping to have this cove to yourself?" Lily asked Walker, her tone prodding.

"Never." Walker had inherited his father's charm, but unlike the former senator, he was not a particularly skilled liar. My gut said that he hadn't known we would be here. He certainly hadn't come looking for us.

"How's your mama?" Lily asked quietly.

There was a beat of silence. "She's just fine."

Walker didn't want to talk about his mama. That made two of us. Charlotte Ames was not a member of the Sawyer fan club. Given that she believed me to be the product of her husband's adultery, I was pretty sure she'd wished me six feet under more than once.

"Is it bad?" Lily asked Walker, her voice muted. He didn't reply, and she pushed off the Jet Ski and glided through the water toward him. I averted my eyes as she wrapped her arms around his neck.

Lily Taft Easterling was a properly bred young lady, a Southern miss to her toes. But right now, her hair was windblown and free, and Walker's chest was wet, and I could not have been more of a third wheel if I'd tried.

"Don't mind me," I said loudly. "Certainly don't refrain from PDA on my part. I'll just be over here minding my own business."

"Very considerate of you, little sis."

Walker's new nickname for me hit me hard. When we'd first met, he'd been in the tail end of a downward spiral and seemed to appreciate that I was immune to his charms. I insulted him, and he enjoyed it. That was our dynamic.

This was the first time he'd referred to me as his sister.

I have to tell him. I did everything in my power not to look from

Walker to Lily. *I have to tell both of them the truth, even if Lily hates me for it.*

But I couldn't make myself do it.

"Don't call me that," I said, and then, realizing that my reaction would probably make him refer to me that way more often, I changed the subject, hard and fast. "I hear the family business is under attack."

"What are you talking about?" Lily said, before turning back to Walker, her arms still wrapped around his neck. "What is she talking about, Walker?"

"It's nothing," Walker told her. "Everything is going to be fine."

"Just like your mama is fine?" Lily asked.

I was starting to regret bringing it up, but I could only compartmentalize so much.

"I don't want to talk about the family business." Walker bent his head forward, allowing his cheek to brush against Lily's, before casting another sidelong glance at me. "That's more Cam's thing these days than mine."

He'd just given me a reason—and an excuse—to get out of here before I said something else I would regret.

"Now that you mention it, Campbell and I are overdue for a little chat." I paddled over to Walker's Jet Ski. The lanyard with the key was still attached to the life vest he'd left on the handlebars. I unclipped the lanyard, attached it to my own vest, and threw his to him.

"Is it me," Walker asked Lily, "or is your delightful cousin stealing my ride?"

"I'm not stealing it," I corrected. "I'm taking it home. Not our lake house—yours. Two coves down, on the point across from King's Island, right?"

Walker shook his head. "You are a strange girl, Sawyer Taft."

"I prefer to think of myself as altruistic," I countered. "This way, you and Lily get some privacy for the latest episode of *Beautiful People in Semi-Functional Relationships,* and I can have a word with your sister."

CHAPTER 6

When I made it to the Ames family's cove, I found Campbell lying out on the front of their dock, her skin glistening with some combination of sunscreen and sweat. She didn't so much as raise her head or flip onto her side as I docked the Jet Ski.

"Not bad," Campbell called out lazily. "For a rookie."

I slid off the Jet Ski and hit a nearby button, which I assumed would either raise the watercraft out of the water or cause everything around us to self-destruct.

"If you're going to stand there dripping wet, could you at least try to drip a little more quietly?" Campbell opened one green eye. "You're spoiling the ambiance."

That was more or less the Campbell Ames version of *hello*.

My version was: "Commit any felonies lately?"

Campbell rolled from her stomach to her back and popped one knee, her right hand taking up position behind her head. "You know what I love about you, Sawyer? You're the only person in this whole state—maybe the entire country—who can say the word *felony* to me and be thinking of what I'm capable of and not that unfortunate mess with dear old Daddy."

That "unfortunate mess" was something she'd masterminded and I'd helped with. Her father was in jail, having pled guilty to several crimes he *had* committed, because we'd framed him for several that he *hadn't*. Campbell's capabilities were, in a word, impressive.

I plopped down beside her, allowing my feet to dangle off the dock. "How are you holding up?"

Campbell had always intended for her father to go down, but I didn't think she'd fully considered the collateral damage, the press coverage, the scandal.

"How am I holding up?" Campbell snorted. "My family has been exiled to the lake since the story broke. Mama's decided that day-drunk is the new tipsy, Walker blames me because he's trying not to blame Lily, and I am starved for civilization. And you?"

Campbell had a flair for the dramatic and a gift for holding people at arm's length, but I could hear the vulnerability buried in her couldn't-care-less tone.

I gave her honesty, tit for tat. "I'm sick of keeping secrets, haven't spoken to my mom in a month, and am getting really tired of people asking me if I'm going to college in the fall."

"Are you going to college in the fall?" Campbell asked innocently.

"I don't know," I shot back. "Are you starting to regret what we did to your father?"

There was a beat of silence. "I don't believe in regrets." Campbell stretched lazily, like a cat, and then stood. "If you want to hear someone mope about the consequences of Daddy's arrest and the journalistic feeding frenzy that followed, I suggest you get on Walker's calendar."

I studied her for a moment. "Was the attempted takeover of your grandfather's company one of those consequences?"

"Do I look like someone who has the inside track on the family businesses?" Campbell asked me. She didn't—and that was the point.

"Spoken like a girl who has a love-hate relationship with being underestimated," I said.

That won me a small, slow, genuine smile—and an answer. "There's blood in the water. The sharks are circling—socially, financially, *whatever*. They think we're weak. But don't worry your pretty little face about it, Sawyer. Our grandfather is tougher than that. He can handle the sharks."

She'd said *our*.

I swallowed. "Campbell?" I was going to regret this, but once I'd started the ball rolling down the hill, I couldn't stop. "There's something I have to tell you."

Whatever reaction I'd been expecting, I didn't get it. Campbell just tossed her damp auburn hair over one shoulder. "So Daddy impregnated a *different* teenager, and I can stop wondering how you and I could possibly share even a quarter of our DNA."

"You can't tell Walker," I said. "He'll tell Lily."

"And why," Campbell asked me coyly, "don't you want dear Lily to know?"

I'd told her who my father wasn't—not who he was and not about the pact.

"Please."

Campbell let the seconds tick by. "I have to admit," she said finally, "I am flattered that you chose to confide in me."

That was as close to a promise to keep my secret as I was going to get. "Side note," I told her, now that I could. "The company that just attempted a takeover of your grandfather's? The man who runs it has the same last name as that teenage girl your dad knocked up."

"Payback?" Campbell arched an eyebrow.

"I don't know." It was a relief to speak openly, no pretending. "But I'd like to find out. Find her."

I expected Campbell to ask me why *I* wanted to find Ana, but instead, she assented. "Yes," she said, "I suppose there's nothing left to do at this point besides attempting to identify and locate my actual half-sibling and doing *something* about that hair."

"What hair?" I said. *"Ouch!"*

I batted Campbell's hand away from my face in an attempt to keep her from trying to detangle my hair a second time. "There's nothing wrong with my hair."

"Keep telling yourself that." Campbell turned her back on the water and pushed past me, striding toward the ramp that connected the dock to the shore. "And keep up."

If there was one thing I'd had in plentiful supply in recent months, it was makeovers. I'd been poked, prodded, plucked, waxed, exfoliated, moisturized, buffed, highlighted, and conditioned within an inch of my life. Not to mention the makeup and the clothes.

But, as Campbell had just so pleasantly informed me, I didn't have a choice. She knew my secret, and she wasn't above a little blackmail. The fact that I'd known that about her and chosen her as the person to confide in deeply suggested that there was something wrong with me.

Either that, or some self-sabotaging part of me was hoping my secret wouldn't stay a secret for long.

"I'd tell you to keep your voice down inside," Campbell said as she opened the back door to her lake house. "But we could probably do some kind of ritualistic animal sacrifice in the living room and still not merit my mama's attention."

I didn't know Charlotte Ames all that well, but my impression had always been that Campbell's mother was closer to Aunt Olivia's end of the maternal spectrum than my mom's. Hovering was a way of life, holding one's daughter to impossibly high standards was practically their religion, and acting the part of the perfect hostess was a darn near spiritual calling.

Over the muted sound of a television some distance away, I heard what could only be described as a belch.

Campbell ignored it as she herded me into a nearby bathroom to stand in front of the mirror. "Luckily for you, I can work around those unfortunate in-lieu-of-therapy bangs," she said. "Far be it from me to point out that there are far more pleasant ways of working out tension and personal issues, so long as you can find a willing and attractive partner." She pulled back the shower curtain. "Here ends the relationship-advice portion of our Betterment of Sawyer lecture series. Hop in the shower. Wash the lake out of your hair. Once you're done, work a quarter-sized dollop of conditioner through that mess and leave it in. I'll get you something to wear."

Campbell Ames was the last person I would have gone to for relationship advice, especially given the identity of her last *willing* and *attractive* partner.

Nick.

"You're really going to blackmail me into a makeover?" I asked, refusing to give life to any of my other thoughts.

"You really let me go on for weeks thinking we were sisters?" Campbell retorted, then she flashed me a sharp-edged smile. "The conditioner will minimize frizz when you're out on the water, which in this humidity with *that* hair is a must. And you'll need clothes for tonight. I'm assuming you and Lily received one of these as well?"

She reached into a nearby cabinet and brandished a matte black box, long and thin and flat, with a card affixed to the front and Campbell's name embossed on the card.

The White Gloves.

"We can hardly rely on Lily to get you ready for your *real* debut in society," Campbell said. I opened my mouth to reply, but she put a finger to my lips to hush me. "Things work differently at the lake. Lake formal basically translates to 'you cannot wear a bathing suit.' Semiformal means that you have to wear some kind of sundress *over* your suit. In either case, your makeup has to pass the boat test: if you can't wear it on the water, you don't wear it at all."

"So you're going to this White Glove shindig?" I asked when she finally stopped talking.

She shrugged. "Who am I to turn down a pity invite?" It was unlike Cam to admit to even the slightest bit of weakness. She was the kind of person who could come in last in a race and convince every person there that she'd won. "At this point in my exile, I will gladly let people gawk at the pitiable, scandalous Ames family to their hearts' content, so long as they offer me some form of diversion as they gawk."

"What kind of diversion are you expecting tonight?" I asked.

Campbell smirked and gestured to the shower. "You strip," she said, "and I'll talk."

I made the executive decision to undress in the shower. I'd shed my swimsuit and started in on washing my hair when Campbell deigned to hold up her end of the bargain.

"Think of the White Gloves like the Junior League—by way of Skull and Bones. They tend to recruit from the debutante sets in a three-state area, but the initiation process is notoriously risky and risqué. A total adrenaline rush, from what I've heard." Campbell paused for a few seconds. "Anyone can be born with a silver spoon in their mouth, but not every country-club girl is White Glove material."

Lily had been excited to receive an invitation. As I stepped under the spray and rinsed the shampoo—and the lake—from my hair, I had the distinct sense that Campbell was relieved.

She needed this.

"Done yet?" Campbell demanded. I barely had time to wrap a towel around myself before she pulled the curtain. "Try this luminizer." She slapped a container into my hand.

"What the hell is luminizer?"

Without answering, Campbell left the room and returned with a dress she'd selected for me: white cotton, with a gathered neckline and spaghetti straps. "I'll send the dress home with you in a watertight bag. I'd recommend a bright-colored bathing suit to go underneath. You're not trying to hide the fact that you're wearing one, so you might as well go big or go home."

I reached for the suit I'd worn here.

Campbell blocked my arm. "Not that one." Having issued that edict, she disappeared back across the hall.

With a roll of my eyes, I studied the "luminizer" she'd handed me, determined it to be some kind of glittery lotion, and mentally filed it under *hell no*.

"What is *she* doing here?"

I turned to see Charlotte Ames standing in the doorway. Campbell's mama wasn't wearing makeup, and I could smell the alcohol on her breath from four feet away. Her question was clearly directed toward Campbell, but she stood facing me.

I could not help feeling that wearing nothing but a towel didn't put me in the best position for a standoff.

"Isn't it enough that your father's in prison, Campbell? Do you really hate me so much that you would invite *this* . . ." Even inebriated, Charlotte Ames was not the type to fling about vulgarities or slurs, so she settled on simply referring to me as *this*. ". . . into my home?"

Maybe I should have felt attacked or degraded or, at the very least, condescended to, but the only thing I could bring myself to actually feel in that moment was pity.

This woman's husband *had* cheated on her. Repeatedly. He *had* knocked up a teenager years ago. And even though that baby wasn't me, I *was* one of the people responsible for her husband's arrest. Campbell, Lily, Sadie-Grace, and I had planned his disgrace down to the last detail, and as a result, Charlotte Ames had spent much of the past month splattered on front pages right alongside her husband.

"I'll go," I said.

"No." Campbell stepped into the hallway and blocked my exit. "Stay, Sawyer. After all, you're my sister." Given that she knew now that I wasn't, I could only assume that Campbell and her mother were not currently on the best terms. "Blood is thicker than water—isn't that what you always say, Mama?"

Charlotte's sharp intake of breath was audible. "I didn't raise you to talk to me that way, Campbell Caroline."

"You raised me to be a lady," Campbell countered lightly. "And ladies play to win. It's not my fault you're slipping, hiding out here with your tail between your legs like we have something to be ashamed of."

"I am not having this argument with you," Charlotte said, her voice low in a way that would have sounded a lot more ominous if she weren't drunk enough to slur her words.

"Then don't," Campbell replied simply. *Don't argue. Don't make a scene.* Campbell turned back to me and held out an electric-orange swimsuit. I took it.

Charlotte straightened, doing a passable impression of someone who wasn't fall-down drunk, and shifted her attention wholly and pointedly to me. "I suppose that I should offer you a beverage."

"That won't be necessary."

Charlotte stared at me so hard that I could feel her gaze on my skin. "It's only a matter of time before your roots start showing, you know." Her voice was strangely pleasant. She barely even slurred the words. "It doesn't matter how they dress you up, or what little tricks you learn, or how well you think you can blend. You are what you are, sweetheart, and you'll never be anything else."

She took a long drink out of the glass in her hand—whiskey, by the smell of it.

"You can tell your mama I said so." She smiled daggers at me and shook Campbell off when her daughter tried to lead her back down the hall. "Or better yet, pass the message along to your aunt."

CHARLOTTE AND LIV
SUMMER BEFORE SENIOR YEAR
TWENTY-FIVE YEARS EARLIER

"*L*iv?" For years, Charlotte had prided herself on knowing the right thing to say in every situation. She was the sensitive one. Julia was the blunt, take-no-prisoners type. And Liv . . .

Liv hadn't been herself since they'd buried her daddy.

Charlotte hovered in the doorway to the late Mr. Taft's home office, her eyes fixed on the silhouette in the window.

"You can't stay cooped up in here all day, Livvy," she said delicately.

"I can do anything I want to." Liv's tone was calm, with just the slightest lilt. "That's what he used to say. 'Sky's the limit, Bug.'" There was a pause. "He called me *Bug.*"

"I know." Despite her best efforts, Charlotte could not find any words of honeyed comfort beyond that.

Liv probably didn't want to be comforted.

"Come on." Liv pushed off the window frame and stalked past her second-oldest friend.

Second-best, a voice inside Charlotte always whispered.

"Call Julia and tell her to meet us at the cemetery," Liv ordered.

She'd always been the charismatic one, enough so that people— male and female, young and old—did what she suggested.

Under any other circumstances, Liv being Liv might have gotten under Charlotte's skin, but not today. Not when Liv Taft was finally starting to sound like herself.

"Don't just stand there, Char. Get a move on. We can raid the liquor cabinet on the way."

CHAPTER 7

*T*here was a board nailed across the door to The Big Bang, like the whole place had been condemned. I had to look twice to determine that it was for show.

"Mama would have a heart attack if she knew where we were," Lily said beside me, straightening her dress. "Or worse, a conniption."

We'd told Aunt Olivia we were spending the night with Sadie-Grace. For good measure, I'd also passed along Charlotte's regards, which seemed wiser than saying, *Campbell's mama sends vague insults and whiskey-laden predictions about the future.*

"Do you want to open the door?" I asked Lily. "Or should I?"

She took a deep and cleansing breath. "Here's to a legendary evening."

She pulled the door open, and a cacophony of country music, loud voices, and what sounded like a live piano hit me all at once. The lighting inside the bar was dim, but there were colored Christmas lights strung along the entire perimeter of the open room, and a massive crystal chandelier hung from the ceiling. There was a baby grand piano on the far side of the room, and behind it, silvery curtains that had been drawn to reveal the bar's name in a spotlight on the wall. Gas station memorabilia hung along the other three walls, with a dozen or more signs for filling stations deeming themselves *The Last Chance*.

The entire place looked like it had been decorated by a couple, one of whom had read *The Great Gatsby* a few too many times, and the other of whom had a fondness for all things mom and pop.

"It shouldn't work," someone said behind me. "But it does."

I turned to see Campbell. When Lily had dropped Walker off and picked me up earlier, Cam hadn't said a word to either of them about what I'd told her. She was good at keeping secrets—if she wanted to.

"I take it you've enlightened your cousin as to the score?" she asked now.

Horror seeped through my body, weighting it down limb by limb—then Campbell smiled and made it clear that her question had been targeted at Lily and that the "score" she'd been referring to wasn't my secret.

"Parts of Regal Lake are Martha's Vineyard," Campbell *enlightened* me. "And parts are *Duck Dynasty*, and ne'er the twain shall meet, except in fine establishments like this one."

Half of the bar-goers in this room looked like they would have been right at home at The Holler. The other half looked like they'd come straight from the yacht club. The common denominator was that nearly everyone in the building was young—and as we stood there, more than a few of them turned to look in our direction.

It took me a moment to realize that they were looking at Campbell.

"Notoriety suits me," Campbell said, but her usual bravado fell flat. "Don't you think?"

"I think we're supposed to be in the back room," Lily said, nudging Campbell in that direction. "Come on."

Before I could follow them, I noticed a disturbance a few feet away. "You two go ahead," I told Campbell and Lily. "I'm going to rescue Sadie-Grace."

Sadie-Grace Waters was what my old boss, Big Jim, would have referred to as a *looker* and what my grandmother referred to as a *sweet girl*. She wasn't particularly skilled at standing up for herself or recognizing sexual innuendos. I managed to push my way through her thick ring of current admirers just as one of them was saying something rather questionable about apples.

"Hi, Sawyer!" Sadie-Grace greeted me cheerfully. "People here are so friendly."

I snorted and gently maneuvered her away from the crowd.

"Where are you going?" one of the men called, disappointed.

Sadie-Grace, bless her heart, bounced to the tips of her toes. "I can't tell you," she called back. "It's a secret!"

The back room was bigger than I'd expected. Round-top tables lined the walls, a half-dozen candles burning on each table, the only light in the room. I'd spent a chunk of my childhood obsessively calculating the maximum occupancy of every building I entered, and my guess was that the room could hold forty and was pushing that number. Every person here was female. Most were dressed like us—sundresses layered over swimsuits, hair strategically windblown—but I counted eight who wore what appeared to be white shifts and elbow-length white gloves under floor-length scarlet robes. Their hoods were up, casting their faces in shadow.

"Don't be shy," one of them told Sadie-Grace and me. "Pick your poison." She gestured to the table beside her, which was filled with martini glasses. Each glass bore liquid of a different color—an entire rainbow of *poisons* to choose from.

Sadie-Grace went for a purple one. I circled the table to grab the only clear drink I saw.

"Do you like it when things are transparent?" the hooded girl asked me. From this angle, I could see her better. Her hair was dark and thick, her skin the same medium brown as her eyes.

I took a very small sip of my drink. "I don't like anything too sweet."

A second or two passed, then the dark-haired girl turned and disappeared into the crowd.

"I can't believe she came tonight."

"I can't believe they invited her."

"Wasn't that nice of them?"

My default would have been to ignore the duo murmuring behind me, but the next thing one of them said was: "It would only be polite to go say hello."

They made their way around me—and that was when I realized they were headed for Campbell. Poor, pitiable Campbell Ames, whose family was embroiled in scandal.

"Should we warn her?" Sadie-Grace asked me. She paused. "Or warn *them*?"

My money was on Campbell being able to take care of herself.

"Lily's with her," I told Sadie-Grace. "She won't let things get too ugly."

Just before the girls reached Campbell, I heard a thump, followed by another and another. Someone was stomping—and soon, multiple people were, creating a steady, rhythmic drumbeat.

"The Candidates are many." Those words were spoken to carry. "The Chosen are few." The speaker stepped onto a chair, and I recognized her as the one who'd told us to pick our poison. "You received an invitation to tonight's little soiree," she said, "because at least one among us thought you had . . . *potential*." She lingered on that word, just for a moment. "You might have noticed that there are eight of us and significantly more of you. For now, you don't need to know our names. All you need to know is what we offer. Eight spots for eight of you. Tradition dictates that at the start of her senior year in college, each White Glove picks her own replacement from among the incoming freshmen at her institution."

There was a pause—a calculated one.

"But this summer, we decided to shake things up a bit and bring the competition to you a little early. Handy, isn't it, that Regal Lake brings together society from three states and twice that many metropolitan areas? You have fourteen weeks to impress us. This may be my first summer at Regal, but it's already clear that it offers a variety of avenues for making an impression." She raised the martini glass in her hand. "Here's to the first."

"The Candidates are many," another hooded girl called out, and then all of them raised their voices in unison. "The Chosen are few."

CHAPTER 8

*T*hree things became apparent over the next hour. The first was that none of the White Gloves were really drinking—nothing more than the occasional sip. The second was that the murmurs I'd overheard about Campbell weren't an isolated incident. And the third was that there was no doubt among the Candidates that this was a competition—and no reluctance whatsoever to oh-so-sweetly compete.

I wondered how many of the girls in this room would deep-six lifelong friends, just to make an *impression*.

"You're friends with Campbell Ames, right?" A White Glove appeared beside me. Lily and Sadie-Grace were mingling on the other side of the room. I'd lost sight of Campbell. "She's causing quite the stir tonight. I knew she would." The White Glove sounded pleased with herself.

"You the type of person who likes causing stirs?" I asked.

"I have a certain appreciation for chaos." The girl shed her hood, revealing a head of dark blond hair underneath. "I know Victoria said no names, but I'm Hope."

"I'm—"

"Sawyer Taft." Hope finished for me. "Former auto mechanic,

prodigal granddaughter of Lillian Taft, and the fifth-most-interesting Candidate here."

During my Debutante year, *interesting* had been used mostly as an insult dressed up in compliment clothing. I didn't sense any of that from Hope.

"Do I want to know how you know that I used to be a mechanic?" I asked.

Hope smiled. "In your shoes, I'd be far more curious about the four Candidates who make your backstory seem tame."

I couldn't help thinking that she didn't know the full story.

Another White Glove appeared beside Hope. "Causing trouble?" she murmured. Unlike Hope's, her hood was still in place.

Hope neither confirmed nor denied the accusation. "Nessa, Sawyer. Sawyer, Nessa."

"No names," Nessa reminded Hope.

"White Gloves don't take orders," Hope replied lightly. "Not even when the person issuing them is one of our own—and that includes the illustrious Victoria Gutierrez."

It took me a moment to process the name, and then I felt like a bomb had been detonated in the room. I couldn't hear anything but a ringing in my ears and the name that Hope had just very pointedly dropped. *Gutierrez. Victoria Gutierrez.*

I scanned the room for the White Glove who'd said that we didn't need to know their names—the dark-haired girl who'd told me to pick my poison. Unfortunately, in this lighting, with most of the White Gloves' hoods still up, she wasn't easy to spot.

What are the chances that Victoria Gutierrez is related to the Victor Gutierrez who made a move against Davis Ames? What are the chances she's related to Ana?

I tried to catch Campbell's attention but couldn't. A nearby White Glove turned. *Not Victoria.* Counting Hope and Nessa, that was three down. A fourth was facing me on the far side of the room. *Not her.* Turning, I saw a hooded girl exiting back into the bar. Glancing through the party, I was able to rule out two more based on height and build. That gave it even odds that the one who'd just left was Victoria Gutierrez.

I decided to take my chances. Once I made it to the main bar, my target wasn't hard to spot. A scarlet robe didn't exactly blend. I followed the hooded girl through the crowd. Despite the music— courtesy of the piano *and* the loudspeakers—very few people were dancing, unless you counted swaying and drinking to one of the dueling beats.

Victoria—if that *was* Victoria—sauntered up to the bar. It was in the middle of the room, elevated and roped off with red velvet ropes.

I tried to follow, but a bouncer stopped me before I could.

"I'm going to need to see some ID." He was small and compact, with a humorless gaze and biceps he probably spent most of the day flexing.

"I'd be happy to show you my driver's license," I replied, "just as soon as you circumvent the fight that's about to break out between Inebriated Frat Boy . . ." I nodded to our left. "His friend, Drunken Heir to the Family Fortune . . ."

The bouncer turned to look.

"And the guy they just bumped into for the third time, who we'll just call Are You Boys Looking for an Ass Whupping?"

The bouncer turned back to me, folded his arms over his chest, and humorlessly demanded my ID a second time.

"Are you boys looking for an ass whupping?" someone demanded—loudly—from our left.

The bouncer made a beeline for the frat boys. Sometimes, it paid to be observant. I moseyed on by the ropes and helped myself to a barstool right next to the White Glove. I still couldn't see her face. She was leaning forward, elbows on the bar.

"Can I get you something?" someone asked her.

I recognized the voice that had asked that question a second before my eyes settled on familiar hazel ones behind the bar.

"Nick," I said. I hadn't expected to see him here. I told myself that was why I felt a jolt, borderline electric, as the ghost of our single shared dance solidified in my memory. At the time, he'd been a fish out of water, the boy at the country club dressed in a T-shirt and faded jeans. Now he'd traded the jeans for shorts—or possibly a swimsuit. His T-shirt was threadbare and worn.

Soft, some part of me thought, imagining the feel of it beneath my touch.

The girl beside me chose that moment to let her hood fall back. *Victoria Gutierrez.* "Another half-dozen drinks," she told Nick, commandeering his attention. "Same deal as before."

"Pretty, colorful, and watered down," Nick said, stealing a sideways glance at me. "Coming right up."

He had the kind of voice that made everything sound a little ironic. When he turned to fill Victoria's order, I tore my attention from the back of his head—and the back of the rest of him—and reminded myself that I'd come here to talk to *her*.

"You two know each other?" Victoria asked me once Nick was out of earshot.

"Something like that," I said, refusing to allow him any more real estate in my mind. Instead, I searched Victoria's features for some resemblance to the Ana I'd seen in pictures. Their hair was different, but they had the same eyes—same shape, same color.

"He's cute," Victoria commented offhandedly. "If you go for the rough-around-the-edges, angry-at-the-world type, which I suspect you do."

I didn't go for any type. I preferred flying solo—and Nick had reason enough to avoid girls like me.

"You asked him to water down the drinks," I observed evenly.

"We're not looking to get anyone drunk," Victoria said.

"You just want them to think they are," I inferred. "It's amazing how people start to act drunk as soon as they *think* they've had a lot of alcohol."

"You're a perceptive one, aren't you?" Victoria almost but didn't quite smile. "Enjoying yourself tonight?"

Eyes on her. No looking behind the bar, Sawyer.

"By some definitions," I said, and then I cut to the chase. "How old are you?" If she was a senior in college, she was probably too old to be Ana's baby, but I had to ask.

"Twenty-one." She arched an eyebrow at me. "Why don't you ask me what you really want to know?"

I wasn't sure what she was expecting—maybe for me to ask for the inside track on how to prove myself worthy of the White Gloves—but I took her up on the invitation to be blunt. "Are you related to Victor Gutierrez?"

"Are you asking on your own behalf?" she said mildly. "Or on behalf of Campbell Ames?"

It took me a second to parse that response.

"I hope she knows that business is just . . . business," Victoria said lightly. "Whatever my father's intentions or grand plans, I assure you, they have nothing to do with me."

Nick appeared then with the first three bright-colored drinks, setting the martini glasses down on the bar in front of her.

"I'll be back for the others," Victoria told him. She glanced at me. "And for you."

As she retreated, I lost my excuse not to look at Nick. I let my eyes travel in his direction, but reminded myself that if he'd wanted to contact me in the past month and a half, he could have.

"Long time no see," I said.

"Last I checked . . ." Nick grabbed a rag and ran it over the bar between us. ". . . you're not old enough to be on this side of the ropes, Miss Taft."

I wondered what Emily Post had to say about telling a guy to take his sarcastic use of the word *Miss* and shove it up his—

"Oh, yeah," Nick continued, in a way that made me pretty damn sure he was trying to get a rise out of me, "you're not really big on rules—or laws. Are you?"

It was hard to tell how much of that was a compliment—and how much was an insult.

Nick had played a key—and largely unwilling—role in Campbell's plan to take down her father. The four of us hadn't exactly endeared ourselves to him, given that the plan had involved him being arrested.

Twice.

Then again, it wasn't like he'd been forced at gunpoint to say yes when I'd asked him for that dance.

It wasn't like he hadn't enjoyed it.

"Pretty sure you're not old enough to be back here, either," I commented, giving Nick a look. "Legally. By the rules."

"I'm not drinking." Nick flashed me a smile more akin to a poker player laying down a winning hand than any kind of invitation. "I'm serving."

"Not very well." Inebriated Frat Boy slid in at the bar beside me. Based on his intact appearance, I assumed the bouncer had managed to defuse the fight in time. "How many rounds do I have to buy to get a little service around here?"

"You can have a little service once I have your keys." There was nothing overtly challenging in Nick's tone or his stance, but it was clear as glass that what he'd just said was nonnegotiable.

"My keys?" The frat boy leaned forward in what I could only assume was meant as a loom. "You think you can tell me not to drive?"

"I think," Nick replied, "that anyone who orders more than three beers in an hour gets to give me their keys. House rules."

I could have told the frat boy not to bother arguing—and not just because of the line of tension now visible in Nick's jaw. His brother was in a coma because of a drunk driver. *Campbell's father.*

"I want to talk to the manager," Frat Boy blustered.

Nick arched an eyebrow at him. "That would be me."

If Frat Boy had been in possession of even half the sense God gave a goose, he would have seen the glint of warning behind Nick's hazel eyes.

"Then I want to talk to the owner."

Nick placed his elbows on the bar and leaned his weight onto them. "Also me."

Now it was my turn for raised eyebrows. "You own this place?"

Nick cut a glance toward me and shrugged, his shoulder muscles pulling at the confines of his shirt. Frat Boy slammed his keys down on top of the bar.

Wordlessly, Nick took them. "What can I get you?"

I had to wait a full minute before he circled back around to me.

"Since when do you own a bar?" I asked.

"The owner put it up for sale a few weeks ago." Nick began making Victoria's remaining three drinks. "I had a friend who worked here. Nice guy. He had a new baby. Couldn't afford to be out of a job."

"So you bought the bar?" If I'd been talking to Walker, that might not have surprised me. But Nick? "Where did you . . ."

"Get the money?" Nick saved me the trouble of saying the *m*-word myself. "Your grandpa paid me off. You know what they say about blood money—it really does burn a hole in your pocket."

Blood money. I shouldn't have been surprised that the Ames family had paid him off. The senator's guilty plea would have opened them up to all kinds of liability on the accident that had put Nick's brother in a coma—not to mention the cover-up.

"Davis Ames is not my grandfather." Of all the ways I could have replied, that was the one that pushed its way past my lips without so much as a by-your-leave. In the past month, I'd thought a lot about what the revelation of my true parentage meant with respect to my relationship with Lily, with John David, with Campbell and Walker.

I hadn't thought about what it might mean for my relationship—or lack thereof—with Nick.

I'm not related to the person who put your brother in that coma. That blood money? It has nothing to do with me.

"Right," Nick replied tersely. "Forgive me for speaking an inconvenient truth."

"The truth," I said, my voice low and every muscle in my body tight, "is that my mom lied. I'm not an Ames." I swallowed, and the only thing that let me continue was the fact that the noise level in this place was so high. "I'm an Easterling."

Nick stared at me. For the first time since I'd recognized him standing behind the bar, I felt like he was really seeing me, and I reminded myself that when it came to the opposite sex, no good came of being seen.

"Easterling," Nick repeated. "Isn't that . . ."

My cousin's last name.

Before Nick could press me further, Victoria reappeared. With one last, long look at me, he turned to her and nodded to the drinks he'd just made. "I'll put these on your tab."

Someone else came up to place an order then, and whatever had been brewing between Nick and me—if anything was—receded, like a boiling pot set back to simmer.

Like a dance where neither person said a word.

Good, I thought as he turned his back on me. *It's just as well. I didn't come here to see him.* I needed to focus on Victoria. I doubted I'd made much of an "impression" tonight. This might be my one and only White Glove soiree.

My only chance to ask, "Are you related to Ana Gutierrez?"

"Why all of this interest in my relatives?" Victoria retorted.

"Ana Sofía Gutierrez," I reiterated. "She'd be in her thirties now. Your sister, maybe? Or a cousin?"

Before Victoria could reply—or decidedly *not* reply—someone pushed between the two of us, forcefully enough that I stood up from the stool I'd been sitting on.

"Where are my keys?" Frat Boy had returned. Based on his volume and tone, I had to wonder if he'd drunk the entire last round he'd purchased himself.

No way was Nick giving this guy back his keys.

"Call a car," I advised him. "Or get a ride."

The second he turned to face me, I knew that drawing his attention my way had been a mistake. He reached out, brushed the hair out of my face. I tried to step back, but his sweaty palm settled on my neck, holding me close.

"Hands to yourself." Victoria surprised me. Her voice was steel. Not pleasant—not even pretending. "Ask before you touch. Got it?"

Frat Boy ignored her. "What's your name?" he asked, his grip on my neck tightening as he brought his mouth closer to mine. I could feel his breath on my face.

I could smell it.

"Ask before you touch," I said lowly, "is a very good rule."

He was probably expecting me to push him away, but I didn't grow up at The Holler without learning to use expectations—not to mention momentum—to my advantage. As he leaned closer still, I hooked my ankle through a barstool, jerked it between us, grabbed his arm, and pulled.

Two seconds later, Frat Boy was sprawled on his stomach, and my heel was digging into his back.

"Nice," Victoria told me appreciatively. I felt and heard Nick leaping over the bar but didn't turn to look at him as he came to my side.

Let him wonder what the hell had just happened.

Let him remember that I wasn't just some poor little rich girl.

I applied a tad more pressure to the drunken a-hole beneath my foot and offered Victoria a smile. "I try."

LABOR DAY, 3:22 A.M.

"*S*awyer? I think I can feel my shoulder."

"Can you feel your hands?"

"No."

"What about your legs?"

"No."

"Can you move?"

"Let me check . . . Also no."

"Then what good could it possibly do us that you now have feeling in your shoulder?"

"I don't know, Sawyer. But I think I hear someone coming, and you're the one in charge of coming up with plans."

THIRTEEN WEEKS
(AND THREE DAYS) EARLIER

CHAPTER 9

*T*he Friday after Memorial Day was marked by the end of forty-eight hours of record-breaking summer storms, mildly less tension on Aunt Olivia's part as she packed for another weekend trip to the lake, and a cryptic text that Lily and I received at the exact same time.

@) - -'- , - - -

It took me several seconds to realize that if you held the phone sideways, the image resembled a rose. The text that arrived on the rose's heel was more immediately recognizable.

~ ~ ~ ~ ~ ~8<

A snake. Together, the two symbols left very little doubt about who the messages—and a third text that followed from the same blocked number—were from.

Falling Springs. 2:30 a.m. Tonight.

"What's Falling Springs?" I asked Lily.

She shushed me. Once she'd glanced back over her shoulder to verify that Aunt Olivia was still absorbed in cross-referencing two of her lists, Lily pulled me into the foyer. "Falling Springs is a cove on the other side of the lake," she said softly.

"Is it a *scandalous* cove?" I asked in an exaggerated whisper.

Lily realized halfway through nodding that I was joking. She pointed her manicured index finger at me in a manner that I assumed I was supposed to find forbidding.

"Okay, okay," I replied. "No jokes."

"It's not the cove associated with Falling Springs that's scandalous," Lily whispered in a tone that told me I'd been begrudgingly forgiven. "It's the cliffs."

That night, wearing swimsuits and the barest of cover-ups, we snuck down to the dock at two in the morning, lowered the smaller of the family's two boats into the water, and glided silently backward into the darkened cove. Picking up Campbell and Sadie-Grace on the way, we made for Falling Springs.

"So . . ." Campbell took up position next to me. "What's the plan?"

She'd kept her voice low, but I still cast a glance at Lily, who was focusing on driving the boat, and Sadie-Grace, who was "helping Lily focus," before I supplied a response. "The plan," I murmured, "is to talk to Victoria again."

I'd caught Campbell up on the conversation I'd had with Victoria Gutierrez at The Big Bang. Cam was as invested in finding Ana's baby—her half-sibling—as I was. And that meant that she was just as interested in what Victoria had to say.

"I didn't actually expect you to answer my question," Campbell murmured beside me. "It was more of a courtesy question, really. You were supposed to ask what *my* plan was."

Having seen one of Campbell's schemes up close and personal, I was almost afraid to ask. "What's your plan?"

"Talk to Victoria." She smiled, her teeth a flash of white in the dark. "No offense, but I'm better at talking than you are."

"Me too!" Sadie-Grace appeared between us. "I'm so good at talking that sometimes, once I start, I can't even stop!"

Neither Campbell nor I had a reply for that. We sank into silence, my brain working overtime calculating the likelihood that Cam could get more out of Victoria than I had.

"There," Lily said suddenly. She eased off the gas, allowing momentum to push the boat farther and farther into a long and narrow cove shaped—appropriately—like a snake.

Following Lily's gaze, I understood why she hadn't wanted her mother to even *hear* the words *Falling Springs*. I could make out five or six boats, each marked with a single light on the front, tied together in a line, front to front and back to back. As we approached, someone picked up a pole that one of the lights was fixed to, and used it to wave Lily to the far side of the line.

That wasn't the wild part.

Velvety darkness had settled over the water, but the bobbing lights on the boats and a white and glowing half-moon overhead cast just enough light to illuminate the nearby shore. Cliffs stretched up overhead, five or six stories at least. The farther up I looked, the steeper the incline got, until at the top, the drop-off was sudden and complete.

In isolation, what I was seeing wouldn't have struck me as ominous—or ill-advised. But as Lily had explained to me hours earlier, the term *Falling Springs* wasn't just synonymous with this cove and these cliffs.

It was a shorthand for the activities the cove and the cliffs were most known for. *Parties. Debauchery. Liquid courage.*

And *jumping.*

CHAPTER 10

"How many of you have jumped off Falling Springs before?"

Victoria stood on the front of the largest boat in the line, the one that was anchored and holding all of the others in place. Her voice traveled along the water. In the silence of the night, I could practically feel it all around us, even from my position three boats away.

"Show of hands," Victoria continued, before repeating her question. "How many of you have jumped off Falling Springs?"

Across the other six boats, I could hear motion but couldn't make out exactly how many Candidates' hands there were in the air. Beside me, Campbell's arm was fully extended.

"And how many of you have jumped off Falling Springs in the dark?" A light breeze caught Victoria's dark hair. In daylight, you might have been able to see shades of brown in it, but at night, with scant lighting, her long, thick waves might as well have been shadows.

Beside me, Campbell's hand was still raised. Lily shifted slightly. Even on a boat, after having snuck out and arguably committed grand theft naval, she sat with her knees together and her feet poised on the floor beneath us, just so. *Perfect posture. Perfect manners.*

Based on Victoria's questions, I could only conclude that those things wouldn't give my "cousin" much of an advantage here.

"And how many of you," Victoria continued with a cunning smile that I could hear in her voice, if not quite see on her face, "have jumped off Falling Springs *naked*?"

"When she said *naked*," Sadie-Grace whispered behind me, "what exactly do you think she meant?"

The four of us, along with our fellow Candidates, had made our way across the line of boats, climbing from one to the next until we reached the one closest to the shore. I was about to supply Sadie-Grace with the definition of the word *naked* when Hope saved me the trouble.

"You can leave everything but your swimsuits here, ladies," she announced. "You'll ditch the suits before you jump."

"Oh," Sadie-Grace said. "That kind of naked."

My primary concern had less to do with what we'd be wearing when we jumped than it did the height we'd be leaping from—and the depth of the water we'd be plunging into.

"Scared?" Campbell asked beside me.

"I don't do scared," I told her. "I also don't do broken necks."

"People jump off Falling Springs all the time." Lily held her head high as she stripped down to her swimsuit. I wasn't sure if she was trying to convince me or herself. "These aren't the only cliffs at the lake; they're just the only ones at a spot where the water gets deep really fast."

"I cannot help but notice that you ladies are still fully clothed." Victoria appeared beside us and zeroed in on me. "Of course, disrobing *is* optional. Totally your call."

The Candidates were many. The Chosen were few.

"Will you be joining us?" I asked her. Whether Campbell made good on her plan or I went with mine, *talking* required face time.

Victoria studied me for a moment. "That depends," she said with an arch of her eyebrow. "Are you four planning to jump from one of the lower ledges—or the top?"

Climbing to the top of Falling Springs required looping around and navigating a wide path through the brush and rocks along the side. Behind me, Campbell fell in beside Victoria. I let her, keeping my focus on the climb. The incline ranged from mild to the occasional vertical that required finding a steady tree limb or stone to grip for support. I'd just grabbed on to a rock and tested it as a handhold when Victoria latched her fingers onto its side.

I glanced back and saw Campbell trailing by five or six feet. I was betting that meant her attempts at conversation had been less than fruitful. I'd just about decided on a way to bring up Ana when Victoria saved me the trouble.

"I don't have a sister named Ana," she informed me without prelude. "Or a cousin. My mother is my father's second wife. He was in his sixties when I was born, so if you're looking for a Gutierrez in her thirties . . ."

She very purposefully trailed off and pulled past me. I barreled onward, pulling even with her an instant before the path narrowed to allow only one of us through at a time.

Victoria took the lead. "I will admit, something about the way you said that name—*Ana Sofía Gutierrez*—got me curious, so I called up the least overprotective and dictatorial of my many much-older brothers and asked if he knew of an Ana in the family."

"Got any rogue Anas running around?" I asked. I could see the ground leveling out ahead. We were almost to the top. Campbell, Sadie-Grace, and Lily were only a few feet behind.

"My brother hung up on me," Victoria informed me, "but not before ordering me to never so much as *think* that name again."

I didn't know Victoria, but I was willing to bet that her brother could not have stoked her curiosity more if he'd tried. I offered her a bit of information, in hopes that she'd be able to do something with it. "Ana was a Debutante with my mom. Midway through the year, the whole family moved."

"That would be my brother Javier and his wife, Freja," Victoria supplied, "which I know, because after Javier shut me down, I called my second-least overprotective and dictatorial older brother. He wouldn't tell me what happened, but he did tell me who Ana was."

"Black sheep of the family?" I guessed. It was a familiar story, close enough to my mom's—and mine—that the answer mattered to me, viscerally.

"I didn't even know Javier had a daughter," Victoria replied as we came to a plateau. "He won't talk about her. According to Rafi, no one in the family has heard a word from her in twenty years."

Twenty years. Since she got pregnant. Before I could say anything, Lily and Sadie-Grace made it to the top of the cliff and took up positions beside us. Campbell followed, and without so much as a glance back at Victoria and me, she walked over to stand right at the cliff's edge.

"What do we do with our suits?" Lily inquired politely. You would have thought she was asking about a coat closet, not the particulars of how and where we should strip.

"Leave your suits here." Victoria gestured to the base of a large oak tree. "I'll make sure someone fetches them for you. *After.*"

Sadie-Grace was the first one to ditch her bikini. Campbell was next, followed by Lily, whose experience with *Secrets* made her strangely adept at casually positioning her arms for maximal coverage.

"Pretend you're getting a massage," she advised me.

I made a face. Massages, saunas, spa days, and casual nudity were all things I could have done entirely without. But if I wanted an opportunity to get closer to the Gutierrez family, Victoria was it. And if I wanted to stay in Victoria's orbit . . .

I needed the White Gloves.

So I got naked. And I jumped.

CHARLOTTE, LIV, AND JULIA
SUMMER BEFORE SENIOR YEAR
TWENTY-FIVE YEARS EARLIER

"*J*ulia. *Joo-lee-uh.*" Liv drew out the name.

Charlotte tried to catch Julia's gaze to impart a silent warning, but the other girl, in true Julia style, didn't have time for such nonsense.

Have it your way, Jules, Charlotte thought.

"Are you drunk?" Julia cut straight to the meat of the situation as she ignored Charlotte in favor of Liv.

Story of Charlotte's life.

"Julia Ames." Liv waved regally at Julia, like she was wearing a tiara and riding a Bison Day float, not slumped up against her father's tombstone. "Took you long enough to get here."

Julia finally spared a look for Charlotte. "Is she serious?"

"*Deadly* serious." Liv beat Charlotte to an answer. "Get it? Deadly."

"Liv." Charlotte cut in before Julia could reply. Julia Ames was not a particularly sensitive individual. She was smart. She was merciless. She was Liv's *best* friend. "I know you're hurting, Livvy, but, sweetie . . ."

Liv stood—without stumbling, with far more grace than she should have been able to muster. "I'm not feeling *sweet.* I'm tired of *sweet.* Aren't you, Julia?" Liv barely paused. "I'm tired of the rules. I'm tired of this place. I want . . ."

Charlotte watched as Liv spread her arms out to the sides, like she was soaking in the sun. Like she could fly.

"I want everything." Liv closed her eyes. "People live, and they follow the rules, and then they die. Don't you want more than that, Jules?" Liv's voice dropped to a whisper as her hands fell back to her side. "I do."

"We should get her home." Julia ignored Liv in favor of speaking directly to Charlotte—for once.

We should, Charlotte thought. *We should take Liv home and put her to bed.* The grief was intense now, but it would get better. Liv would get better.

And things will go right back to the way they've always been.

Charlotte stepped toward Liv, responding to her—not Julia. "I do," Charlotte said. "I want more, Liv. Your daddy said you could do anything you wanted to do in this life. Just this once . . ."

Charlotte knew this was a bad idea, but there was something buzzing inside her—power, maybe, the kind that came from knowing that she could finally break out of the role in which she'd been cast when her family moved to town in the fourth grade.

She didn't have to be the good girl. The sensitive one. The *sidekick.*

She didn't have to be Liv's second-best friend.

"Just this once," Charlotte repeated, "I want to break all of the rules."

CHAPTER 11

The summer air was warm, even in the dead of night. But as I bulleted downward, gathering speed, goose bumps rose on my skin. I didn't have time to think about all the reasons that jumping off a cliff naked, in the dark, into a blackened body of water was a bad idea. My feet hit first, but I felt the sting of contact ten times more in my arms when they slapped the surface of the water, and my entire body plunged down into the deep. I'd thought it was dark outside, but that was nothing compared to the sensation of being completely submerged, unable to breathe, feeling my movement slowing, all too aware how easy it would be to forget which direction, in the pitch black, was up.

I kicked. It was only a matter of seconds—could have been two, could have been twenty—before I broke the surface. I gasped for air, even though I knew on some level that I hadn't gone without it for long. From the moment I'd jumped until now, time had seemed to stretch sideways. My heart was thumping. I could hear other girls breaking the surface all around me, gasping and giggling. Adrenaline surged through my body.

And before I knew it, I was laughing.

"Anyone want to go again?"

•••

We stayed in the water until someone had fetched our clothes. Most of the other Candidates had jumped off one of the two lower ledges. Victoria was the only senior member of the White Gloves who'd joined us at the top.

"That was . . ." Lily was pulling her swimsuit on beside me on the shore. They'd turned off all of the lights on the boat but one—for modesty's sake.

Because we're all so very modest.

"That was *amazing*." Lily was giddy. "I thought we were going to die!"

"I didn't," Sadie-Grace said seriously. "I thought the rest of us were going to be fine, but Campbell was going to die."

"What?" Campbell demanded. "Why me?"

"I thought that maybe you had a heart condition that you didn't know about." Sadie-Grace paused. "Is this what Greer means when she says I let my imagination get the best of me?"

"No," I replied before Campbell could. "What Greer means is that maybe you *imagined* her wearing a fake pregnancy belly. She'd give anything to convince you that you don't know what you know."

In the ultimate irony, Sadie-Grace's stepmother—the third participant in my mom's pregnancy pact, who'd lost her baby and hung the others out to dry—was currently faking a pregnancy. None of us had any idea how she thought that would work out, given that her August "due date" was quickly approaching.

"It's not Greer's fault she's grumpy." Sadie-Grace was the world's most understanding stepdaughter. "Faking the third trimester is *exhausting*."

"You have *got* to tell your dad," Lily said for probably the hundredth time.

Campbell sidled up beside me.

"Later," I told her quietly. *I'll tell you what Victoria told me later.*

"Everybody decent?" Hope didn't wait for a response to the question she'd just called out before she yelled, "Let there be light!"

One by one, the boat lights came back on—and then some. An instant later, music was booming from the direction of the boats.

There wasn't much of a shoreline directly beneath the cliffs, but on either side, girls stood shivering on rocky ground. I could feel bits of sand and gravel pressing themselves into my own feet. The beat of the music was impossible to ignore.

Every inch of skin on my body felt *alive.*

"The Candidates are many," Victoria called out. She was standing in the light now, her black hair soaked, the weight of the water pulling it straight. "The Chosen . . ."

"Are few." The last words were yelled by more than one person.

"You know who else is few?" Campbell murmured beside me. "People with ovaries enough to jump off the . . ."

Top. My brain filled in the end of her sentence, but instead of finishing it, she screamed. The sound was horrible—piercing and guttural and without end.

"Campbell?" My heart rate had just stabilized, but I could feel it ticking upward, feel the chill of something in the air, the way I had on the way down.

Beside me, Sadie-Grace started screaming, too.

"Oh dear," Lily said, preternaturally calm in a way that freaked me out more than the screams. "That's . . ."

The rest of the sentence caught in her throat. I followed her gaze, to the place where the lake met the shore. Water sloshed gently against the rocks, and scattered among them . . .

. . . was a skull.

LABOR DAY, 3:23 A.M.

"She's almost here, Sawyer!"

"Close your eyes."

"What?"

"Just do it, Sadie-Grace. Pretend you're still unconscious. Until we can move, until we can fight back, the name of the game is *stall.*"

ELEVEN WEEKS
(AND *THREE DAYS*) EARLIER

CHAPTER 12

*T*here were numerous downsides to discovering human remains while cliff-jumping, naked, in the middle of the night. For example: explaining to the cops the circumstances surrounding the discovery and becoming acutely aware that your body and *the* body had been in the lake—in close proximity—together. Two weeks had passed, and I still didn't feel like I'd showered enough.

I also hadn't stopped wondering about the corpse—how old it was, *who* it was, how long it had been in the depths of Regal Lake before the storms had dredged it up.

As a bonus, I'd also spent the past two weeks "not grounded." To say that my aunt had not been pleased when the Lake Patrol had escorted us home that night would have been an understatement. Since Lily and I were legally adults, Aunt Olivia had contented herself with very pointedly *not* scolding us and *not* punishing us, while simultaneously foisting so much family togetherness upon us that leaving home without her company had quickly become a fond memory and nothing more.

I'd taken to hiding out on the roof just to get a moment of peace. That was where I was when my phone rang. I answered it quickly, lest it announce my location to the occupants of the house. "Hello?"

I half expected it to be one of the White Gloves.

"Sawyer." The voice on the other end of the phone paused after saying my name. "It's Nick."

The sound of his voice had me flashing back to The Big Bang and the moments after he'd jumped the bar.

"So I'm not *Miss Taft* anymore?" I asked pointedly, remembering the exact expression on Nick's face as he'd taken the drunk frat boy off my hands: pissed at him, reluctantly appreciative of me and my ability to damn well take care of myself.

"Once someone starts a bar fight in my establishment *and* offers pointers on my tossing-out-dirtbags technique, we're pretty much on a first-name basis by default."

"I didn't start the fight. I finished it. And if you keep tossing people out like that, you're just asking for a case of tennis elbow."

"Message received," Nick told me. "Loud and clear."

We descended into silence then. I thought about the way he'd looked tossing Frat Boy out on his ass. The clenched jaw, every muscle in his body tight.

"You still there?" he asked on the other end of the line.

"Yup," I replied. After another second or two, I issued a reminder. "You called me."

Another pause, shorter than the last. "I need a favor."

Of course you do, I thought. Of course he hadn't called just to reminisce about my endearing knack for self-defense. He'd had my number for months. If he'd wanted to call—at any point in time— he could have.

"What kind of favor?" I asked.

"Before we get into the specifics, I'd like to remind you that you owe me."

"Debatable."

"You don't really believe that."

He was right. After everything I'd helped Campbell put him through last spring, I *did* owe him. "What do you need, Nick?"

He replied, but I couldn't make out what he was saying.

"I'm sorry," I told him, "but I don't speak incoherent mumbling."

"There's a party next weekend," Nick gritted out. He did not appear to be relishing that statement. "A fund-raiser Davis Ames is throwing at the Arcadia hotel." He said *Ames* like it was a curse word. "I need you to go with me."

I'd never been much for dating, only partially because I'd never been the kind of girl that boys dated. I could handle catcalls and propositions and rumors about what might or might not have happened under the bleachers, but anything beyond that was virgin territory.

No pun intended.

"Sawyer?" Nick prompted.

"And here I thought you were going to ask me to plan a jewel heist," I quipped, because quipping was easier than thinking about what he *had* asked in any level of detail.

"If I wanted to plan a jewel heist," he retorted, "I would have called Campbell."

Hearing him say her name didn't hurt, even knowing their history. *Thank God.* My utter lack of an urge to wince reinforced for me that I was still on the right side of the fine line I'd spent my life skirting. Flirting was fine. Thinking was fine. Physicality, even, I could handle.

Just not feelings.

"Why *didn't* you call Campbell?" I asked. They'd been each other's method of blowing off steam, once, and if I owed him, she owed him *big*.

"Because," came the reply. "I called you."

That—and the way he'd said it, his voice softening—wasn't something I had any intention of letting my mind linger on for long.

Luckily, Nick chose that moment to enlighten me as to why he wanted to go to some party badly enough to call in a favor. "I have a sister. She's fifteen. Lives with our grandmother. Wants to do the stupid Debutante thing in a couple of years."

He sounded so disgruntled at the idea that I grinned. "And this requires me going to a party with you why?" I asked.

"I have money now." He sounded disgruntled about that, too. "I just don't have the connections she needs. Or the reputation."

"Are you asking me to make you respectable?" I said, enjoying this more than I should have. "What is this, a Jane Austen novel?"

"I like Jane Austen," he replied evenly. "And you owe me."

I did—and as long as I owed him, that was all this had to be. A debt I could pay. Maybe we'd get another dance in.

Maybe I could get him out of my system.

"You have yourself a deal," I said. *"Mr. Ryan."*

Before he could respond to my use of his last name, Aunt Olivia called out for Lily and me from inside the house, and I stifled a groan.

"What was that?" Nick asked.

My traitor lips ticced upward. "Goodbye, Nick."

I hung up just in time to hear Aunt Olivia trill out, "Who wants to make personalized memo boards? And then I'll show y'all the absolutely *darling* little outfits I got for Greer's shower."

My desire to make a memo board for a dorm room I hadn't even agreed to live in yet ranked only slightly above my utter lack of inclination to attend a baby shower for a baby who I knew for a fact *did not exist.* I'd been expecting Sadie-Grace's stepmother to have a "miscarriage" for months. When we'd received the invitation to the shower, I'd even tried telling Aunt Olivia that Greer was faking her pregnancy.

Aunt Olivia had shushed me. *"Don't be silly, Sawyer. I'm sure you simply misunderstood."* Personally, I thought witnessing a woman strapping on a fake pregnancy belly was the kind of thing that was pretty darn hard to "misunderstand," but Aunt Olivia wouldn't hear a word about it. *"To think that any woman would do such a thing! Pshaw. I've had enough ridiculousness for one summer, thank you very much. We're going to that shower. End of story."*

"Don't you think the girls have been punished enough?" Uncle J.D. asked, right inside the window. As much as I agreed with the sentiment, the fatherly tone with which he'd said *girls*, plural, hit me like the sound of fingernails on a chalkboard.

"Are you implying that time spent with me is a punishment, John?" Aunt Olivia only called him by his first name when she was annoyed.

"They're eighteen, Liv. Almost nineteen."

"I'm always Liv when you want something," Aunt Olivia said quietly.

"God forbid I try to talk to you like—"

"Like I'm *her*?"

I'd only heard them fight once before, about some kind of money problem.

Like I'm her. Like I'm her. Like I'm her. Aunt Olivia's words repeated on a loop in my head. Who was she talking about? Did she think he was having some kind of affair? Or worse, had she found out what he'd done with my mother?

"Keep your voice down, Olivia." J.D. followed his own advice, lowering his volume so much that I had to strain to hear him, even though they were standing right next to the window now.

"So I'm *Olivia* again?"

The question was met with silence—and then the sound of footsteps.

"Where are you going?" she called after him.

This time, my "uncle" actually answered his wife's question, his words shot through with an emotion I couldn't quite peg. "I'm going to the lake. If you're going to keep the family home, someone has to check on the boats."

CHAPTER 13

J.D. still wasn't back the next morning when Aunt Olivia, Lily, and I left for Greer's shower.

"Smile, Sawyer," Aunt Olivia instructed me as she rang the doorbell. "You're such a pretty girl when you smile."

"She's right," a voice said from the bushes. "You are."

I jumped and turned to see Campbell's cousin—and Sadie-Grace's boyfriend—three-quarters covered in shrubbery.

"Boone Mason," Aunt Olivia exclaimed. "Is that you?"

That was clearly a rhetorical question, but Boone didn't let that stop him. "Yes, ma'am."

"What are you doing in the bushes?" Lily asked, putting a finer point on her mama's question.

"Moral support," Boone replied solemnly. "No men allowed inside, but the bushes are more of a gray area."

"Go on with you," Aunt Olivia told him, but she was smiling.

Before I could tell Boone that nobody considered the landscaping a "gray area," Sadie-Grace opened the front door. She greeted us, sounding like a mix between a robot and a pageant girl. "Hello! We're so happy you could make it. Please come in."

"Don't mind me," Boone stage-whispered. "I'll just be out here, moral-supporting."

Sadie-Grace's feet settled themselves into fifth position, and I considered the fact that she might actually need Boone here—bushes and all. "Please," she repeated, maniacally cheerful. "Come in!"

I'd never been to a baby shower before, but based on what I'd seen in movies, I'd assumed there would be finger foods and an overuse of pastels. What I got was a trained waitstaff serving petits fours and champagne. They offered the latter mixed with "just a smidgen of peach nectar" for those in the mood for a Bellini, or with a "healthy helping of white-peach punch" for those of us too young to drink.

And those of us faking pregnancies.

Greer made a show of taking a teeny, tiny sip from her crystal flute as she mingled. "Olivia, it's so good to see you. Lily, honey, that dress is just darling."

I could not help but notice that Sadie-Grace's stepmother didn't comment on *my* dress. Perhaps her ironclad sense of self-preservation was warning her that the only thing keeping me from blowing this whole charade to smithereens was discretion, which she probably suspected—correctly—was not my forte.

"Miss Olivia." Campbell approached us and greeted my aunt with her sweetest smile. "We've been missing y'all up at the lake."

Campbell and I had talked exactly once in the past two weeks. I'd caught her up on Ana's relation to Victoria and the fact that Ana had been estranged from their family for years. Based on the texts Cam had sent me since then, I was fairly certain she'd spent most of her free time trying to track Ana Sofía Gutierrez down online.

To no avail.

"Campbell." Aunt Olivia gave her a side hug. "Is your mama here, sweetie?"

"Mama sends her regrets," Campbell lied smoothly. She turned to Sadie-Grace. "I'd just love to see the nursery." She gave me a look so pointed it could have pierced ears. "Wouldn't you, Sawyer?"

She knows something, I thought.

"We'd *all* love to see the nursery," Lily said before I could reply. Given that she hadn't figured out the roof trick yet, I could only assume that she was dying to get away from her mama.

"After I show y'all the nursery," Sadie-Grace said as she led us through the party and up the stairs, "you three can help me practice my toast. I'm the hostess. I have to toast Greer and the baby."

"The baby," I emphasized, *"who does not exist."*

Right on cue, we came to the threshold of the nursery. I'd thought the situation with Greer's "pregnancy" had already reached maximum ridiculousness, but as I took in the infant wonderland spread out before me, I could only conclude that I'd been wrong.

"It looks like Pottery Barn Kids threw up in here." Campbell was, as ever, a sensitive soul.

"It's lovely," Lily corrected. And it *was.* The room was fully furnished, complete with an antique rocking horse, a mobile, window treatments, and framed pictures above the crib. The walls had been painted a very pale blue. The changing table was already outfitted with supplies.

"Greer does know she's not *actually* having a baby, right?" I said.

Sadie-Grace rose to the tips of her toes, a sure sign her anxiety levels were rising, too. "Maybe?"

I could sense a *rond de jambe* coming on.

"You need to tell your father the truth," Lily told her yet again.

"But he's so *happy* about the baby. . . ."

"Forget Greer." Campbell had clearly expended the sum total

of her ability to pretend to care about the nursery, the "baby," or Sadie-Grace's family drama. "Who wants to know what I found out about the Lady of Regal Lake?"

That wasn't what I'd expected when Campbell had suggested we'd come up here.

"The who?" Lily responded.

"That's what people are calling the body we found. The Lady of the Lake. She's female, obviously." Campbell stepped into the nursery and turned back to face us, like a player on a stage. "The authorities think the storms we've been having dredged her up. I heard they dated the remains back a couple of decades." Campbell met my eyes. "Female," she reiterated. "Dead around twenty years."

It took me a moment to realize what she was getting at. *Twenty years ago, Ana Gutierrez left town. Her family hasn't heard from her. There's not a trace of her online.*

"Am I missing something here?" Lily asked, looking between Campbell and me.

"What could you possibly be missing?" Campbell asked innocently, knowing quite well that her tone would stoke Lily's interest more than quell it. "Aside from my brother, who I'm pretty sure has only been to visit you twice in the past two weeks."

"Where did you hear about the body?" I asked Campbell, saving Lily the trouble of trying to come up with a retort.

Cam toyed with the ends of her hair. "The local sheriff's department is trying to keep a tight lid on the investigation, but they're a total podunk operation, and since my family has been exiled to living at Regal full-time, I've taken the opportunity to make some friends. Deputy-type friends."

I waited for Lily to realize that Campbell might have a reason beyond having discovered the body to want an inside look at the investigation, but that didn't seem to register. Without another word to Campbell, Lily turned her back on the conversation and walked over to get a closer look at one of the window treatments.

Cam's comment about Walker must have really gotten to her.

"Nice fabric," Lily commented, touching the curtains. "What's the nursery theme?" In true Taft-woman style, she answered her own question. "Geometric shapes. It's understated, as themes go."

"I wanted elephants," Sadie-Grace replied. "And possibly giraffes, but Greer said—"

"That her entire pregnancy is a hoax?" I suggested.

"Is that really your biggest concern right now?" Campbell stepped up behind me and whispered directly into the back of my head, her voice too low for the other two to hear. "Not the fact that the body we found could be the girl my dad knocked up?"

Ana's family hasn't heard from her, I thought. *That doesn't mean she's missing.* But still, the muscles in my stomach tightened, and a ball of nausea rose in the back of my throat. What if Campbell was right?

Female, dead twenty years.

"Sawyer." Lily was staring out the window. She turned to face me, looking a bit like she'd just taken a rapier to the gut. "Do you know who I just saw walking up the sidewalk?" Another question to which I was quite certain she would supply her own answer.

Lily didn't disappoint. "Your mama."

CHAPTER 14

More than once since the night of my debutante ball, I'd thought that if my mom had been up front with me, I could have gotten past the choices she'd made when she was my age, regardless of how messed up those choices were. But she'd lied to me about it. It was hard not to feel like that made me just one more person Ellie Taft was willing to manipulate and mislead and use.

I don't want to talk to her, I thought, staring down at the sidewalk below. *I don't want to see her.*

So why did I bolt from the nursery and head for the stairs? The doorbell chimed. Greer went to open it just as I arrived. She froze when she saw who was on the other side.

"Greer," my mom drawled. "You look fantastic. Why, you've barely put on a pound. If it weren't for that baby bump, I'd swear you weren't pregnant at all."

Subtle, Mom. Real subtle.

As if she'd heard my thoughts, my mom turned to look at me. I could see her wanting to say something, on the verge of saying something—but she didn't get the chance.

"Ellie." Greer's grip on the door tightened, but she didn't shut it.

One did not slam the door in the face of one of Lillian Taft's daughters—in front of witnesses.

My mom had grown up in this world. She knew how the game was played, but as she maneuvered her way through the room, chitchatting with other guests, she kept at least half of her attention on me. When the party moved to what the Waters family referred to as "the Great Room," she fell in beside me and spoke. "You look good, Sawyer. Happy."

Happy? She thought I looked happy? *Happy that you're here? Happy that you slept with Uncle J.D.? Happy to have recently discovered a decades-old corpse?*

I couldn't even muster a proper response.

The Great Room furniture had been removed and replaced with a cluster of eight-top tables, each set with different china. I only half heard Greer telling people that this set was her mother's, and that set was her grandmother's, and oh, that one belonged to Great-Grandmother Waters.

Why are you here, Mom? What do you want?

My mother took a seat at the table with the Waters china and stared up at me expectantly. Before I could decide whether to join her or back away, Aunt Olivia appeared beside me and steered me into a seat, placing herself squarely between my mom and me.

She must have sensed that this could go to hell in a handbasket—fast.

A woman I recognized took a seat across from Aunt Olivia. "It's been an age," Julia Ames—Boone's mother—declared. "How have you been, Liv?"

"She goes by Olivia now." My mom could weaponize smiles

with the best of them. She'd told me once that after their father had died, Aunt Olivia had run away. Back then, she'd gone by Liv. When she'd come back, she was Olivia, practically perfect in every way and not interested in sharing her sister's grief in the least.

She abandoned you, so you slept with her husband. If my mom was here to give me excuses, I didn't want to hear them.

Campbell took the seat on my left. "You're not happy to see her," she murmured. "I get it. Believe me, I do, Sawyer. But you have to talk to your mama."

Campbell Ames was the last person in the world I expected to be brokering parent-child reunions—especially given that she *knew* my mom had lied to me.

And then Campbell made her reasoning apparent. "See if she knows anything about Ana."

There's no logical reason to think that the Lady of the Lake is Ana Gutierrez. I got why Campbell had gone there—Ana had been pregnant with Sterling Ames's child, and we all knew Cam's dad wasn't exactly a trustworthy guy. The fact that his teenage mistress had seemingly disappeared didn't look particularly good.

But the past year had taught me to look before I leaped.

"I don't know how Boone broke his pinkie finger!" Sadie-Grace's perky statement snapped me back into the moment. She appeared to be addressing Boone's mother. "I'm sure whatever he was doing at the time, it was totally PG."

"Sawyer." My mom cleared her throat. "Could I borrow you for a minute?"

Brunch was just being served. Mini muffins, mini cinnamon rolls, mini quiches, and mini cucumber sandwiches. So many tiny foods, so many reasons *not* to talk to my mother.

"Please."

A flash of vulnerability crossed her face, and my chest tightened. Campbell gave me a look, and I stood. I couldn't undo a lifetime of loving the only parent I'd ever had—and for better or worse, I couldn't ignore her forever.

CHAPTER 15

"Well?" I said. I'd gone outside. My mom had followed. Now the two of us were standing in the backyard. The only sound, other than my question, was the tinkling of water over the infinity edge in the pool. "Why are you here?" I asked.

My mom caught my gaze and held it. "You're not allowed to hate me." She softened the declaration with a small, lopsided smile. "I've thought about it, and I've decided. I love you too much. You're not allowed to hate me."

She'd never had any trouble telling me that she loved me. Even when she was barely more than a kid herself, even when our little family was struggling—I had always known that I was loved.

"Am I allowed to be upset that you lied to me?" I asked. I didn't want to feel like my throat had turned to sandpaper. I didn't trust the sting in my eyes.

"You could be," my mom offered. "You could be *extremely* upset with me—or you could forget about that for a minute and tell me what happened at Regal Lake."

That brought me up short, and for a moment, I let myself really wonder if Campbell was onto something. If the body *was* Ana.

"You heard about the body?" I asked.

"I've been calling Lillian every week. To check on you." My mom and Lillian had issues. I had the sense I was supposed to take those phone calls as some kind of grand gesture, but it fell flat.

"Lillian said you girls were the ones who found the body." My mom reached out to touch my shoulder. "That couldn't have been fun, Sawyer."

I stepped back from her touch. "Campbell thinks it might be Ana."

Whatever she'd been expecting from me, it wasn't that. She stared at me. When her response did come, it was only two words. "My Ana?"

I hadn't realized until that second that as ill-conceived and ridiculous as the pact was, it meant something to her. *Ana* meant something to her. Once upon a time, Greer had, too.

"Her family hasn't heard from her in twenty years," I said, feeling the weight of that more strongly now than I had when Victoria had told me.

"If she wasn't with her family . . ." My mom looked like I'd hit her. "If she didn't leave town with them, why didn't she come to me?"

"Did she know where you were?" I asked. "Where you went when you got kicked out?"

"No." My mom's hand went to her stomach, like she was pregnant still. "I had to leave town so fast—but she had my number. When Greer lost her baby, Ana and I agreed to tell our parents we were pregnant. We picked a night. I told Lillian. You know how that went." She shook her head. "I called Ana afterward, but her phone was disconnected. I went by her house—her entire family was gone. They just . . . moved. Her grandfather was some big deal in Dallas. I always assumed Ana's parents went back home. Ana, too."

Not Ana.

"She never got in touch with me, Sawyer." My mom pressed her lips together. "Why would you think that body is hers?"

I don't think that, I told myself. *Campbell does.*

"Davis Ames knew Ana was pregnant," I said out loud. I swallowed. "He told me that he handled the situation." Looking back, that conversation sounded even worse.

"Not the kind of thing he'd tell anyone if he'd killed her," my mom pointed out, sounding incredulous and overwrought and, somehow, like she was about to start cracking jokes.

"That wasn't what I thought he meant, either," I said.

My mom got very quiet. "Ana wouldn't have gotten an abortion, if that's what you're implying. She wanted that baby. She loved her."

The way you loved me. I couldn't keep that from hurting, but I didn't let myself dwell on it. "Ana's baby was a girl?" I asked.

"I don't know," my mom admitted. "I was further along than she was. It took Ana longer to get pregnant."

I wondered how many times she'd slept with Campbell's father. I wondered if she'd loved him. But my mom was still talking, so I didn't ask.

"Ana didn't know *she* was having a girl. The baby could have been a boy, I suppose." There was something almost wistful in her expression. "We just always imagined having girls."

I had to turn away, then, from the reminder that my mom had wanted me. She'd *imagined* me. Hell, she'd practically willed me into being. She'd imagined me being a girl. She'd imagined having a person who would always love her, no matter what.

I love you too much. You're not allowed to hate me.

I walked away. I didn't go far, just a few steps closer to the pool, but that was enough that when I turned back to face my mom, I could see past her into the Great Room. Through the massive, floor-to-ceiling windows, I could see Greer opening presents. As I watched, she picked up a white package adorned with a pale blue bow.

"Do you think Greer knows anything?" I asked. "About what happened to Ana?" It was easier to talk about that, to tell myself that I was doing this for Campbell as much as for myself.

"No," my mom said. "She wouldn't have. Ana and I tried to support her when she lost her baby, but she wasn't even sad. She told us we were on our own, that she didn't need us anymore. . . ."

And now she's having a fake baby shower for a fake baby.

"Are you ever going to forgive me, Sawyer?"

It would have been easier if the raw emotion in my mom's voice didn't sound so much like everything I'd been feeling myself.

Don't think about it. Don't think about her. I breathed in and held the breath. *Think about Davis Ames. Think about the fact that he's the one throwing the fund-raiser Nick needs an escort to. Think about the fact that the old man "handled" the situation with Ana.*

Think about the fact that he may have been the last person who saw her alive.

I let out a breath and walked past my mom toward the house. I answered her question but didn't turn around. "I don't know."

LABOR DAY, 3:25 A.M.

"Is she gone?"

"I think so. For now."

"You know how I said I could feel my shoulder? Good news: I think I can almost, maybe, kind of, sort of feel a tiny bit of my arm."

TEN WEEKS
(AND *TWO DAYS*) EARLIER
CHAPTER 16

*A*rcadia was a lakeside resort. From what I'd gathered, it had been built in the fifties. Stepping through the grand entrance into the lobby felt like stepping back in time. Granted, part of that was probably what we were wearing. Aunt Olivia might not have been a fan of the lake—or the activities Lily and I had partaken of on our last trip up here—but she and Lillian were both big fans of theme parties. Tonight's fund-raiser was Big Band themed, and they'd insisted we go vintage.

Full-on, straight from the forties, stop-and-stare *vintage*.

My dress was red, with buttons at the waist and capped sleeves. Lily's was a floral print. Both had skirts that flared and modest, fitted tops. Our hair was curled. We were given bright lipstick. The only concession, other than knee-length dresses, that Aunt Olivia had made to the fact that this was a lake party was that neither one of us was wearing heels.

Sandals, apparently, fully qualified as lake formal.

I had the general sense that the tuxedo Nick was wearing did not. He stood near a column at the side of the lobby, his back toward the door. Even from behind, I recognized him in a heartbeat: his stance, the way he had his hands shoved into his pockets, the lines of his body, only partially masked by the tuxedo jacket.

Everything about him screamed that he'd rather take that jacket off.

Tamping down on that thought, I excused myself from the family as they made their way to the ballroom and started toward him.

Lily followed. "You didn't tell me you had a date tonight." That might have come off as an admonition, if she hadn't sounded so intrigued.

"It's not a date," I told her as Nick shifted to lean against the column. "More of an arrangement."

Nick turned toward us moments before we reached him, like he'd known exactly where I was from the moment I walked in the door. He let his eyes roam over my dress, then glanced briefly at Lily's.

"Nice outfits." He balled his hands into fists inside his pockets. "I'm overdressed."

The fact that I'd noticed what his hands were doing inside his pockets probably meant that I was watching him a little too closely. *Too close for comfort.*

"A pair of khakis would have been just fine," Lily told him delicately. "Things aren't as formal up here. You could try taking off the jacket?"

Yes, please. I quashed that reaction and shifted to problem-solving mode. "Forget the jacket. What clothes do you have in your car?"

Nick ended up in a pair of jeans and his white undershirt—shirt tucked in, hair teased back. Under Lily's instruction, I did the teasing.

"A little more," she told me.

Nick's neck was bent, his head bowed. As I brought my hand back up, he angled his eyes toward mine. I tried to view this situation objectively. Objectively, he had the longest eyelashes I'd ever seen on a guy. Objectively, his expression was annoyed, borderline pained.

Objectively, that expression changed when I touched his hair.

"Use both hands," Lily said, and I did, pushing my fingers along his scalp, separating locks of hair until Lily decreed that we'd reached ideal levels of mussed.

Nick didn't look away from me once, and if I'd let myself, I could have imagined exactly what it would feel like to curl my fingers in his hair, tighten my grip, pull his head back.

Bring my lips to his.

Instead, I stepped to the side, trying not to think too much about my hands and where they'd been a moment before.

"If anyone asks," Lily told Nick, "you're James Dean in *Rebel Without a Cause*."

"Wrong decade," Nick responded.

I shrugged and offered him a crooked grin. "That's how you know you're a rebel."

He *almost* smiled back.

"It's better than the tux and theme-adjacent," Lily said firmly. "As long as you're with Sawyer, you'll be fine."

"And what am I supposed to do . . ." Nick glanced at me, and I wondered if he was thinking about the feel of my hands in his hair. ". . . with Sawyer?"

"Mingle." Lily smiled softly. "A dance or two or seven. Maybe a stroll out onto the patio." She leaned her head slightly to one side. "Just pass the time."

I turned my attention to her, keenly aware that Nick's was still on me. "Are you talking about us," I asked Lily, "or you and Walker?"

"Walker Ames?" Nick said. I didn't need to glance his way to know that his expression had darkened.

"Is it so wrong to want things to be the way they used to be?" Lily asked me wistfully. "For just one night, I want Walker to forget about—"

"Lily." I cut in before she could say anything about Walker's father or the events of the past year. She stared at me for a moment, then glanced toward Nick. Her brown eyes widened.

"I apologize," she said. "I wasn't thinking about your brother, Nick. You must think I'm absolutely—"

"No," Nick said, interrupting her. He looked down at the ground, then back up at Lily. "It's not wrong to want things to be the way they used to be," he told her gently, "just for one night."

I liked him more for biting back his resentment of the Ames family and assuring her of that than I'd liked anyone, regardless of gender, in a very long time. Somehow, that felt a hell of a lot more dangerous than running my hands through his hair.

As the three of us made our way back to the lobby and the double doors leading to the ballroom, neither Nick nor I said a word. He stopped right outside of the doors. "I hate parties," he grumbled. Then he pushed the door inward. "And I am the best damn brother in the world."

As the dull roar of the gala washed over us like a wave, I couldn't help thinking that maybe he was.

"Don't be such a baby," I told him. Once upon a time, I might have been right there with him, grumbling and feeling ten kinds of out of place, but tonight, I found that I didn't hate parties at all.

The first thing I saw inside the ballroom was the band. A male singer was crooning. A female singer with turquoise hair stepped up to the mic beside him. My thoughts flicked briefly to the dance

Nick and I had shared, but before I could even entertain the idea of a repeat, I saw a familiar figure on the dance floor that banished all other thoughts from my head: Walker Ames—and he was dancing with a girl I immediately recognized as Victoria Gutierrez.

I'd been told once that the Ballad of Lily Easterling and Walker Ames was epic. At the moment, a more appropriate descriptor would have been *awkward*. Lily was too polite to kick up a fuss about one little dance. Walker was too charming to let on that he realized, 100 percent, that she was bothered.

The entire dynamic set Nick's teeth on edge. The thin white shirt he wore made it easy for me to see the tension in his muscles every time Walker so much as opened his mouth. Walker wasn't the Ames who'd put Nick's brother in a coma—but for a year, Walker had believed that he was and hadn't done a thing to make it right.

I couldn't expect Nick to get over a thing like that. How was it Victoria had referred to him? *Rough around the edges. Angry at the world.*

"Come on," I said, placing a hand on the back of Nick's shoulder. "Let's go."

A moment passed, and then I felt his shoulder muscles loosen under my touch. He let me lead him away from Walker—and Lily.

"Is this the part where we mingle?" he asked gruffly. "Or dance?"

I'd come into this evening open to the possibility of a second dance, but that was before I'd touched his hair. Before I'd noticed those long, long lashes.

Before he'd been kind to Lily, even though it meant fighting back his resentment toward Walker.

"Beats me," I said flippantly. "If you were looking for a tour guide who actually understands high society, you could have chosen better."

That got a begrudging smile out of him. "I think I chose okay."

Objectively, that wasn't high praise. So why did it feel like it was?

Ultimately, the two of us didn't mingle *or* dance. We milled, in silence more comfortable than it should have been. There was space between us, inches. One second, it felt like too much, and the next, I was damn near certain it wasn't enough.

Looking out at the crowd, I spotted the evening's host on the other side of the ballroom. Davis Ames was holding court and shaking hands. My grandmother had taken up position at his side.

"If I have to listen to one more person tell me what a *cozy* get-together this is, or what a *good man* my grandfather is, I will not be held responsible for my actions." Campbell didn't bother with *hello* as she sauntered up. "*Cozy* is just a way of saying this year's event isn't half as well attended as last year's," she continued, "and talking about what a good man my grandfather is? That's code for how lucky Mama, Walker, and I are that he hasn't disowned us all." She paused, but only for an instant, then turned her attention to my companion. "Hello, Nick."

If I'd needed a reminder that the two of them had been friends with benefits, heavy on the benefits, her coy tone would have done it. Thankfully, I managed not to study *every* detail of Nick's expression as he responded.

"Isn't this what you wanted?" he asked her. "Daddy in prison at your hands?"

"I'm a complicated person," Campbell shot back. "I'm allowed to hate the things I want." She turned to me. "So is this a thing now?" she asked, nodding to Nick. "The two of you?"

No. Yes. Only for tonight. My brain supplied a string of answers, rapid-fire.

"Do you have a problem with that?" Nick asked, beating me to an actual response.

"None in the least. But I am afraid that I'm going to have to borrow Sawyer from you for just a minute. We have some things to talk about, and I'm afraid they're need-to-know." Campbell went for the kill shot. "Sister things."

Nick shrugged.

"He knows we're not sisters," I informed Campbell. "I told him."

Nick smirked. "I suppose I didn't *need* to know . . ."

"But you do," Campbell finished. "Lovely." She flashed him another smile. "In that case, should I assume Sawyer has also told you that we found a twenty-year-old body that might have ended up at the bottom of Regal Lake at the hand of an Ames?"

No. I hadn't.

Nick's eyes narrowed. "What the hell is she talking about, Sawyer?"

"The Lady of Regal Lake," Campbell supplied.

"I know about the body," Nick said, his eyes still on me. "I run a bar. I hear things. What does Campbell mean about someone in her family being responsible for the body?"

If stoking Nick's enmity toward her family had been Campbell's goal—well, goal achieved.

"Campbell is jumping to conclusions," I said. I couldn't leave it there, though, because Nick deserved better than for me to let her dangle the possibility like a string in front of a cat. As much as I wanted to, I couldn't dismiss the idea Campbell had planted in my mind the week before, and I couldn't lie to Nick. "But there was a teenage girl that her father knocked up. As far as we can tell, no one's heard from said girl in twenty years."

Nick ran a hand roughly through his hair, then forced a smile for anyone watching. "Do you two even hear yourselves?" he asked. "You get that this isn't normal, right?"

"What isn't normal?" a voice asked cheerfully.

I turned to see Sadie-Grace. Beside her, Boone held out his hands, as if framing a picture around my face. "Lo," he called out dramatically, "thereby a vision in red came upon me, and her name was . . ."

I shot him a look that *almost* proved effective in preventing him from finishing that sentence.

"*Sawyer,*" he whispered. "*Her name was Sawyer.*"

Boone's last name might have been Mason, but he was an Ames, and though Nick didn't have anything against him specifically—as far as I knew—I couldn't help thinking that my "date" was probably reaching his limit with all things Ames.

He probably wished—like I did—that we were back at his car, my hands teasing his hair.

If wishes were horses, then beggars would ride. Turning that idiom over in my mind, I looked away from Nick—and the rest of the group. On the other side of the room, an immaculately dressed couple approached Lillian and Davis Ames. The man looked to be in his seventies—at least; the woman he had his arm around didn't look all that much older than my mom. Her skin was a glowing, medium brown; his was lighter. They both resembled their daughter, enough so that I might have pegged them for Victoria's parents, even if she hadn't mentioned their notable age difference.

The expression on Victoria's father's face as he shook Davis Ames's hand was inscrutable.

"Earth to Sawyer?" Campbell said. I had no idea what I'd missed.

"We were just about to discuss how incredibly debonair I look in this hat," Boone informed me, sliding his fingers along its brim. "I was born to fedora."

I wasn't sure whether the pained look on Nick's face was the result of Boone's use of the word *fedora* as a verb or the conversation he, Campbell, and I had been having before we'd been interrupted.

"I'm sorry to do this," I told him. "But I have to go—just for a few minutes."

On the other side of the room, words were being exchanged between Victor Gutierrez and the man whose company he'd attempted to topple. *If it was personal, if he targeted the Ames family because of Ana . . .*

"I'll be back soon," I told Nick. "Think you can stomach a dance then?"

Campbell responded before Nick could. "I'll go with you," she volunteered. I wasn't sure if she'd clued in to what I'd noticed, or if this was just another attempt to get under Nick's skin.

"No," I said. Whatever Campbell's intention was here, I'd never told her the exact words her grandfather had used when he indicated to me that he'd *handled* Ana. Cam might have had complicated relationships with her parents, but she loved the old man.

I needed to talk to him alone.

"Will you be okay?" I asked Nick, because he still hadn't replied to anything I'd said, including the question about the dance.

"I'm a big boy." Nick didn't even have half a smile for me now. "I can take care of myself."

Like me, he had probably been born taking care of himself. If you didn't rely on other people, they couldn't disappoint you. Hadn't that been my own mantra, once upon a time?

I'll make it up to him, I told myself as I started weaving through the crowd toward the Ames and Gutierrez patriarchs.

"You, too, would look excellent in a fedora," I heard Boone tell Nick behind me.

"Is now a good time for a subject change?" Sadie-Grace asked, in a rare moment of social acuity. I told myself she had the situation in hand, but the last thing I heard as I stepped out of earshot was "Because I think my stepmother might be planning to steal a baby."

LABOR DAY, 3:25 A.M.

"Let's play a game. How deep do you think this hole is?"

"That's not a game, Sadie-Grace."

"Not with that attitude, it's not."

"Seriously?"

"Come on. Please? How deep do you think this hole is?"

"Deep enough that it's going to be a pain in the ass to climb out—*if* we even can."

"Well, I've decided I like our chances. Because I'm an optimist, *and* I'm pretty good at giving boosts."

TEN WEEKS
(AND TWO DAYS) EARLIER

CHAPTER 17

By the time I reached Davis Ames, Lillian and Victoria's parents had been swept up in other conversations. Pushing down the urge to look back toward Nick, I wondered what Mr. Gutierrez had said to the Ames family patriarch. *Idle chitchat? Not-so-friendly doublespeak? A warning?*

"You have the look of a woman on a mission," Davis told me.

I nodded toward the man I assumed to be Victor Gutierrez. "What did he want?"

"To say hello."

That was a nonanswer if I'd ever heard one. "What else did he want?"

Davis cocked his head slightly to one side, then laid a heavy hand on my shoulder. "Escort an old man out for a breath of fresh air," he said, "will you?"

The deck outside the ballroom faced the water. Down below, a hundred or more boats were docked. Farther out, the lake glistened in the twilight. I could hear the sound of water rhythmically washing over the shore.

"If I thought she would agree," Davis told me, leaning up against the deck's railing, "I would ask your grandmother to dance."

That wasn't what he'd brought me out here to say, and it certainly wasn't what I wanted to talk to him about, but I'd been a part of the world he and Lillian inhabited long enough to know that this was how the game was played. "She said she met my grandfather at a party like this one."

Davis nodded back toward the ballroom. "In that very room." He ran his thumb over his forefinger, and I noticed that he still wore a wedding ring on his left hand. "There was a time that I thought one dance with your grandmother might make all the difference in the world." He was quiet for a moment, listening to the sound of the water and the faintest traces of music from inside. "It is out of courtesy to my relationship with her that I will ask you exactly once to stay out of my dealings with Victor Gutierrez."

There was something in his tone and posture that reminded me that he'd grown up with Lillian, in a town where my grandmother claimed that people had to fight to survive.

I wasn't deterred. "His granddaughter was the teenage girl your adult son knocked up." I rested my forearms on the railing and took in the way a muscle in his jaw had just ticced. "So it isn't just business," I said, reading into the tell. "Your dealings with Victor Gutierrez—and his with you—*are* personal."

"What they are," he emphasized, "is none of your concern."

"You told me that you took care of the situation with Ana," I said, studying the lines of his face, looking for another tell. "I assumed that meant you paid her off."

That seemed to be the go-to move in the Ames family playbook. Davis had helped to cover for the accident that had put Nick's brother in a coma, back when he'd thought that Walker was the one driving.

He'd paid Nick off once the truth about the senator's involvement had come out.

"I believe," Davis said, "that I've had enough fresh air." He started back for the ballroom.

"Campbell thinks Ana is the body that's been sitting at the bottom of Regal Lake for two decades." I dropped that bomb, stopping him in his tracks. "She thinks someone in your family killed her."

Davis Ames turned back to face me, his expression inscrutable, his posture impossible to read. "And why the hell would she think that?"

I kept expecting someone to open the door and join us on the deck, to interrupt this conversation, but no one did. It was just the two of us, out here, alone. "Campbell doesn't have the highest opinion of your son," I said. "Or her mama. Ana's pregnancy was awfully inconvenient, and as far as Campbell and I have been able to tell, neither Ana's family nor anyone hereabouts has heard from her in twenty years." I held his gaze. "It doesn't look good."

He stared at me for a moment, then let out a huff. "Too much like your grandmother for your own damn good," he muttered, before getting down to business. "How much have you told Campbell?"

"I didn't tell her that you *handled* Ana," I said, "if that's what you mean."

"I didn't kill the girl," Davis said, "and you damn well know that." He shook his head. "I spoke to her about her situation just once. I told her she had options."

"Options," I repeated, making no attempt to downplay the skepticism in my voice. Davis Ames did not strike me as someone who sat back and let other people make their choices, completely free of input and coercion.

"Yes, options. Alternatives. Choices. And I suggested that she'd have a hell of a lot more of them with money."

Of course he had. "You bought her off."

Davis Ames didn't seem insulted by that statement in the least. "I scared the hell out of that girl, and then I offered her a way out. Money up front, and more once the baby was born."

The latter half of that statement surprised me. "Once the baby was . . ."

He gave me a look. "I have a reputation for being a real bastard—well earned, I might add—but if there's one thing I care about, it's my own flesh and blood. Yes, I wanted to protect my son, but that child was my blood, too. I had hopes that once Ana realized her parents weren't going to support her, she'd see her way to an adoption."

I stared at him for a moment. This was a man who made decisions, a man who liked control. "You probably had adoptive parents all picked out."

Davis didn't deny it. "That's neither here nor there. Ana took my money, Sawyer. She left town. And I never heard from her again."

CHAPTER 18

Within moments of reentering the ballroom, I was
waylaid by Campbell.

"What just happened?" she asked. "And don't tell me that you
and my grandfather were simply overcome with a need for fresh air
and chitchat."

"He didn't want me asking about his interaction with Victor
Gutierrez in public." I let that sink in, then imparted the other piece
of information I'd gained. "Your grandfather admitted to paying
Ana off. He was trying to bribe her into an adoption. A quiet one."

"You should have let me come with you," Campbell insisted. "I
could have gotten him to tell us more."

"There might not be any more to tell," I replied. "If Ana took
his money, if she was keeping the pregnancy quiet . . . what motive
would anyone have had to hurt her?"

Campbell didn't have an immediate response. I glanced around
the room, looking for the others, and realized that Sadie-Grace and
Boone were on the dance floor.

"Where's Nick?" I asked Campbell. I had a sinking feeling about
what she was going to say before she replied.

"He said to tell you that you suck at favors, and then he left." She made a tsking sound. "Don't look so disappointed. Nick's not a boy you rely on, Sawyer." She gave the faux sympathy a rest and offered me a wicked smile. "But he *is* an awful lot of fun."

I wouldn't know. Before I could dismiss the alien sense of disappointment that accompanied that thought or tell Campbell that Nick and I weren't *really* dating and she could stop marking her territory, a third party entered our conversation.

"Did someone mention *fun?*" Victoria said, sliding in between us.

Campbell eyed her. I wondered if she was thinking about Ana, but what came out of her mouth was: "Done flirting with my brother?"

Victoria was undaunted by the question. "It was just one dance," she said. "And Lily doesn't own him."

Sometimes, I thought, *a dance is more than a dance.*

"And I suppose your interest in Walker has *nothing* to do with whatever ax your family has to grind against mine?" Campbell asked Victoria sweetly.

"No more than my interest in you," Victoria replied. She tilted her chin up slightly. "For the record, I didn't come over here to talk about Walker." She brought her hand to her lapel, and I realized that she was wearing a pin. *Silver. A snake wrapped around a rose.*

"Kind of hard to top our last rendezvous," I commented dryly.

Campbell batted her eyelashes. "Discovering a twenty-year-old corpse really does have a certain flair."

"Twenty-five," Victoria corrected.

"What?" I said.

"My father's been keeping tabs on the investigation," Victoria told us casually. "The body has been dated back twenty-*five* years. And, yes, the authorities do suspect foul play."

Not twenty years. I tried to wrap my mind around that. *Twenty-five.*

Victoria let her hand go to the pin on her lapel again. "You two and Sadie-Grace might want to check out the valet stand," she advised us. "And don't tell Lily."

CHARLOTTE, LIV, AND JULIA
SUMMER BEFORE SENIOR YEAR
TWENTY-FIVE YEARS EARLIER

"We should call the boys." Liv addressed that statement to Julia, but Charlotte was the one whose gut twisted in response.

The boys. Liv knew how Charlotte felt about Sterling Ames. *Of course she knows. And of course she wants to call the boys.* Hadn't Charlotte told her that she wanted more? She could taste the words on the tip of her tongue, even as her stomach flip-flopped at the thought of Julia's twin brother. The golden boy of their senior class. *Just this once, I want to break all the rules.*

"And what are we going to tell the boys?" Julia asked dryly. "That we're going on a drunken adventure?"

"*I'm* drunk," Liv corrected. "You're not, because you're driving. And Charlotte's not—yet—because I want her sober when *she* calls the boys."

Boys, plural. Charlotte could manage a call to J.D. He and Liv had been together since the beginning of the summer. Sterling Ames, however, was another story.

"I'll call my brother," Julia volunteered suddenly. "He has a new friend. *Thomas.* He worked for Daddy this summer. He's a little rough around the edges."

Liv cackled. "Just the way you like them, Jules."

CHAPTER 19

"Twenty-five years," I told Campbell. "Not twenty. Whoever the Lady of the Lake is, she died five years before Ana disappeared."

"Is this the part where you tell me I told you so?" Campbell asked.

"No," I said. I'd wondered—and suspected—too.

"Good," Campbell replied. "In other news, I vote we get Sadie-Grace *after* we visit the valet stand, because the good Lord knows the girl's sweeter than she is discreet. Now, do you want to distract the valet, or should I?"

Campbell could go from zero to full-on Southern belle in half a heartbeat. Luckily for us, she could also go from Southern belle to seductress and back again in a heartbeat and a half. The poor valet was going to get whiplash.

But at least she had his attention.

I ducked behind the valet stand, telling myself that I was doing this for Campbell—because I owed her one, and she needed the White Gloves.

She needed *something*. I knew what that was like.

The valet stand had a cabinet built into the back. It was, not surprisingly, locked. I grabbed a pin from my hair and went to work.

"But what do you do," I could hear Campbell saying, "when a car is too big to fit in a spot? Or too . . . *powerful* to handle?"

I rolled my eyes and continued jimmying the pin in the lock. The mechanism clicked, then gave, and a second later, I had the cabinet open. Inside, there was a Peg-Board, with easily a hundred numbered pegs. Valet keys hung on a good three-quarters of them. I scanned the rungs, trying to figure out what Victoria had meant when she'd said that we should check out the valet stand.

"Personally, I'm a bit of daredevil. You won't tell, will you? I just like to go fast, is all."

There. Three rows down, there was a key on a familiar-looking chain. *A snake wrapped around a rose.* I plucked it from the board and then saw two others. I grabbed them, too—seconds before I heard someone coming out the front door of the Arcadia hotel.

Keeping low to the ground, I shuffled toward the entrance and then popped up beside the group as they exited. When Campbell saw me, she cut the valet loose, and two minutes later, we'd made it far enough away from the building to examine our loot.

The three key chains were identical. The keys that hung on them were different, but all three had one thing in common.

Size.

"Golf cart keys," Campbell said. "One for you. One for me. One for Sadie-Grace."

Right after Victoria had pointed us to the valet stand, I'd been more focused on the bombshell she'd dropped about the Lady of the Lake than her parting shot. *Don't tell Lily.*

"If Lily's out, I'm out," I told Campbell. I'd never cared about impressing the White Gloves in the first place, and I didn't think there was any more information to get out of Victoria.

"What if Lily weren't out?" Campbell asked me.

I wasn't sure what she was getting at. "Victoria just said . . ."

Campbell smiled. "I happen to have an in with one of the other White Gloves," she said. "One who isn't overly fond of Victoria Gutierrez."

CHAPTER 20

I texted Lily and Sadie-Grace. Campbell texted Hope, who met us—all four of us—at the front of the hotel. I didn't know what Campbell had texted her, but she didn't bat an eye at Lily's presence.

"The golf carts are parked around back," she said. "You obtained your keys?"

"Easy as pie," Campbell replied.

"Apple pie," Sadie-Grace added confidently. Then, in the interest of full disclosure, she continued. "Or so I assume. I wasn't there."

"We only have three keys." I phrased my question carefully. "Is that going to be a problem?"

I was keeping secrets from Lily. If and when the truth about my parentage came out, she might hate me, but I wasn't going to sit back and let anyone else hurt her if I could help it.

"Not a problem," Hope replied cheerfully. "Each White Glove picks her own replacement. Victoria can't cut any of you as long as I'm interested."

Apparently, she hadn't found Lily interesting enough to keep around on her own, but if she was part of a package deal with me and Campbell—so be it.

What are the chances that Lily can change any of the other White Gloves' minds tonight?

Lily must have sensed something was off with me, because she squeezed my hand as we rounded the back of the hotel. "Don't worry," she whispered as a line of a dozen golf carts came into view. "I won't let them cut you."

Hope was as good as her word. Victoria didn't say a thing about Lily's presence. I counted sixteen other Candidates present, along with the eight White Gloves.

"Keys, please," Victoria told us. I handed them over. She tossed one to Sadie-Grace. "You're with Nessa's group. Hope, you can have Campbell." Another key toss. Victoria waited a moment and then closed her fist around the last key. "Sawyer and Lily are with me."

Each golf cart had two seats—one front-facing and one back. I ended up behind the wheel of our cart. Lily was sitting beside me, and Victoria had taken up a perch on the backseat.

On the carts around us, the other White Gloves and Candidates chattered. Every single one of them was dressed to the nines.

Golf carts? Check? Formal wear (lake version)? Check.

"What exactly are we doing tonight?" I asked.

The answer, it soon became apparent, was *off-roading*. Victoria directed us past the hotel, past the ramp down to the docks, past the golf course and the tennis courts, past the condos, down a gravel road. . . .

After that, things got rural, fast. Our drive ended outside a gate. The grating beneath it prepared me for the possibility of cows.

"Sawyer." Victoria nodded toward the gate. "Would you do the honors?"

She probably expected me to be horrified of the mud or the fact that the headlights on the golf cart couldn't compensate for how quickly things had gotten dark when the summer night had finally lost its sun.

But darkness I could handle. Mud I could handle. I had a healthy respect for—and accompanying wariness of—cows.

Trespassing I tended to take on a case-by-case basis.

"We have to cut through here to get to the woods." Victoria took note of my hesitation, however brief. "There's already a trail from point A to point B. Having second thoughts, Taft?"

"Sawyer doesn't have second thoughts!" Sadie-Grace insisted from the golf cart behind us, loyal to the bone. "Sometimes, she doesn't even have first thoughts!"

Thank you, Sadie-Grace. I jumped out of the cart and opened the gate. Mud flicked up onto my lower calves as I walked back to the golf cart. Aunt Olivia was not going to be happy about the state of my sandals.

Once I was situated behind the wheel again, Victoria leaned between Lily and me and waved me forward.

"The Candidates are many," a White Glove called out behind us. "The Chosen are few!"

Victoria didn't sit back down. Instead, she braced her hands against the frame on either side of the cart, her arms and legs forming an X that I could only partially see when I glanced back at her in the dark. She angled her face skyward, her long hair waving behind her, lost to shadow, as I gave the golf cart a little more gas.

"Let the games," Victoria murmured, "begin."

CHAPTER 21

*I*t became clear pretty quickly that the primary game in question was *chase*. The woods were vast, uneven, and littered with rocks, trees, and the kind of dense underbrush that a golf cart could only plow through going full speed—and only because these particular golf carts had a lot more horsepower than the kind you'd find on a golf course.

"Truth or dare?" Victoria yelled in my ear as we hit a bump that sent us airborne—and swerving to miss a tree. Behind us, I could hear another cart full of girls shrieking—and closing in.

"Really?" I shouted back, easing off the gas just enough to hang a turn. "You want to play Truth or Dare *now*?"

Our headlights illuminated the woods for just three or four feet in front of us. I aimed for what I hoped was a bit of a clearing and gave the cart enough gas to tear through the brush.

Victoria may have tightened her hold on the cart, but she didn't show any signs that her heart rate had ticked up even a beat. "My mother is thirty-five years younger than my father. I'm the family scandal *and* the much-beloved baby. It's called multitasking. Truth or dare, Taft?"

"Truth!" Lily yelled as we picked up speed. The shrieking behind us got louder and our pursuers closed in. "She'll take truth."

"Excellent choice," Victoria commented. I hauled it ninety degrees to the left, hit a clear patch, and managed to circle back behind the other cart, flying past them before they'd registered what was happening.

Victoria chose that moment to let loose her question. "Why did you ask me about Ana?"

"Who's Ana?" Lily said beside me.

This time, I took a major bump on purpose. Golf carts didn't come with seat belts, so we all bounced upward, fast enough and far enough to nearly hit our heads on the cart's roof.

Unfortunately, once we'd righted ourselves, it became clear to me that neither Victoria nor Lily was letting go of the question.

"Ana," Victoria told Lily, "is my niece—and a friend of Sawyer's mother, and yes, my father really is *that* old."

Though we'd left our closest pursuers in the dust, I could hear at least two more carts nearby. I steered us away from the noise.

"Your turn," Victoria told me. "Truth. You don't have secrets from your cousin, do you?"

She'd boxed me into a corner, and she knew it. If I didn't answer her question, that would only make Lily *more* suspicious.

"Ana was my mother's friend," I reiterated, "and I wanted to know what happened to her, because last anyone heard of her, twenty years ago, she was pregnant."

I couldn't risk looking away from the "road" long enough to ascertain which one of them had the more marked reaction to that statement, but Victoria was the one who recovered first.

"That explains some things. Knowing all six of my much-older brothers, not to mention my father, if the family knew she was pregnant, there was probably a lot of blustering about convents—they're very fond of hypothetical convents."

"Are they fond of kicking people out of the family?" I asked pointedly.

"Your mama had a friend who was pregnant twenty years ago?" Lily grabbed my arm, then seemed to realize I was still driving and let go of it.

"Yes," I said.

Victoria countered that question with one of her own. "Back at the gala, why did you step outside alone with Davis Ames?"

"I thought we were playing Truth or Dare," I said pointedly. "Doesn't that mean it's *my* turn now?"

"*If* we were taking turns," Victoria said, her voice low and silky, "I'd pick dare. There's nothing I won't do, with proper motivation."

I wanted to ask her what she was *doing* with Walker—what her father's *motivation* in approaching Davis Ames had been. But she hadn't chosen truth, and even if she had, Lily was right beside me.

"What if I dared you to jump off this cart?" I threw out the question, allowing the pedal to creep back to the floor.

"Is that a hypothetical dare . . . or a real one?" Victoria asked.

"Sawyer!" Lily yelled beside me.

I realized too late that we were going too fast. The cart hit what I thought was a bump, but when we went airborne, I realized that it wasn't a bump.

It was a ledge.

CHAPTER 22

*E*verything hurt.

The cart must have flipped. That was my first thought. It felt immediate, like less than a second had passed since we'd gone over the ledge, but that couldn't have been true, because, somehow, I was lying on muddy, damp grass, sticks and rocks digging into the flesh bared by my vintage dress.

"Lily?" That was my second thought as I pushed up to my elbows, my entire body objecting. The lights on the golf cart had gone out. I couldn't see either of my companions. "Lily, are you okay?"

That question was greeted by a moan. I crawled toward the sound until I hit a figure lying prone. *Not Lily,* I realized belatedly. *Victoria.*

"I'm fine," she said before I could ask.

I wanted to tell her that she wasn't fine, that she was an idiot, that we all were, because what did we expect to happen, off-roading in a vehicle that wasn't meant for off-roading with limited visibility and unpredictable terrain?

I heard Victoria sit up before my eyes could process what little movement I was able to see. There was a shuffling sound, and then there was light. "Let's hear it for dresses with pockets," she said, brandishing her phone.

Flashlight mode let me see just far enough that I was able to spot Lily. She'd landed much farther from Victoria and me than either one of us had been from the other. My brain said that didn't make sense. Lily had been sitting right beside me. Victoria was the one who'd been in the back.

As I crawled carefully toward Lily, I let my thoughts race, let my brain outline all the reasons that if I was in one piece, Lily had to be, too.

"Lily." I reached her. "Are you okay?"

Unlike Victoria, she didn't moan. I told myself that it was because Lily was too much of a stickler for manners, and she found moaning uncouth.

"Lil—"

"*Sawyer.*"

For a fraction of a second, I was terrified that Victoria was the one who'd said my name, even though it had come from Lily's direction, even though I was close enough to her body now to practically feel the words on my face.

"You're okay?" I said.

Lily let out a long and wobbly breath. "I'm in significantly better condition than my dress."

Leave it to her to be thinking about our clothing at a time like this.

"Victoria?" Lily asked.

"I'm fine." Victoria punctuated that statement by flooding us with light—not from her phone this time. She'd managed to find the cart. The roof had been knocked clean off, and two of the four bars that had been holding it up were demolished.

At least the lights still worked.

"You're bleeding," Victoria stated. I thought she was talking to me, but she quickly corrected that misapprehension. "Not you. Her." She jerked her head toward Lily, who was still lying on the ground, and who, I could see now, had blood smeared across her face and temple.

"I shall choose to believe," Lily said, forcing herself into a sitting position, "that *her* is Victoria's version of an affectionate nickname."

I reached out. "Your head."

Lily swatted my hand away. "Head wounds bleed. It's what they do. I'm okay."

"What's your name?" I asked her. "What's today's date? Who's the president?"

"As long as we're asking questions," Victoria said beside me, "Sawyer could enlighten us as to why she and Davis Ames felt the need to step outside back at the gala."

"What is your deal with the Ames family?" I said at the exact same moment that Lily attempted to climb to her feet and deal with Victoria herself.

"Sawyer has her reasons," she said, unsteady on her feet. "She and Mr. Ames have . . . a lot in common."

The vise around my chest loosened slightly. If Lily was with it enough to infer that the reason I'd stepped outside with Davis Ames was because—as far as she knew—he was my grandfather, her cognitive capacities were clearly intact.

The fear that her condition was serious gave way to guilt more intense than any I'd felt in the past few weeks. "Lily," I said. "Don't."

Don't defend me. Don't remind me that I'm a liar.

Lily pursed her lips. "Sawyer, you've been acting . . ." Even with a head wound, Lily couldn't bring herself to use a descriptor as ill-mannered as *weird* or *strange*. ". . . at odds with yourself for weeks. What is going on with you?"

I looked toward Victoria—and the demolished golf cart. "We need to get the cart upright and get out of here. If someone else comes over that drop, we're toast—or they are."

Victoria handed Lily a strip of fabric. "Press this to your head and try to stop the bleeding. Sawyer, help me with the cart—and answer the damn question. Mine *or* your cousin's, I'm not bothered much as to which."

Getting the cart upright again was the easier task. I could have ignored Victoria's instruction. I could have told Lily that I was fine, but I just kept thinking of the seconds when I hadn't been sure I'd ever be able to talk to her again.

Up until now, I'd been keeping secrets from Lily, but I hadn't lied to her.

Campbell knows that her father isn't mine. She's not going to keep it from Walker forever. One way or another, that much of my secret was coming out.

Better that Lily heard it from me.

"I was talking to Davis Ames," I said, the cuts and scrapes on my legs, arms, and chest throbbing as Victoria and I coordinated our movements and got the cart back on its wheels, "because his son was the father of Ana's baby." I glanced at Victoria. "I'm guessing your father knows that, and his takeover attempt earlier this summer was somehow related."

"My niece was pregnant by Campbell's father?" Victoria asked, eyebrows jetting up.

"The senator—" Lily stopped, then tried again. "Sterling Ames," she corrected herself, and then she finally just said, *"Two?"*

As in: *He got two teenagers pregnant?*

"What do you mean, *two*?" Victoria asked.

I directed my answer to my cousin. "Not two, Lily. My mom, what she told me that night at the Christmas party about Sterling Ames, it's not true."

"She lied to you?" Lily said. "But Campbell's mama as good as confirmed it."

"A case of mistaken identity," I explained. "Wrong pregnant teenage girl."

"And it's just a coincidence that your mother and her friend both got pregnant?" Victoria asked.

I walked around to the back of the golf cart. "Help me push this," I said. "It's either that, or we leave it here."

For a moment, I thought Victoria would press for answers, but she didn't. "We need the light." The White Glove was remarkably calm under pressure—and far more logical than I would have anticipated. "Phones don't get a signal out here, so we're on our own for getting back to the party. The headlights do a hell of a lot more than a cell in flashlight function."

I listened but couldn't hear even a trace of the other groups. How far into the woods had we gone? How big were they?

"Push," Victoria told me. "Lily, if you need to ride . . ."

"I can push."

Somehow, I had a feeling that after Victoria saw this side of my very proper cousin, getting an invitation to the next White Glove event wouldn't be a problem for Lily.

We'll be lucky if the next one doesn't kill us.

"Do we even know which direction we're going?" Lily asked five minutes later.

I was on the verge of responding, but Victoria beat me to it. "I always know exactly where I am. It's a family trait."

"Stop," I said suddenly. They complied. "Listen," I told them. The silence had given way, and in the distance, I could hear something—*people*. Talking. Laughing.

"Over here!" Victoria yelled. Lily and I added our voices, to no effect.

"We could go in that direction," I said, eyeing what I could see of the terrain. "But we'd have to leave the cart behind. The brush is too dense, and the trees are too close together. We'll never make it through that way pushing."

We fell into silence and, again, heard laughter. It was faint, but it was there.

Victoria turned her phone back to flashlight mode. "I guess this will have to do."

Lily and I followed closely on her heels. Eventually, the sounds of the others grew louder, and when there was finally a break in the trees, I could make out the outline of a golf cart ahead. It took until we got much closer for me to realize it was parked—and empty.

A second later, I heard the voices again and realized, with a start, that one of them was male. I looked to the key, still in the golf cart we'd found. Closer inspection showed that it had a key chain, but not one of ours.

No snake, no rose.

Victoria shone her flashlight on the key, and I saw that the key chain was a Mercedes.

A stick snapped up ahead of us. Victoria pivoted, and so did the light. One second, I spotted clothing slung carefully over a low-hanging limb on a nearby tree, and the next second, a naked man stepped into view and turned in the direction from which he'd just emerged.

Beside me, Lily let out a strangled whisper. "Daddy."

I'd thought, in passing, that Lily's father might be having an affair, but there was a difference between thinking something in the abstract and seeing it in the flesh. *Literally.*

I briefly entertained the ridiculous idea that maybe Aunt Olivia was out here with him, but the next second, a woman stepped into view. She saw the flashlight, even though Uncle J.D. was too involved in what he was doing—and her—to notice.

"J.D.," the woman said softly.

I stared at her, trying to process what I was seeing. The woman reaching to grab her clothing off the tree had blond hair, but her features and skin-tone bore a striking resemblance to Victoria's.

I know that woman. I told myself I was being ridiculous, that there was *no way*, but the next word out of Uncle J.D.'s mouth put a nail in that coffin.

That word, which he murmured into her neck, was: "Ana."

CHAPTER 23

*L*ily made a mewling sound. Her father saw her, saw *us*. There was frenzied movement as he pulled on his pants, then a string of stammered explanations, none of them worth a damn thing. *Questions, cursing, demands*—and all I could think, through all of it, was that the woman standing next to Lily's father, the very naked woman he was having an affair with, looked so much like she had as a teenager.

Ana Sofía Gutierrez. She wasn't dead. She wasn't missing. She was here, pulling a dress over her head. She was looking at Lily and at Victoria and at me.

"Lily's bleeding." Victoria somehow managed to sound, if not calm, then at least somewhat in control of the situation. "We crashed. She hit her head. Hard."

"Lily . . ." Uncle J.D. choked on her name. "Sweetheart, what—"

"No." Lily's voice wasn't quiet, exactly, but I had to strain to hear it.

"No," J.D. repeated. "You didn't hit your head?"

"Stay away from me." Lily took a step back. Her entire body was shaking. "Don't talk to me. *Don't touch me.*"

I crossed in front of her, between them. I had about a million questions, but right now, it didn't matter that the woman was Ana—or that Campbell and I had been looking for her. It mattered that Lily was bleeding, figuratively and literally.

It mattered that she was shattered.

"Sawyer." J.D. turned his attention to me. "What happened?"

I hated him for doing this to her, the way I hadn't ever quite been able to hate him for myself.

Behind me, Lily gripped my arm. At first, I thought she was using me as a shield.

And then she went down.

Lily regained consciousness just as we made it out of the woods. She didn't say anything—not when the other White Gloves mobbed us, not when Campbell and Sadie-Grace got close enough to ask us what was going on, not when Ana emerged from the forest, too, and the whispers started.

Lily was silent on the way to the car.

Silent on the way to the hospital.

I stayed with her, even though that meant staying with J.D. Campbell texted that she and Sadie-Grace were going to follow. I called Lillian. What else was I supposed to do? In the ER, the doctors sent Lily for a CT scan, just as Campbell and Sadie-Grace arrived.

"Is Lily okay?" Campbell asked, and then, because she couldn't be caught caring too much, she continued, "Inconveniencing others with an unruly head injury is awfully impolite for Miss Manners."

"Lily isn't okay," I said. Campbell did me the favor of not asking if I was.

"Is Lily . . . *dead*?" Sadie-Grace asked, horrified.

"She's getting a CT scan," I clarified.

A second or two passed before the next question came, and in that time, it took everything I had not to look back at Uncle J.D., who was filling out forms.

"What happened?" Campbell said. "Who was that woman?"

I realized then that I'd never shown her the pictures I had of Ana. Now that Lily was out of earshot, now that the emergency was under control and there was nothing more I could do for her, the enormity and ridiculousness of the situation hit me.

"That," I told Campbell, "was Ana Gutierrez."

"I'm not one to throw stones, but . . ."

Campbell's disclaimer was a clear and direct indication that stone throwing was imminent.

Since this situation was more messed up than she even knew, I saved her the trouble. "But Ana seems to have a type?"

"Tall men with thick hair and side parts?" Sadie-Grace suggested guilelessly.

Married men, I thought, but I didn't say it, and neither did Campbell.

"We should talk to her," Campbell told me. "Ask her if she had the baby."

Even thinking about talking to my uncle's mistress made me feel sick and disloyal to Lily. This was such a mess.

I reached for my phone. I looked down the screen—no new texts, no missed calls. *Nothing from Nick.* It was easier, for once, to think about him than it was to think about anything else. My whole life felt like it was imploding, but the fact that I'd ditched him before he'd walked out on me was simple.

Of course he hadn't been waiting on me when I got back. *I could text him. To apologize.*

"Sawyer?" Campbell prompted. "Don't you want to talk to Ana?"

I did, and I didn't. Nothing about this was okay. *I* wasn't okay.
So I sent the text to Nick, and then I waited.

The hospital had a room for Lily. The nurse showed us back as
we waited for her to finish the CT scan—family only. We left
Campbell and Sadie-Grace in the waiting area and I found myself
alone with Lily's father.

Our father.

"How long?" I asked him, my voice devoid of all emotion.

He looked at me, no more disheveled than if he'd just stepped
off the golf course or out of a boardroom. "They'll bring her back
as soon as they—"

"How long have you been sleeping with Ana?"

"We're not discussing this, Sawyer," J.D. said.

"Would you rather *not discuss* the affair you're having now," I
asked him, eyes narrowed, "or the one you had approximately nine
months before I was born?"

The implication underlying my question landed like a punch.

"You . . ."

"I know," I said. "I know that you slept with my mother. I know
that you got her pregnant. I know that you're the kind of person
who could pretend, all this time, that I was just your niece."

"Does Lily—"

I didn't let him finish the question. "You are aware that Ana was
a friend of my mom's, right? Did you know that they got pregnant
together? That they planned it?"

"Sawyer." J.D.'s hand closed around my forearm. "This isn't the
time or the place." He might have said something else, but then his
gaze caught on something behind me.

Someone.

I turned to see Ana Sofía Gutierrez standing in the doorway. I couldn't believe she'd had the gall to come to the hospital, let alone Lily's family-only room. I definitely couldn't believe that the moment Lily's father saw her, he stopped talking to me and crossed to take her hands in his and whisper something in her ear.

I stared at the two of them. For ten or fifteen seconds, I stood there, frozen, and then a strange, numb fury settled over my body, extremity by extremity and limb by limb. I'd spent months *not* acknowledging the truth of my relationship to the man, and now that I had?

He'd walked away.

I didn't remember taking a single step toward the two of them, but the next thing I knew, I was within an arm's length.

"I should go," Ana was murmuring. I didn't know why she'd come to the hospital in the first place, why she'd followed us out of the woods, in a way sure to inspire questions and start the rumor mill churning.

"I'll be okay," J.D. told her.

That was about all I could take. "Really don't think whether or not *you* are going to be okay is the real issue here."

"Hey," Ana said, looking directly at me for the first time since she'd appeared in the doorway. "Ease up. We're all worried about Lily."

"You don't even know Lily," I snapped. "And clearly, she isn't much of a priority to either one of you."

"Sawyer," Uncle J.D. said lowly. "Please."

"Please what?" I retorted. "Please don't make a scene?"

Before he could reply, a doctor appeared and pulled him aside, and the two of them began talking in muted tones. I wanted to hear what they were saying, but I couldn't quite convince my body to turn my back on the woman opposite me.

The woman who was having some kind of affair with my aunt's husband. The other participant in the pregnancy pact. A woman Campbell and I hadn't been able to find a trace of.

"Everything is going to be fine," she told me.

That snapped me out of it. "You don't get to tell me that things are going to be fine," I said, enunciating every word. "And you don't get to 'worry' about Lily. You're banging her father, who, as goes without saying, is a fetid piece of rotting—"

"I get it," Ana interjected softly. She tucked her blond hair behind her ears, her dark brown eyes oozing understanding. "I do, honey, and I'm leaving. I just . . . I needed to make sure y'all got here okay."

I should have let her go. I should have told her to get the hell away from me. But some ghosts can't be banished that easily, and my mom's past—*my past*—had been haunting me for months now. Campbell's statement in the waiting room, her assertion that we should ask Ana about the baby, wouldn't be banished.

Somehow, what ended up coming out of my mouth next was: "I know who you are. You're Ana Sofía Gutierrez."

If she was surprised that I knew her full name, she didn't show it. "These days, I go by Olsson—my mother's maiden name."

I wondered how long she'd gone by a different name. I wondered if she'd made herself difficult to find on purpose.

"I'm Sawyer," I told her. "Ellie's Sawyer."

For a moment, something like nostalgia crossed Ana's features. "Ellie always said that's what she was going to name you, even if you ended up being a boy."

I breathed in and breathed out and then spoke again. "You always imagined having girls," I said, the words coming out hoarse.

Emotion flickered over her features, but she washed her face clear of it a moment later.

"I know about the pact." I waited for a response, but the only thing I got in return for the statement was silence. "Where have you been, all of these years?" I asked. "What are you doing here? Why would you sleep with *him*?"

Ana had been one of my mother's closest friends. She had to have known who my father was. Didn't she? Either way, she must have known that J.D. was married.

"It's complicated, Sawyer."

"Then uncomplicate it."

Ana tried stepping past me again, but this time, I reached out and touched her arm. I didn't grab her, but she ground to a stop like I had.

"Campbell Ames is in the waiting room," I said. "She's a friend of mine. And Lily's. You know her father." I let that sink in. Even though I felt like I'd swallowed cotton, I made my mouth form the question. "What happened to your baby?"

Three things occurred in the wake of that question. The first was that a nurse brought Lily back from her CT scan; the second was that Lillian and Aunt Olivia arrived.

And the third was that Ana Gutierrez placed a hand softly against my cheek, leaned forward, and whispered the answer to my question.

LABOR DAY, 3:26 A.M.

"*S*awyer? I just wiggled my feet! And my hands! And my temple!"

"Your temple? As in your head?"

"No. As in my *lady temple*."

"Your lady . . ."

"Temple. Like how it says in the Bible that your body is a temple?"

"Oh, God. Can we just go back to the part where you were talking about your hands and feet?"

EIGHT WEEKS
(AND SIX DAYS) EARLIER

CHAPTER 24

"*L*ong time no see, Sawyer Taft." Walker greeted me the same way he had every time I'd seen him exiting Lily's room for the past nine days.

Somehow, I'd found myself living in a strange alternate universe where Lily's boyfriend was allowed to be in her bedroom with the door shut, and I wasn't allowed in her room at all—the former by my grandmother's edict and the latter by Lily's. If Lily could have kicked me out of the house, she would have. Lillian was blaming it on the head injury, but she hadn't seen the look on Lily's face when she'd seen me standing there with her father's mistress's hand on my face.

"How is she today?" I asked Walker.

I wasn't asking about the stitches or the concussion, and he knew it.

"She's angry," Walker said. "It's a better look for her than sad."

Lily didn't, as a rule, let herself get truly angry. She didn't lose her temper. Anything she could repress, she did. But this wasn't the old Lily we were dealing with here. *This* Lily's father had moved out. Her mother was insisting on pretending that he was just being considerate, and once the gossip blew over, everything would go back to normal.

I knew, the same as Lily did, that there was no normal now. And while she'd had Walker to lean on, I'd been left out in the cold. She wasn't talking to me. Nick hadn't returned any of my texts.

"You know what the doctors said," Walker told me.

"They said she might be irritable." I parroted the interpretation Lillian had been trying to sell me. "They said she might behave in uncharacteristic ways."

They'd said it was temporary—but they didn't know what Lily had seen in the woods.

"If you ask me, it's good that she's feeling things this strongly," Walker said. "You're taking this personally, Sawyer, but it's not you. It's everyone and everything."

"Except for you," I replied.

Whatever problems Walker and Lily had been having, whatever issues and emotions he'd been dealing with since his father had been arrested—those had been put on hold. Now that Lily needed him, he was there.

"Give it time, Taft." Walker looked like he was on the verge of saying something else, but then his phone rang. He looked down at caller ID and then dismissed the call.

"Campbell?" I asked. She'd been calling me almost every day. "Or your mama?"

"Neither," Walker replied. "I should go before traffic hits."

This time, my phone was the one that went off—not a call. A *text*. On the other side of Lily's door, I heard her phone buzz as well. I expected the message to be from Sadie-Grace, who'd taken to sending both Lily and me random pictures of puppies four or five times a day, but as I went to check the message, three others arrived, back-to-back.

@) - -' - , - - -

~ ~ ~ ~ ~8<

Tonight.

Stay tuned.

CHAPTER 25

*L*illian's preferred method of coping involved tending the garden, drinking wine, and continually drafting me into joining her at the former.

I would have preferred the latter—if tequila could have been substituted for the wine.

"Do you know what today is, Sawyer?" my grandmother asked me.

"Tuesday?" I replied dryly.

"The third of July." Lillian leaned forward to prune a rose with the exact same sense of determination with which she was tending to our conversation. "The last time this family missed the Fourth of July celebration at Regal Lake was the year your grandfather got sick and passed on." *Trim. Trim. Trim. Clip. Clip.* "I did what I could for the girls, but I was mourning, too. By the end of the summer, your aunt was gone and your mama had taken to dressing only in black."

According to my mom, Aunt Olivia had run away for almost a year in the wake of their father's death, and once she'd returned, my grandmother had refused to acknowledge that she'd ever gone missing.

Denial wasn't just a stage of grief; it was practically a family tradition.

"Is that your way of asking me if I'm going to start dressing in all black?" I asked Lillian.

She put her gardening shears down, removed her gloves, and plucked her glass of wine from the deck. "Lily's mourning, Sawyer. I cannot help but notice that you're not."

"I don't get to be upset about this." I set my jaw. When she didn't reply, I elaborated. "They're not *my* parents."

Even with respect to Uncle J.D., that felt true now. What did it matter that I carried half his DNA? Just look what he'd done to the daughter he loved.

"You're a part of this family, Sawyer Ann. If you want to play the part of the stoic, I'm hardly the one to stop you, but don't you tell me that this doesn't affect you."

All things considered, I preferred our conversation the previous day, which had focused entirely on the way that my bangs were growing out. "Can we talk about something else?"

Lillian returned her attention to the roses. "Certainly." She adopted a serene expression. "I've decided that it would be wrong to have your uncle killed. I'm still debating on the issue of kneecaps."

I was 90 percent sure she was joking.

"Davis Ames seems like he might know some kneecap-busting types," I volunteered. "Then again, Campbell said he won't talk about anything related to Ana."

I'd repeated to Campbell the single sentence Ana had given me back at the hospital. *My baby deserved the world, and I deserved a chance to start over—alone.* Cam and I took that to mean that the baby had been adopted, but for all that conversation with Ana had cost me, it hadn't told me enough to know by whom.

"Incoming! Hostile at forty-four degrees! Duck, Mim! Sawyer—man down!" John David didn't give me time to process whether that was supposed to be an order, a warning, or a threat before he army-crawled to my feet, swept them out from underneath me, and sent me flying.

"Man down," I repeated, getting ready to give as good as I got.

"Oh, Sawyer," my grandmother said indulgently. "He's just having a bit of fun."

John David wasn't Lillian Taft's grandson for nothing. He hopped to his feet and started blathering on a new topic in hopes of forestalling my revenge. "I love Fourth of July. It's my favorite, isn't it, Mim? This was going to be the year I won the golf cart parade *and* the pie-eating contest up at the lake. William Faulkner, too."

"William Faulkner was going to win a pie-eating contest?" I asked.

Still channeling Lillian, John David gave me a look. "Don't be ridiculous, Sawyer. There is no canine pie-eating contest. William Faulkner was going to win the costume contest, which is part of the parade."

"I mean, sure," I said, nodding. "Who doesn't celebrate American independence with some kind of dog costume contest?"

"And parade." John David could not have emphasized those words more.

"I know you miss your father," Lillian told him. "And I know you're missing how things usually are."

"No one's missing anything!" Aunt Olivia stepped onto the back porch, an honest-to-God apple pie in her hands and a stars-and-stripes apron tied neatly around her midsection. She looked like something out of either a Norman Rockwell painting or an Alfred Hitchcock movie, depending on how soon she snapped. "Now, what's this nonsense about us skipping the Fourth of July festivities? I certainly never said a word about that."

Lillian arched an eyebrow at her. "You've never been overly fond of the lake, Olivia."

"Go on with you, Mama. I love the lake as much as anyone in this family. I just don't care much for the heat or the humidity or actually going out on the water. *But in any case*, we're going. To the lake. For Fourth of July."

That was unexpected. My mind went immediately to the texts that Lily and I had received. There hadn't been any details, just enough to know that the White Gloves had plans for tonight.

"Is Dad coming?" John David asked tentatively. I couldn't remember if he'd ever called J.D. *Daddy* the way that Lily did, but either way, he said *Dad* like a word that had lost nine-tenths of its shine.

"I'm afraid he can't make it, sweetheart." Aunt Olivia brandished the pie like she expected that to soften the blow. "But guess who *is* joining us?"

"Who?" John David asked, inching toward the pie.

Aunt Olivia beamed at me in a way that made me think she definitely hadn't forgotten—or forgiven—the moment she'd seen me with Ana.

"Sawyer's mama!"

CHAPTER 26

*T*hat was all of the warning I got. Within three hours, we'd made it most of the way to the lake, all of us in one car. Including my mom. And Lily. And every ax Lily had to grind with me.

I'd never been claustrophobic, but ignoring my mother while Lily ignored me was suffocating. *Think about something else,* I told myself, and my brain obliged.

I thought about my hands in Nick's hair.

I thought about leaving him at the gala.

I thought about the fact that he hadn't replied to any of the texts I'd sent him since. Presumably, he still needed an in to polite society. He needed me. I'd seen *My Fair Lady.* I'd seen *Pretty Woman.* This wasn't a one-off kind of thing. And if he still needed my help . . .

If he still *wanted* it . . .

Even if it meant nothing, at least it would distract me from everything else. As much as I wasn't of the Campbell Ames school of thought on working out issues, the idea of touching Nick's hair again—touching *him* again—wasn't entirely without appeal.

I looked down at my phone. *Headed to the lake.* My fingers typed out the message. *Let me know if you need an escort for Fourth of July.* I hit send right before looking up and catching sight of my mom. She would have been thrilled to know that I was texting a boy.

The thought made me sick to my stomach.

How many men had I seen her fall for? My childhood was filled with optimistic starts, followed alternatingly by boredom and broken hearts. Texting and dancing and touching wasn't for girls like me.

I put my phone away and my brain on lockdown. Fortunately, we arrived at the lake house before my memory could start torturing me with anything else.

"Ellie, why don't you and Sawyer take the turret room?" Lillian deftly avoided allowing Lily to kick me out of our formerly shared room, as the lot of us exited the car.

"Lily can bunk in my room," John David hollered, even though he was standing maybe four feet away from the rest of us. "I'll mostly be in the garage, working on the golf cart. I'm going to need someone to take me to Walmart to get supplies. *Lots* of supplies. This parade won't win itself, people."

"I'll go," I volunteered. *Less time with Lily, less time with my mom.*

"There's no need to put yourself out, Sawyer," Lily told me. "I'll take John David."

That was the first thing she'd said to me in two weeks, and the subtext hit me harder than an insult. There was *no need to put myself out*, because I wasn't family.

Not her family.

Not anymore.

The view from the turret room hadn't changed. Even though it was the middle of the week, there was already plenty of traffic out on the water.

"There'll be fireworks tomorrow." My mom threw her bag on one of the beds. I heard her flop down beside it. "Hundreds of boats will be anchored in that cove to watch. I'm sure John David is looking forward to the F-16 flyover—or at least, that's what he'll be looking forward to after the golf cart parade."

"And the pie-eating contest," I said, turning away from the window. I spotted a rose sitting at the end of my bed and another one sitting at the end of Lily's. There were envelopes attached.

Details about tonight, I thought. Considering that the last White Glove event had ended with Lily in the hospital and the one before that had led to the discovery of a human corpse, I wasn't sure opening those envelopes was worth the risk.

"Do I want to know?" my mom asked, glancing at the roses.

The hopeful note in her voice told me she did want to know. She wanted me to talk to her. She wanted me to be her best friend and confidante and vice versa.

I wasn't sure if Aunt Olivia had invited her here to punish me for the way I'd interacted with Ana, or if, in the wake of Uncle J.D.'s infidelity, my aunt had somehow decided it was time to bury other axes.

Ultimately, it didn't really matter.

"Sawyer," my mom said. "I'm trying here. Really trying. Just tell me what I can do."

Go back in time, and tell me the truth. I couldn't say those words. I couldn't even think them without feeling guilty. That was the most impossible thing about this whole situation. No matter what she'd done or hadn't done—what she did or didn't do going forward—part of me would always feel like it was my job to make it better.

My job to love her.

"Did Aunt Olivia tell you her husband is having an affair?" I asked, managing to keep my voice even and not betray the emotions churning inside me, threatening to erupt.

"She did, in fact," my mom said. I could see her bracing herself for me to say something to the effect that this wasn't the first time.

I didn't. I was so tired of being angry. I didn't want to hurt her any more than I wanted loving her to hurt.

So instead, I let my fingers curl around the windowsill for a moment, and then turned back to her. "Did Aunt Olivia tell you the person he's having an affair with is Ana Gutierrez?"

CHAPTER 27

"*A*na gave her baby up?" Of everything I'd told my mom in the past hour, *that* was what surprised her the most. "Why would she do that? Did her parents make her? Did she . . ."

"Did she *what*?" I asked when my mom trailed off.

"I don't know." My mom looked younger than she had at the beginning of this conversation, and a little lost. "It was one thing when Greer had a miscarriage." Still sitting on Lily's bed, she pulled her knees up and tucked them close to her body. "But Ana just deciding to give her baby away? That wasn't the plan."

I remembered the pictures I'd seen of the three of them, white ribbons tied around their wrists or wound through their hair. *That wasn't the pact.*

"You left after your fight with Lillian," I pointed out. "And Greer had hung both of you out to dry."

"I tried to get in touch with Ana on my way out of town," my mom said defensively. Then she wilted. "Maybe I didn't try hard enough. I felt like she'd abandoned me. This whole time, what if she's felt the same?"

I shouldn't have felt for her, not about this. Maybe I wouldn't have, if Lily and I were still speaking. *Greer and Ana were Mom's people, and then they were gone.*

"I still don't understand why she didn't look for me," my mom continued. "Maybe someone threatened her. The baby's father or *his* father or his wife . . ."

Before my mom could continue to speculate, there was a knock at the door. I recognized it immediately: *light, crisp, three taps.*

My stomach twisted.

"Lily," I told my mom, assuming that she'd know that meant that we should stop tossing around words like *baby* and *pact* and, most of all, *Ana.*

The last thing I needed was to throw gasoline on that particular fire.

"Come in," my mom called.

Lily opened the door. She looked thinner than she had two weeks ago. Her hair clearly hadn't been conditioned in a while. Her entire face was makeup-free, and though her skin had tanned early in the summer, right now, she looked wan.

"May I speak with Sawyer?" she asked my mom. "Alone?"

An hour earlier, if you'd told me that Lily wanted to talk to me, I would have felt a mix of trepidation and hope. But after a one-on-one with my mom, I couldn't afford either. *If you don't expect anything of anyone, people can't disappoint you.*

When my mom left, Lily sat in the exact spot she had just vacated. "It's John David," she said without preamble.

That was all it took to snap me out of my head and into the moment. "What's wrong with John David?"

"Picture this," Lily told me, her gaze focused on her own hands. "We're in Walmart with an overflowing cart of supplies. My brother is elbow-deep in streamers and trying to convince me that he needs a minimum of two thousand sparklers to truly bring his golf cart vision to life. And then, out of nowhere, he says, 'Hey, Lily? You know how Mama says little pots have big ears?' And I say yes. And then he says, 'And you know how she also says that eavesdroppers never hear any good of themselves?' And I say yes, and then he continues with 'And how Mama always says that this is a one-party consent state with respect to audio recordings, so it's completely legal to record any conversation you're a party to?'"

"Pretty sure Aunt Olivia has *never* said that last one," I opined.

"Even if she *had*," Lily replied, "John David's version of being 'party' to a conversation apparently doesn't involve being a participant in that conversation, so much as eavesdropping while eating cake and/or pie to fulfill the 'party' quotient."

I read between the lines there. "Aunt Olivia has been grief-baking a lot lately."

"Not just lately," Lily replied quietly. She held up a phone. I recognized immediately that it wasn't hers. Lily's phone didn't have a camouflage cover. "He's been spying on my parents and recording their conversations. For more than a month."

More than a month. As in, since before we discovered the affair?

"Sawyer?" Lily held the phone out to me. "You have to listen to this."

With no further ado, she played the audio files for me—not all of them, but three in particular.

"Could you grab the other end of the sheet?" Aunt Olivia's request on the tape sounded absolutely ordinary. She waited a second, and then added, *"I think I've figured out why we're having so much trouble finding the money to finish the remodel."*

She still sounded pleasant enough, but before this summer, the one argument I'd ever heard them have was on this topic.

"I told you," J.D. said on the recording, *"we're fine, Olivia. It's going to be fine. Our assets—"*

"*Just aren't liquid right now. So you've said, repeatedly. But I had a bit of time between projects with the girls, and I took a peek at the books—ours and your company's.*"

On the bed, Lily sat perfectly still. I knew this wasn't her first time hearing these recordings, but she was listening the way a starving person ate.

"*Leave my job out of this,*" Uncle J.D. snapped.

"*Certain filings are a matter of public record. You know that.*"

"*Stop telling me what I know, Olivia.*"

"*You've exercised a lot of stock options in the past six years.*" Aunt Olivia's voice had taken on just the slightest hint of an edge.

"*We agreed that was the right call. We used my trust—from my family—to do it.*"

"*At first,*" Aunt Olivia said firmly.

There was a long pause. "*No matter where the money came from, we agreed about buying the stock, Olivia.*"

"*That's the thing, John. We agreed about exercising your options, but when I compared the public filings to our balance transfers, every single time you convinced me to fund a stock buy, you took a little off the top. And by a little, I mean a very large sum.*"

"*I'm not talking about this.*"

"*Yes, you are.*" Now, Aunt Olivia didn't sound pleasant at all. Her voice was low enough that I wondered if John David had been hiding *under* the bed in order to get audio as good as he had. Either that, or he'd purchased some pretty high-tech spy equipment off the internet. "*It's one thing for you to have your fun between the sheets, though I confess that I've always found your choice of paramour rather . . . odd.*"

"*Don't you dare talk to me about Ana.*"

My gaze darted from the phone back up to Lily. Her dark brown eyes were intent and smoldering. She wouldn't—maybe couldn't—look at me.

"*You've been giving her money. And I'm stupid—so stupid—that I didn't know it until now.*"

"*You're very, very stupid,*" J.D. said, his voice every bit as low as his wife's. "*And you don't get to say a word to me about any money that I might or might not have given to Ana.*"

After that, the audio cut out. Lily still wouldn't look at me. I sat down beside her on the bed, my own mind reeling.

"She knew, Sawyer." Lily shook her head, like that might make what she was saying less true, like she was waiting for me to tell her that she was jumping to conclusions, when she very clearly wasn't. "Mama already knew about Ana, and she didn't care."

How much of the anguish Lily had been through in the past two weeks was out of guilt, for what we'd discovered? For the fact that because of us, her mother had learned the truth, too?

"She cared that he was paying her." I said that so that Lily didn't have to.

"I thought . . ." Lily didn't finish that sentence. Instead, she scrolled through the audio files and selected another one to play.

"*I want a divorce.*" This time, there were no clues on the tape about where the conversation was taking place—or where John David might have been hidden when his father issued that statement.

"*Of course you do.*" Aunt Olivia didn't sound particularly fussed. "*But, J.D., honey, we can't always get what we want. Some of us take our commitments seriously. Some of us don't make promises unless we're dead set on keeping them.*"

I had a feeling—a very vague one—that there might have been more than one meaning to those words. Her husband's next statement did nothing to weaken that particular bit of intuition.

"Let me go. Olivia, please . . ."

"Nice manners from a man who's cheating on his wife." She'd taken the gloves off more quickly this time.

The second she did, he lost it, at low volume. "You blackmailed me into marrying you in the first place!"

"What?" I said out loud to Lily. She didn't act like she'd heard me at all.

"I was young," her father continued on the tape, "and I was scared, and I let you."

"But now you're done? Suddenly, you don't care if the truth comes out?"

"For God's sake, it was an accident!"

I managed not to say *What was an accident?* out loud, but only just.

"You won't tell anyone what happened," J.D. was saying now. "You have as much to lose as I do if the truth about that body comes out."

The mention of the body sent an electric chill down my spine. I told myself that I must have misheard.

"Did you ever even try to love me?" Aunt Olivia asked on the recording, her voice quiet and rawer than I'd ever heard it. "I have been nothing but a good wife to you and a wonderful mother to Lily and John David. Even you have to give me that."

"You love our children. If I had any doubts whatsoever on that score, I wouldn't have kept up this charade for as long as I have."

The admission didn't seem to calm her. If anything, it had the opposite effect. "That's all it ever was to you? A charade? When are you going to understand that I'm better for you than she ever was?"

"Say her name."

"Excuse me?" Aunt Olivia was retreating to form—manners, manners, manners.

"Just once. Say. Her. Name."

"You're being ridiculous, John."

"Liv—"

All of a sudden, their voices were blocked by the sound of a familiar—and very deep—bark. Then there was a series of noises that told me some major tussling was going on in the background, and then I heard John David yelp, *William Faulkner, this was not a part of the mission!* and the recording cut off.

I tried to process what I'd just heard, but the parameters would not compute. "What was *that*?" I asked Lily. She didn't even try to form an answer in reply. "He said that she blackmailed him into marrying her." Repeating that didn't make it sound any more plausible. "He mentioned . . ."

"A body." Lily finished my sentence for me.

You have as much to lose as I do if the truth about that body comes out. That statement rang in my ears. Before Ana had shown up, alive and well, it had seemed, if not plausible, at least *possible* that the body at Falling Springs was hers. I'd already let myself come far too close to jumping to conclusions once.

And yet, I had to ask: "Do you think this has something to do with the Lady of the Lake?"

Lily's only response was to play a third recording. It was significantly shorter than either of the others.

Lily's father said, *"You're not going to tell anyone the truth, Olivia. You might have, once. But now? I don't think so."*

Aunt Olivia replied, *"Maybe you're right. And maybe you should consider that I don't have to tell anyone your oldest, darkest secret to ruin your life. All I have to do to destroy your world is tell Lily the truth about Sawyer."*

CHAPTER 28

*I*n the grand scheme of things, the final recording wasn't as shocking or significant as the ones that had come before. But somehow, hearing Aunt Olivia say my name—knowing that Lily had heard it—dulled the cacophony of other questions in my mind.

"I got mad at you," Lily stated quietly. "Back when I found that old photo of your mama's, and you told me that you thought my daddy might be yours."

I felt like I'd swallowed sandpaper and was in danger of throwing it back up. "Lily . . ."

"And I got mad at you again when I saw you talking to *that woman* . . ." She swallowed and corrected herself: "Ana."

One second I was standing by the bed, and the next, I was sitting beside her. I wanted to make this better for her. I wanted to fix it.

"And none of that," Lily continued, her voice trembling, "*none of it* was your fault."

I'd been waiting for the guillotine to fall for months. I'd set the ball rolling myself when I'd told her that Sterling Ames was not my father. If she hadn't spent the past two weeks ignoring me, this moment—and the question she was on the verge of asking—might have come long before now.

I've been punishing myself. I've been letting her punish me—because of this.

"You heard Mama on that tape." Lily swallowed. "She threatened to tell me the truth . . . about you."

Aunt Olivia knows. I'd been so focused on what Lily had heard on the recordings that I hadn't really processed the fact that her mother was the one who'd implied the truth. *How long has she known that her husband slept with her sister?*

How long has she known that he's my father?

"You're my sister," Lily said quietly. "Aren't you?"

Answering that question shouldn't have been this hard. "I wanted to tell you."

"My daddy . . ." Lily pressed her lips into a thin line, her brown eyes flashing. "My *father*—he slept with your mama when she was in high school."

This time, all I could manage was *yes.*

"You knew." Lily's lips folded inward this time, like she was blotting her lipstick or biting the inside of her mouth. "That's why you've been so weird the past couple of months."

"That's part of it." This was all so much more messed up than she knew. Hell, given what we'd just heard on those recordings, there was a good chance that this situation—and this family—were way more messed up than *I* had previously thought, too.

"Who else knows that my father is also yours?" Lily asked quietly. "You didn't tell me. You didn't feel like you could. Who *did* you tell?"

I'd only told one person.

"Nick," I said. Before the gala, before he'd called in any favors, back when I could count the total number of times we'd had anything resembling a conversation on one hand, I'd told him some-thing that no one outside of this family had any business knowing.

"Are you two . . ." Lily trailed off, then course-corrected. Right now, what Nick and I were—or more accurately, given his radio silence, what we obviously *weren't*—was beside the point. "He's the only one who knows?" Lily asked instead.

I pressed my lips together and shook my head. "Lillian knows, too, but I didn't tell her."

Lily brought a hand to cover her mouth, like she could take whatever she was feeling and snuff it out. After several seconds, she lowered her hand. "And Campbell? You two have been thick as thieves this summer, whispering every chance you get."

I hadn't realized that she'd noticed—or cared. "I told Cam that her father wasn't mine. That's all."

"Okay. Tell me everything," Lily said, her voice hollow and her eyes strangely bright. "And, Sawyer? Don't you dare leave a damn thing out."

CHAPTER 29

*E*xplaining the circumstances surrounding my conception took a while. But once Lily seemed to have wrapped her mind around the abbreviated version of Sawyer's Messed-Up Origins 101—the pact, Greer's involvement, exactly what I'd been talking to Ana about at the hospital—the decision to go back through the recordings with a fine-tooth comb didn't take us long.

We started back at the beginning—not just the three recordings Lily had played for me, but every conversation John David had caught. The rest of them were fairly run-of-the-mill—no mention of bodies or blackmail or how and when Aunt Olivia had discovered that her husband was my father.

"I can't stay here," Lily told me once we'd finished. "I just . . . I can't be in this house right now, Sawyer."

I let my gaze travel to the roses the White Gloves had left us—and the envelopes.

"I'm with you," I told Lily. "Let's get the hell out of Dodge."

King's Island. 10 p.m. That was all our invitations said. Once we ascertained that John David was occupied with decorating his golf cart—and once we had *promised* to return in time to put the finishing touches on it in the morning—we did get the hell out of Dodge, via Jet Skis.

Riding separately from Lily, I leaned into the wind as we cut across the main channel. *As far as we can, as fast as we can.* I'd missed Lily these past weeks. I'd missed being *us.* Whatever she needed from me, I'd give her.

Anywhere she ran, I'd run, too.

Water sprayed the right side of my body as Lily sped past me. We wove in and out of a larger boat's wake. *Farther. Faster.* I could feel the sun on my face and forearms and the tops of my feet.

But no matter how loud the roar of the engine beneath me was, no matter how free I should have felt, I still couldn't outrun the realizations of the past hour: that Aunt Olivia had known about her husband's mistress—not to mention the truth about my paternity—for an indeterminate amount of time; that Uncle J.D. had apparently been giving Ana money; that years ago, long before either Lily or I had been conceived, Aunt Olivia had blackmailed her husband into marriage.

You won't tell anyone what happened, I could hear Uncle J.D. saying. *You have as much to lose as I do if the truth about that body comes out.*

Right after the Lady of the Lake had washed ashore, Aunt Olivia had gone on a strike against weekend trips to Regal Lake. She'd filled our days with crafts and togetherness and left zero time for us to follow up on what we'd stumbled into. That wasn't suspicious per se.

Not in isolation.

That body . . .

I hoped Lily was having an easier time outrunning her thoughts than I was having with mine. Barring that, I was cautiously optimistic that whatever the White Gloves had planned for this evening would do the trick.

It was still light outside when Lily and I made it to King's Cove. We stayed out on the water until the sun started its descent. As daylight began to give way, we cut our engines and waded into the shallows, throwing the entire weight of our bodies into pulling the Jet Skis up onto the shore.

King's Island wasn't more than a hundred yards across. There was no dock and only one crumbling building, made of siding and wood. The closer we got to it, the more apparent it became that, at some point, there had been a fire here. Parts of the house had burned and had never been replaced.

There was no roof.

"What time is it?" Lily asked me.

I wasn't wearing a watch, so I made my best guess based on the sun's position, sinking down past the horizon. "Eight thirty, eight forty-five?"

"That gives us another hour to kill." Lily placed her hand on the wall of the abandoned house. She stared at it for almost a minute, then headed inside. I followed. "If I asked you to fight me," she said softly, "would you?"

My stomach dropped, like an elevator whose cables had been abruptly cut, and a chill crawled up my spine. I'd thought that I'd been forgiven. I'd thought Lily and I were us again. Even when she'd been giving me the silent treatment, I'd never thought she wanted to hurt me.

Not physically.

"What?" I managed to say.

"I've never fought anyone before." Lily sounded far too reflective for my liking. "Never really gotten physical—unless you count that time you ended up turning the hose on Campbell and me." She laid her hand lightly on the wall, and then, before I could stop her, she pulled the other arm back, curled her fingers into a fist, and drove it into the charred wood.

Hard.

She reared back and did it again. I checked the impulse to grab her and keep her from punching the wall for a third time. Walker had told me that she was angry, but this was fury. Rage.

It was *hers*.

"All these years," she gritted out, plowing her hand into the wall again. "I thought my family was perfect." *Another hit*. "I thought I had to be perfect for *them*."

She was scaring me now. The silent treatment hadn't been pleasant, but it had been in character. This was something else.

"If I agree to fight you," I said, eyeing the blood now dripping from her fist, "will you stop hitting the wall?"

Lily let her hand drop to her side and turned to me. "Mama likes for things to be perfect. And Daddy . . ."

She couldn't finish that sentence.

"I was mad at you for *them*, Sawyer." She shook her head. "But now? I think I'm mad for me." She swallowed hard, bringing her hand up and resting a bloody knuckle against her mouth. "You didn't even give me the chance to choose you. And maybe I wouldn't have. Maybe you were right not to trust me, but that doesn't make it hurt any less."

She turned back to the wall. Her entire body shook, then tensed.

"I'm not good at trusting people," I said. My voice came out ragged and low. "That's not your fault. This whole situation? It's not your fault, and it's not mine. It just *is*." I could have left it there, but then she reared back for another hit. "Put your thumb on the outside of your fist when you punch," I advised. "Otherwise, you're just asking to break it."

"Advice for the ages," a voice commented behind us.

Lily froze, then let both hands drop to her sides. I turned sharply and saw Campbell standing in what had once been the doorway.

"Don't let me interrupt you," she said airily. "Please, go on."

Lily cast a sidelong glance at me. "It's not her fault, either, but perhaps a flying tackle would not go astray?"

"Bring it on, blondie." Campbell smiled. "I'm an Ames. We're taught how to fight dirty from the crib."

Lily was not at a loss for a response for long. "Speaking of Ames family members and cribs—I understand that Sawyer isn't your sister and that your real half-sibling is still out there somewhere."

"Adopted, presumably," Campbell replied smoothly.

Sadie-Grace chose that exact moment to stick her head in through the doorway. "I can't talk about adoption," she said solemnly. "Greer told me that I'm not allowed to say that word."

CHAPTER 30

By the time the rest of the White Gloves and Candidates arrived, the four of us had made our way out of the remains of the house and around the perimeter of the island. Three-quarters of it was walkable, but the northmost stretch featured a series of steep drop-offs and a heaping ton of debris.

It was like Mother Nature had been using the island for her castoffs: dead wood and decomposition and trash dredged up from the deep.

"Candidates, there are half as many of you as there were a month ago." For once, a White Glove other than Victoria took the lead. Hope let her gaze linger first on Campbell, then on me. "And there are twice as many of you as there will be a month from now."

The Candidates are many. The Chosen are few. I waited for someone to chime in with the phrase, but not one of the White Gloves did.

"Do you know why you're here? Why you've made it this far?" Hope let the question hang in the air. "Do you know what the White Gloves really are?"

"Maybe you've heard rumors," Nessa chimed in. "But you've only heard what we want you to hear."

"You've heard," Hope continued, "that we come from a certain kind of background and a certain kind of family." That would have elicited an eye roll from me—and possibly a gagging sound—except that she followed that sentiment with these words: "Maybe you think that makes us powerful."

"But you're not here because you're *powerful.*" Victoria didn't bother trying to project her voice, and it was almost lost to a sudden gust of wind. I felt, as much as saw, the Candidates pulling in tighter, closer together as she continued. "You're here because you know what it's like to feel powerless. Everyone you see here has been given every privilege that money can buy, but at the end of the day, there are some privileges that money can't buy. Money doesn't keep people from telling girls who look like me to go back to the other side of the border. And no matter what your family name is, or how white your skin, I'm willing to bet that there are still people who tell you to smile, because you look *so pretty* when you smile." She paused, just for an instant. "We all play by rules our brothers will never even have to know.

"You want to know why we go cliff-diving and off-roading and drag you out to abandoned islands in the night?" Victoria's voice was no louder, but her delivery was suddenly crystal clear. "Because we can. Because when people say that well-behaved women rarely make history, they leave out the little tidbit that the women who do make history rarely do so alone."

If they'd pitched the White Gloves to me this way from the get-go, I might have been in it for more than the distraction and the opportunity to cross-examine Victoria Gutierrez. Forget tradition and secrets and symbols. All they would have had to do was send me a note scribbled on scrap paper that said *Smash the patriarchy? Circle one: yes or no.*

"The reason that you're still here isn't just that you take risks."

Hope took over again, where Victoria had left off. "It's not just that you've stepped up to the challenges we've handed down. You're here because we believe that there's more to you than meets the eye."

"You're here because you have secrets," Nessa elaborated.

"You're here because, on some level, in some way, you want to keep up appearances *and* burn it all down." Victoria gave some sort of signal with her hand. There was a flurry of movement on either side of her, and within a heartbeat, flames exploded into the air.

Torches? Check. Abandoned island? Check. Highly flammable ruins? Check.

"In a moment, you'll receive three cards with your name on them and a pen." Victoria's features were lit by torchlight. "Tonight's challenge is simple: three secrets, one on each card. I'm not going to tell you that you have to push down the urge to hold back your deepest and darkest. The secrets you choose are up to you. But what I can and will say is that this is a sisterhood. This is real. And what you choose to write down on those cards? It matters."

CHARLOTTE, LIV, AND JULIA
SUMMER BEFORE SENIOR YEAR
TWENTY-FIVE YEARS EARLIER

"It's official." Julia smiled. "The boys will meet us at the lake."

Charlotte bit her tongue to keep from pointing out that Julia wasn't the only one who'd made a phone call, thank you very much. Charlotte was the one who'd called J.D.—for Liv.

"Are they meeting us at your family's house or mine, Jules?" Liv was sprawled across the passenger seat of Julia's car. Charlotte had been relegated to the back. She told herself that didn't matter, just like it didn't matter that *her* family didn't have a house at Regal Lake.

Just like it shouldn't have mattered that Julia had somehow gotten credit for calling all the boys.

"Who says we have to meet at someone's house?" Charlotte was almost surprised by how steady her voice sounded.

In the front seat, Liv turned around to look at her.

Charlotte popped on her sunglasses and leaned back against the window, mimicking Liv's posture with her own. "Let's have the boys meet us at Falling Springs."

CHAPTER 31

A year ago, I wouldn't have had nearly so many secrets to choose from. Even just a few weeks ago, I probably wouldn't have been tempted to put any of them to the page. But there came a point when secrets just didn't seem worth keeping anymore.

I wrote down my first, in all capital letters: *I AM THE RESULT OF A TEEN PREGNANCY PACT.*

Was admitting that discreet? No. Would Lillian be happy if the truth got out? Probably not. *Oh well.*

The second secret was harder to choose. The identity of my father and everything Lily and I had heard on John David's recording—those didn't feel entirely like my secrets to tell.

So instead, I went with a fraction of the truth for secret two. *I CAN'T STOP THINKING ABOUT THE LADY OF THE LAKE.*

More specifically, I couldn't stop thinking about the way Lily's father had said *that body* on the recording. *That might have nothing to do with the Lady,* I told myself, but I struggled to believe it.

On either side of me, I could hear Lily and Campbell writing on their cards. Someone farther away from us shifted, snapping a twig under their feet.

"If you're not finished yet," Nessa called out, "consider this your fair warning that it's time to wrap things up."

I needed a third secret. My thoughts went to Nick. To the texts I'd sent that he hadn't replied to. And then I thought about my mom. I'd always prided myself on being a straight talker, but there were certain truths everyone struggled to admit, even to themselves.

I don't know how to stay mad at my mom. I'm not sorry Lily's my sister. I've always wanted a family. I've always wanted a place to belong.

I want Nick to text back.

I glanced over at Lily. I could barely make out her face in the dark, but her eyes caught the torchlight. She was staring straight ahead, an odd half smile on her face, like this whole exercise had been therapeutic.

Like some part of her was hoping Victoria had been speaking literally when she'd mentioned the possibility of *burning it all down*.

I chose my third secret.

I wrote it down.

The White Gloves collected the pens, but they let us hold on to our secrets—for the moment.

"Take your first card," we were instructed, "and turn to the person beside you." I was sitting between Lily and Campbell. My instinct would have been to turn to Lily, but she was already turning to her left.

To someone else.

"Trade secrets," Victoria said. "One of yours for one of theirs."

"Well, Sawyer?" Campbell said beside me.

In for a penny, in for a pound. I held my first card out to her, anticipating her reaction. She plucked the card from my grasp, then hesitated before allowing me one of hers.

I saw the exact second Campbell processed the words *pregnancy pact*. "Your mama and Ana?" she murmured. I nodded, and her eyebrows nearly disappeared into her hairline.

Knowing I'd probably get an earful about having held back that information once we weren't surrounded by Candidates and White Gloves, I looked down at the card Campbell had handed me. The torches the White Gloves had lit all around us only provided so much light, but I could still make out every word.

If I could undo it all, I would.

I looked from the card back up to Campbell. Her expression never changed. I knew without asking that the card was referring to what we'd done last spring. She'd been the driving force behind bringing her father to justice. She'd needed, on some level, to take him down.

And if she could take it all back? She would.

"Don't say a word." Campbell's tone was pleasant enough, but I recognized a warning when I heard one. I wasn't sure if she was telling me not to comment on the secret I'd just read or not to share it.

Either way?

"I won't."

All around us, the world settled into silence. There seemed to be an understanding among the Candidates that the words we'd written on our cards weren't meant to be spoken out loud.

"Now take your partner's secret . . ." Victoria said. I waited for her to order us to share them. "Fold it in half."

Hope walked the group, gathering the cards, one by one. "Some secrets," she told us, "should stay secret. No matter how many cliffs we jump off of or dares we issue and fulfill, society will always have its rules, and our power will always come, in part, from knowing when to break them and when to play along."

"There's a time for telling secrets," Victoria translated. "And a time to bury them deep."

Someone brushed past me. My eyes had adjusted enough to the dark to recognize Nessa. She was wearing a scarlet robe now, the hood pulled up over her head.

She was carrying a shovel.

CHAPTER 32

*T*hey put our secrets in a wooden case. Each one of us took a turn with the shovel. The ground was harder than I'd expected, the digging grueling, but eventually, we had a hole: two feet by two feet and three deep.

The case was lowered in, and one by one, the eight White Gloves took possession of the shovel and started covering it with dirt.

"Choose another secret." Victoria waited for her voice to break through the odd reverie that had settled over the group. "And find another partner."

This time, Campbell ended up with Sadie-Grace, and I found myself face-to-face with Lily. I looked down at the second card I'd written, the one about the Lady of the Lake. Before I could decide to hand Lily my third card instead, she took the second from my hand and offered me one in return.

I can't stop thinking about the Lady of the Lake. I watched Lily read those words. It was hard to tell if they resonated with her, if she was remembering and thinking about and obsessing over two little words her father had said on the recordings.

That body . . .

"It's nothing," Lily told me. "It has to be nothing."

For God's sakes, I could hear Uncle J.D. saying, *it was an accident!*

All too aware that the discussions around us were minimal and quiet, I didn't press Lily further. Instead, I looked down at the card she'd handed me. I recognized her handwriting from the *Secrets* blog—tiny and evenly spaced and perfect.

SOMETIMES, MY BODY FEELS LIKE IT BELONGS TO SOMEONE ELSE.

I tried to wrap my mind around that, tried not to find it eerie. *Sometimes,* as in when she was punching her fist into a wall? Or *sometimes,* when she wrote other people's secrets on her skin?

No clarification was forthcoming.

"Take your partner's secret, and fold it in half."

I did as I was instructed, and so did Lily. This time, Hope was the one who came around to gather the cards. "Some secrets," she said wickedly, "are explosive. Sometimes, all a White Glove needs is to bide her time, and then . . ."

The two White Gloves who'd lit the torches earlier dipped them toward the ground now. I realized, belatedly, that while we'd been writing, they'd been assembling brush and debris.

Flammable was an understatement, enough so that I wondered if there had been gasoline or another accelerant involved. Flames flickered through the air, the sound and smell and heat reaching me in waves. I'd spent a few weeks in childhood fascinated with flint and trying to bang various stones together to make fire.

I hadn't realized, until now, how many more colors there were in a flame than orange and red.

One by one, the White Gloves took turns tossing secrets into the bonfire. They never opened them. They didn't read them.

They burned them.

And then they invited us to sit. Even without the heat of the bonfire, the summer air would have been sticky and warm. With it, I felt like we were all under some kind of blanket—or inside a pressure cooker, vents closed.

"One to bury," Victoria said. "One to burn. One for all." I waited for her to tell us to pass our cards in, or instruct us, one by one, to read them out loud. But what she did was produce a card of her own. "Three years from now, those of you who become White Gloves will come back to this island and do some digging. That's the thing about buried secrets—they don't stay buried forever." She looked down at the card she was holding. "Three years from now, it will be your turn to choose a new location for this ceremony. You'll gather your Candidates to bury and burn their secrets. And before you ask them to share the third with everyone present, each of you will share the one you buried years before."

I was used to them putting us through our paces. But this? The current White Gloves giving us something in return for what was being asked?

That was new.

"I'll go first," Victoria said. She paused, for a second, if that. "I'm not in my father's will." She looked down at her card after she said the words, as if to check that she'd said them correctly. "That's all I wrote. Next?"

Hope held her card in both hands. "The cancer came back." She didn't say whose cancer.

No one asked.

Nessa stared at Hope for a moment, shaken, and then read her own secret aloud. "I'm a replacement."

For what? Or who? Again, there was no explanation, no clarification.

A fourth girl whose name I couldn't remember offered only three words: "I said no."

One by one, the other White Gloves read their secrets. Most of them had kept things brief. Some of the secrets were hard to understand without context. Some were pretty damn clear.

You're not here because you're powerful, we'd been told. *You're here because you know what it's like to feel powerless.*

Once they finished, it was our turn. The first Candidate followed their example. She read her card—no context, no explanation. One by one, the others did the same. I barely registered what they were saying, because I was waiting for my turn—and my friends'.

The four of us went last.

"I have a half-sibling I've never met." Campbell had a way of tossing out words like they didn't matter and including just enough of a challenge in her tone to dare anyone to tell her that they did. After a second's silence, she broke the mold the others had set and elaborated. "Though to be fair, I suppose it's entirely possible that I *have* met this person and just didn't know we were related."

That was an angle I hadn't considered—though maybe I should have, given that I'd gotten the distinct impression from Campbell's grandfather that he'd had a plan for the baby, once upon a time.

"My turn?" Sadie-Grace had a habit of turning statements into questions. "I . . . ummm . . ." She was seated, but I would have bet big money that her feet were going crazy. "Okay? Here it goes?" She took a deep breath. "My mama was pregnant when she died."

I heard a sharp intake of breath beside me. I wasn't sure if that meant that Lily hadn't known what Sadie-Grace had just told everyone, or if she was taken aback to hear her best friend actually say the words.

Suddenly, Sadie-Grace's reluctance to tell her father the truth about Greer's "baby" made so much more sense. When Sadie-Grace had discovered the pregnancy was fake, she'd been so sad. I

171

couldn't remember everything she'd said when she'd gotten drunk at our casino-themed Debutante party, but I was pretty sure the words *No sisters for Sadie-Grace* had been included.

I'd known that Sadie-Grace's father had lost his first wife when Sadie-Grace was young. I hadn't realized he'd also lost a child. Knowing that and knowing what Greer was doing to him now made my stomach turn.

No wonder Sadie-Grace can't bring herself to tell him the baby isn't real.

I was next in line to read my secret, but before I could, Lily jumped in to take the attention off of Sadie-Grace. "My turn." She waited a moment, then spoke, enunciating every word. "I don't know what I want anymore."

If I hadn't known Lily, that wouldn't have sounded like much of a secret, but she was, next to Aunt Olivia, the most type A person I'd ever met. Lily always had a plan. She had her whole life mapped out. Even when Walker had broken up with her, even when she'd been dealing with so much suppressed emotion that she'd taken to displaying other people's hidden thoughts and darkest secrets on her own skin, she'd still *wanted* the same things.

To be the daughter Aunt Olivia wanted. To be the kind of granddaughter Lillian could take pride in. To be a credit to her family name.

Walker.

"That's not good enough." Victoria had remained silent through all of the other secrets. I couldn't help wondering why she was speaking up *now*.

"Victoria," Nessa murmured. We'd been told up front that they weren't going to demand our deepest and darkest. They were supposed to accept our secrets and move on.

"Fine," Lily said. I pictured her punching the walls of that ruined house, but when she spoke again, her voice was calm and clear. Too calm. Too clear.

"I don't know what I want anymore," she repeated. "Or who."

CHARLOTTE, LIV, AND JULIA
SUMMER BEFORE SENIOR YEAR
TWENTY—FIVE YEARS EARLIER

*C*harlotte adjusted the straps on her bathing suit. She knew she looked good. She told herself that she looked good.

"You're perfect," Liv told her. "Now hand me a damn pair of sunglasses before my skull actually splits in half."

Charlotte had to go back to the car to find the sunglasses, but she did as she was bid. *This was my idea,* she told herself. *My plan.*

The boys were meeting them at Falling Springs.

Charlotte had jumped off the lower ledges before but never the highest one. She was not fool enough to believe that Liv would accept anything less today.

"Having second thoughts?" Julia asked from the back when Charlotte stuck her head into the car.

"Of course not," Charlotte replied, judiciously avoiding looking at Julia, who was changing into her suit.

"No peeking," Julia needled. "Then again, I'm not the Ames you want to see naked."

Charlotte could feel herself blushing. She grabbed Liv's sunglasses and shut the car door—she shut, not slammed it, because one did not let Julia know when she'd hit the mark.

It's not about seeing Sterling—or touching him or having him touch me. Charlotte could feel a blush rising in her cheeks just thinking the words, and she thanked the Lord that she was fair enough that she could blame any pink tint to her skin on the punishing August sun.

"Thinking dirty thoughts?" Liv was every bit as perceptive as Julia, but most days, she was also twice as loyal and only half as mean. She plucked the sunglasses from Charlotte's hand. "I'm just kidding, Char. You look fabulous. You are fabulous. Sterling won't know what hit him. Drink?"

Charlotte was not sure if that was a question, an order, a suggestion, or a request. She went to grab the liquor, but stopped when she saw the boat pulling into the cove below. On a weekend day, Falling Springs was busy, but during the week?

They were the only ones here.

Charlotte's eyes searched the boat. Sterling was driving, which only made sense, because it was his family's boat.

He wasn't the type to abdicate the wheel.

Charlotte smiled when he looked up at her—not too much, not too little. *Just right.*

Liv was right. She was perfect. And so was he.

"Who the hell is that?" Liv asked suddenly.

Belatedly, Charlotte finished assessing the occupants of the boat. J.D. was there, of course, and there was a third boy whom Charlotte assumed was the rough-around-the-edges Thomas Mason, who Julia had talked her brother into bringing along.

And sitting between them was a girl.

CHAPTER 33

The Ballad of Lily Easterling and Walker Ames was supposed to be a love story for the ages. Or at least, that was what I'd been told.

That was what Lily had always seemed to believe.

"Sawyer." Victoria turned to me, implicitly accepting Lily's second offering as sufficient. "You're up."

The secret I'd written down on my card was only two words long. *I CARE.* I'd spent a lot of my life in self-protection mode. I'd learned early on that it was better not to expect too much of people. I liked to think of myself as someone who didn't have tender feelings for other people to hurt.

If nothing mattered that much, it was hard for anything to penetrate your armor.

But the truth was that I cared. I'd always cared—about the way my mom was the best friend a girl could ask for one moment and off chasing daydreams the next. About the way a subset of people had talked to me and about me in the town where I'd grown up.

About not having a father.

Now I had other people to care about, too. People who could

leave me. People who could decide, if they were so inclined, that I was more trouble than I was worth.

"Sawyer," Victoria prompted again.

I glanced at Lily, who'd just admitted that, for the first time in her life, she had no idea who or what she wanted.

"I wrote down 'I care,'" I said, still looking at Lily. "But since I suspect that won't be *enough*"—I shifted my gaze to Victoria, who might not have chosen to press me the way she'd pressed Lily—"I'll throw in another secret for good measure."

There wasn't much I could have said that would have stood a chance of distracting Campbell from Lily's admission—and everything it implied about Lily's relationship with Campbell's brother. So I went for something just as personal, a corollary to caring—and being well aware of the dangers of caring too much.

"I *do* know what I want," I said. "And I know what I don't want." I'd never actually said this out loud before, but the words came out easily. "I never want to fall in love."

That night, when Lily and I snuck back into the family's lake house and to the turret room, our grandmother was the one who caught us on the stairs.

"Your mama isn't happy you girls pulled a disappearing act," she warned Lily mildly.

"Mama's never happy," Lily said. "Or she always is. Honestly, it's getting hard to tell."

Lillian's expression softened—or at least shifted—as she processed the truth in Lily's words. Without any additional commentary, she turned to me. "Sawyer, your mama might have a bit of a headache in the morning." My grandmother was far too discreet to say the word *drunk*, but she did elaborate. "I believe there were Long Island iced teas involved."

The fact that my mom had been drinking in their presence was enough to get an eyebrow raise out of me. They were lucky she hadn't gotten weepy and started reminiscing about my conception.

Assuming she didn't.

"Come on," I told Lily, nodding toward the turret room. "Ellie Taft sleeps like the dead when there are Long Island iced teas involved."

Since my mom was passed out in one of the twin beds in the turret room, Lily and I both squeezed into the other. It was a tight fit, but we were both spent, and I don't think either one of us wanted to be alone. Her hair ended up spread across our pillow. Mine was bunched up beneath me.

I didn't say a word to her about Walker, and she didn't say a thing to me about love.

CHAPTER 34

*M*orning came early—and by *morning*, I meant *John David*. I awoke to him cannonballing onto the bed Lily and I were sharing. I ended up with what I was fairly certain would turn into a pretty impressive bruise, and Lily ended up on the floor.

John David, on all fours on the bed, made no apologies. *"Golf cart,"* he declared emphatically. *"Parade."*

Due to what he'd termed a "sparkler deficit," John David had opted for themed decorations. The theme he'd decided on was "Star Wars Spangled Banner."

"Does the cart look enough like the Death Star?" John David asked, eyeing his work critically. "Except also like the American flag?"

I thought there was some questionable and assuredly unintentional symbolism at play there for a holiday that was supposed to be patriotic, but who was I to argue with genius?

"It looks exactly like the Death Star," I told him. "And also the American flag."

"Good." John David narrowed his eyes at Lily and me. "Listen up, soldiers. We only have ninety minutes to finish these light-sabers and droids."

It turned out that when it came to arts and crafts, John David was an even stricter taskmaster than his mother. With five minutes to go on our ninety-minute deadline and all three of us sopping wet from sweat, he stepped back to appraise our work.

"Perfect," he declared. "Now all we need is to get William Faulkner into her costume."

Putting pants on a dog was not what one would call "easy." Putting pants on a purebred, hundred-pound Bernese mountain dog who was fairly certain she did not want to wear pants could have substituted for one of the twelve labors of Hercules.

But with enough cajoling and the right bribes, we did it.

"Bless William Faulkner's little doggy heart," Lily said as John David proudly drove past us in the Death Star, dressed like a Jedi, with a canine companion costumed as Uncle Sam.

Including the hat.

There were easily fifteen or twenty carts in the parade, plus bicycles, strollers, and at least a half-dozen other costumed dogs.

"How much do you think he understands?" I asked Lily as John David's cart disappeared from sight, and the two of us melted back into the crowd. "About everything that's happened?"

Lily's blond hair caught in the wind. For once, she didn't try to tame it. "More than he lets on."

Thanks to being drafted as John David's assistants, the two of us had managed to avoid Aunt Olivia this morning. My mom, as far as I knew, was still asleep.

"About last night," I said, but before I could say more or Lily could interject, her phone buzzed—three times. I was close enough to see her screen.

The first text was a rose. The second was a snake. And the third started with the words YOUR CHALLENGE, SHOULD YOU CHOOSE TO ACCEPT IT . . .

"Why," Lily said for the fifth time, "do they want me to enter the pie-eating contest?"

"Not enter," I clarified helpfully, taking a bite of the snow cone I'd just acquired. "Win."

Lily didn't respond to the teasing tone in my voice the way she might have, pre-Ana. She didn't respond at all. The thumb on her left hand prodded the bruised and battered knuckles on her right.

I thought about her second secret. *Sometimes, my body feels like it belongs to someone else.*

"Lily?" I said.

She blinked. "Headache." Before she could return to the topic of the pie-eating contest—or why she cared about meeting the White Gloves' challenge—her posture changed abruptly. She grabbed the snow cone out of my hand.

"Wouldn't advise eating that if you want room for pie." I realized a second later that she had no intention of eating anything. She just wanted something to look at. Something to hold. An excuse to pretend she didn't see Walker and Campbell Ames across the way.

"Do you think she told him?" I asked so Lily wouldn't have to. On the other side of the sprawling lawn, where a group of men was just starting to set up a half-dozen grills, Campbell and Walker were approached by Victoria.

And her father.

"Maybe Walker should date Victoria," Lily said, tightening her death grip on the snow cone. "Dance with her. Talk to her. Kiss her and tell her she's the one."

I had the distinct feeling that Lily saying that was no different than her pressing on bruised knuckles to see if it hurt.

"Before you have your boyfriend and Victoria hypothetically married off and having babies," I interjected, "I'd like to remind you that you're the one who's not sure, and they only danced together once."

"I'm the one with doubts *now*," Lily replied. "Walker was the one who wasn't sure before." She shifted the snow cone to her left hand, and the bruised fingers on her right curled and uncurled at her side. "Walker likes to be needed. He likes to ride in on a white horse and save the day, and he spent the last year thinking he'd never get to be that kind of guy again."

"And you don't want that kind of guy?" I asked.

"I don't know what I want," Lily reiterated as Walker and Campbell spotted us through the crowd. "I thought my mama and daddy had the perfect marriage. I thought they were the perfect couple. I was wrong. I wanted what they had. What does that say about me?"

Walker started making his way toward us, Campbell two steps behind.

"Are you hoping she didn't tell him?" I asked Lily. "Or that she did?"

No reply.

"Happy Fourth of July." Walker greeted her with a quick kiss to the lips. "Care for a stroll?"

He held out an arm, and she took it.

Once they were out of earshot, Campbell turned to me. "I didn't tell him. Obviously."

That was unusually altruistic of her. "What did Victoria and her father want?" I asked.

"To say hello," Campbell replied. "Supposedly." She didn't dwell on that—or allow me to. "Get any texts this morning?"

"No," I said. "But Lily did." Maybe that meant I'd been cut. As fond as I was of patriarchy smashing, that was an outcome I could live with.

"Aren't you going to ask me what my challenge is?" Campbell prompted.

I obliged.

"That's for me to know," came the reply, "and you to provide an alibi for me in regards to later."

"That almost makes me nostalgic," I said.

"Must be in the air," Campbell replied. "Mama informed me this morning that she's been feeling nostalgic, too."

I scanned the sprawling lawn and caught sight of Charlotte Ames, on the far side of the basketball and tennis courts—and right next to Aunt Olivia.

She's probably enjoying the fact that someone else is the scandal du jour. No sooner had that thought crossed my mind than I saw my mother standing underneath a large blue tent, all of three feet away from Greer Waters.

Depending on where my mom fell on the scale from hungover to *really* hungover, this had the potential to get ugly.

"I have to go," I told Campbell.

She caught my arm as I walked past. "If anyone asks tonight after the fireworks, I was with you all morning and afternoon." She smiled. "And, Sawyer? You'll know my challenge when you see it."

CHAPTER 35

I'd made it nine-tenths of the way to the catastrophe-in-waiting that was my mom and Greer when I bumped into Sadie-Grace.

"This heat, I swear," Greer was complaining to a group of women nearby. "Never have an August baby."

As tempting as it was to call out Greer's performance for exactly what it was, years of being my mom's wingman, confidante, backup, and babysitter told me that her doing the same thing—in public—had the potential to blow up in all of our faces.

"Excuse me," I told Sadie-Grace. I went to move past her, but she sidestepped and blocked me.

"No."

I tried to make sense of that. "What?"

"I said no," Sadie-Grace said apologetically. "I have to say no. Not just to you. To everything. I have to say no to everything anyone asks from me, all day. *Because.*"

She put so much emphasis on that last word that I finally connected the dots. "Because that's your White Glove challenge?"

"I can neither confirm nor deny that." Sadie-Grace was serious as a funeral. "But maybe, if you want me to get out of your way, you should ask me *not* to step aside?"

"Whatever you do, don't step aside."

Once she'd cleared the way, I made my way to where Greer had been standing a moment before. Neither she nor my mother was immediately visible. Eventually, I spotted them just outside the tent, back and away from the foot traffic.

"I don't hate you, Greer." I was wired to hear my mom's voice above others, to be able to pick it out of a crowd. "If it weren't for you, I wouldn't have Sawyer. So rest assured, I'm not going to burst your little bubble with respect to your current deception."

"I'm sure I have no idea what you're talking about, Ellie." Before my mom could respond, Greer caught sight of me and nodded in my direction.

My mom turned. She saw me, then let her gaze travel farther into the tent, to Sadie-Grace. "All I'm saying, *friend*, is that maybe you're so set on making life go your way that you're missing out on the ways that it already has."

I'd wondered how hungover my mom was. The answer was apparently *philosophically hungover*, which generally hovered around the midpoint of the scale.

Without responding to my mom's advice, Greer went to make her exit. I watched her go. *Do you know that your husband lost a child when he lost his first wife?* I thought. *Would it make any kind of difference to you if you did?*

Given that she was eight months into this deception, I doubted it.

"She's a piece of work," my mom declared, coming to stand beside me. "Happy Fourth of July, baby."

She hesitated when she called me *baby*, like she wasn't sure she was still allowed to call me that. The hesitation hit me harder than any attempt she'd made to mend things between us.

"Happy Fourth of July," I returned. I might have left it there, but I realized, suddenly, that I knew something that she didn't know.

Something that she probably should know.

"Mom," I started. "Don't do anything rash or stupid when I tell you what I'm about to tell you. Aunt Olivia? She knows."

CHARLOTTE, LIV, JULIA, THE INTERLOPER, AND *THE BOYS* SUMMER BEFORE SENIOR YEAR TWENTY-FIVE YEARS EARLIER

"*D*on't worry," Liv whispered in Charlotte's ear. "You're prettier."

Charlotte wanted to say that she hadn't been worried, but that was a lie. Down below, the boat was anchored. Sterling and the other boys—and the interloper—were making the climb up. The girl might have been wearing a bathing suit, but she was also wearing an oversized T-shirt that made it hard to tell. She should have looked hideous in it, but she didn't.

She shouldn't have been touching Sterling, but she was.

"Hello, hello!" Charlotte forced a smile onto her face, sweet as sugar. She waved, letting her eyes lock onto Sterling's as he helped Miss T-shirt up the incline.

"Who's she?" Julia asked, coming up behind Charlotte and Liv. Charlotte would have liked Julia significantly better if she'd sounded the least bit upset about the unexpected addition.

At least she'd asked the question loud enough for everyone to hear.

"Her name is Trina," Sterling called back. "She's a local. We met her when we went to gas up the boat and decided to invite her along for the ride."

Charlotte could feel Julia assessing the situation. The local girl was getting touchy-feely with Sterling, not Thomas—and certainly not J.D.

Charlotte wouldn't let that be a big deal. She could be gracious. She could be beautiful.

She could be fun.

"Don't worry," Liv murmured beside her. "If she gives you any trouble, I'll happily push her off the cliff."

CHAPTER 36

*A*gainst all odds, my mom didn't do anything rash or stupid when I broke the news that her sister knew exactly who my father was. I could only conclude that she was saving that for after the pie-eating contest.

"The rules are simple." A woman with a microphone was standing in front of a stage that had been erected near the tennis courts. "The first person to finish their pie wins. Of course"—she winked at the crowd—"there is one other tiny detail." She held up what appeared to be a bunch of silk scarves. "Our contestants' hands will be tied behind their backs!"

With quite a bit of further ado, the would-be pie-eaters had their hands bound. Pies were ceremoniously placed on the table in front of each of them. There were nine contestants total, eight of them male. The pies, from what I could see, appeared to be heavy on the whipped cream and/or meringue.

Lily was seated at the very end of the stage. Her posture was impeccable. Her hair had been pulled into a low ponytail at the nape of her neck.

"On your mark . . ." the woman with the microphone said. "Get set . . ."

Lily bowed her head slightly, as if in prayer.

"Go!"

I expected Lily to hesitate, but she didn't. She *buried* her face in that pie at a high enough velocity that pieces of meringue went flying. As she started chomping away, I realized that was the point. Her competitors were eating the pie with their mouths. Lily was quickly turning this into a whole face endeavor. She was eating the pie, but she was also demolishing it.

The important thing about a pie-eating contest, it turned out, was not so much *eating* the pie as it was making sure that your tin was empty first.

"Done!" Lily yelled, lifting her head. To her left, eight men ranging in age from their teens to their forties turned to stare at her. The judge walked over and examined Lily's pie tin, which contained only faint traces of pie.

"It appears," the woman said, casting a mildly horrified look at Lily, whose face, hair, and clothing were covered in pie bits, "that we have a winner."

"Are you sure she's Olivia's?" my mom asked beside me. "Because that was really something."

Up onstage, someone was handing Lily a towel. It took me a second to realize that the person in question was Walker.

He was laughing.

"Sawyer." My mom nudged me. "Your phone."

I made a concerted effort to stop watching Walker and Lily and turned my attention to my own text messages. In quick succession, I received three.

@) - -' - , - - -

~ ~ ~ ~ ~ ~8<

Look to your left.

That didn't seem like much of a challenge to me. Then I looked to my left. Through the slight crowd that the pie-eating contest had attracted, I saw someone milling on the outskirts.

Nick.

My phone buzzed again: a fourth text. *Your challenge, should you choose to accept it: spend the afternoon with him.*

Nick was wearing a navy swimsuit with a ratty red T-shirt. As I approached, he crossed his arms, the shirt pulling against his biceps and shoulders.

Not that I noticed.

"Hi," I said. He didn't say hello back, so I filled the silence. "I always wondered what a grudge personified would look like."

That almost got a smile out of him. "You the reason I got invited to this thing?"

"That would be the secret society that's trying to torture me with your presence."

It felt good to be too honest with someone.

"You're really not great with apologies," Nick commented.

"I already apologized," I replied. When he didn't seem to know what I was talking about, I elaborated. "Via text."

Texts that he hadn't returned.

"I don't text," Nick said.

"You make phone calls," I said, reading between the lines. "Like a civilized person."

This time, the edges of his lips *did* tilt up, ever so slightly. "I didn't come here to do this with you," he said.

"And yet," I replied, casting a look at the Fourth of July Wonderland all around us, "you still need the connections. And the reputation."

He grimaced. "Damned debutante ball."

I said what he hadn't. "Damned debutantes."

That seemed to penetrate, in a way that nothing else I'd said had. "I really did think you were different," he told me quietly.

That hurt, but I didn't let it sting for long. "What kind of person would I be if I prided myself on being different from other girls?"

He studied me for a moment—blatantly, intently. "I wasn't talking about girls. I was talking about . . ." He looked around at the pockets of people all around us. The tennis and sand volleyball courts. The immaculate, sprawling lawn. "All of this."

"It's weird, isn't it?" I asked him. "Being one of them?"

"I'm not." His reply was immediate. The elaboration took longer. "And neither are you."

And just like that, I was forgiven.

"Last time I saw you," Nick said, "you were making noises about that body. What do they call her?"

"The Lady of the Lake," I replied. "And FYI: referring to someone talking as 'making noises' doesn't exactly endear you to the speaker."

Nick tilted his head to the side. "Noted."

I decided not to hold the word choice against him. "The body wasn't who we thought it was. Whoever she was, we have no reason to believe that she was killed by an Ames."

"Well, that's a relief," Nick said dryly. Then he took in the look on my face. "Isn't it?"

We ended up down on a nearby dock. I told him everything Lily and I had heard on John David's recording. I waited for him to decide that I was more trouble and more drama than I was worth, that I was one of *them* in the worst possible way.

"Is there a reason," he asked after a long silence, "that you tell me all of your secrets?"

I heard no judgment in his tone, but there was something in the way he was looking at me that I couldn't put into words.

"Who are you going to tell?" I brushed off his question and looked out at the lake. The water in our cove was choppier than I'd ever seen it. Every once in a while, as we sat in silence, the waves hitting the dock sprayed the two of us.

"Did you ever come to the lake?" Nick was the one who broke the silence. "Before?"

"No," I replied, thankful for the change in subject. "Did you?"

Nick let his feet dangle over the side of the dock. "When I was younger. One of Colt's friends would borrow a car. There's a camping area, close to the Macon Bridge. Even when it's not a holiday weekend, the place is too crowded. Loud. Muddy as hell, if there's been rain."

The smile on his face made it clear. "You loved it."

He looked down at the backs of his hands. "Colt did."

That was the second time he'd said his name. "I'm sorry," I told him. "About your brother."

Nick locked his eyes on the horizon. "He'd be a hell of a lot better at this than me. The parties. Playing nice. Jessi." I assumed that was his younger sister's name, but didn't get the chance to ask before he continued. "You."

I should go. I felt that, like a warning siren going off in my brain. I wanted to say those words to him, but I couldn't.

"You're not doing so bad," I said instead.

Nick turned his head toward mine. I tried to remind myself that he'd had weeks to get back in touch with me and hadn't. That he hated the world I lived in and the people in it. That he'd been involved with Campbell before he ever met me.

That I didn't want to want anything like this.

But all I could think about was my hands in his hair.

"Promise me," Nick said, his voice rumbling and low, "that for the next ten seconds, you're not going to say anything about dead bodies or fake pregnancies or anyone with the last name Ames."

I felt my body listing toward his. My hands moved to his chest of their own volition. "I'll give you seven," I countered.

He brought his hands up to my fingertips, touching them lightly. He leaned forward, his lips stopping a fraction of an inch from mine, then moved his hands to the sides of my face. His fingers were rough and callused.

And warm.

"I can make seven work." He grinned and closed his lips over mine.

I should have pulled back, but I didn't. I shouldn't have lost myself to it—to him—but I did. On some level, I was aware that I suddenly had his shirt fisted in my hands, that I wasn't sitting next to him anymore, but on top of him.

His hands trailed down to my waist as he pulled back from the kiss. "Seven."

My phone buzzed. I ignored the text, but it was followed by another and another. I looked down at my phone. *Lily.*

"Trouble in paradise?" Nick asked me.

I was on my feet before I'd even finished reading the message. "You don't even know."

CHAPTER 37

"Where is he?" I asked.

Lily led me through the crowd, then stopped when we got close to the long line of grills that they'd finished setting up since Nick and I had disappeared. "There."

J.D. Easterling had some nerve, showing up here. When I finally saw him, however, I realized that was an understatement. Lily had omitted one key fact from her text.

"He didn't," I said.

Lily swallowed hard. There were still some noticeable pie bits in her hair. "He did."

The fact that Lily's father had decided to attend the festivities was surprising enough, the kind of move meant to communicate to everyone, but especially to Aunt Olivia, that he was still the same man—Lily's father, John David's father, a prominent member of the circles in which all of these people ran.

But J.D. hadn't just come here. More specifically: he hadn't come here *alone*.

"Why would he bring her?" Lily was practically shaking.

I grabbed her arm and held it. "I have no idea."

Ana was wearing a blue sundress—white shrug with capped

sleeves, sedate ponytail low on the nape of her neck. She looked all-American and wholesome.

I scanned the area for Aunt Olivia. She stood on the other side of the lawn flanked by Boone's mother and Campbell's. Julia Ames had a grip on Aunt Olivia's arm, the way I held Lily's, but I got the distinct feeling that she wasn't so much holding her as holding her back. Charlotte was standing an extra step or two away. She and Aunt Olivia had a habit of exchanging sugary-sweet barbs, and yet, Charlotte was the one who stepped forward, to block Uncle J.D. from Aunt Olivia's view.

"Sawyer." Lily's voice took on a sudden urgency as she dug her fingers into my arm. "Your mama."

I'd expected a scene when my mom had confronted Greer, but hadn't gotten one. A lifetime of experience had taught me I wouldn't be so lucky twice.

"What can I do?" Nick asked beside me. I hadn't expected him to come with me, but his physical presence—and the way I felt the weight of it in every inch of my own body—reminded me that I'd confided in him.

Nick was the only one here who knew everything that Lily and I knew.

"Everyone is watching." My half-sister didn't sound as upset as I would have predicted, like she'd disassociated and couldn't feel anything other than numb.

"Seriously, Ana?"

I could hear my mom from ten feet away. Under any other circumstances, I would have been amused by the way everyone in the vicinity was not-staring. *Staring* was rude, but there wasn't a person nearby who didn't find themselves casually glancing a few feet away from the action.

"Ellie," J.D. said, striking a balance between cajoling and a warning.

"How could you?" my mom asked. Most people probably thought she was talking to him, but I flashed back to the dozens of pictures I'd seen of my mom and Ana and Greer, wearing white ribbons on their wrists or woven through their hair.

Ana seemed to know the question my mom had just asked was for her. "You have no stones to throw here," Ana told her—quietly, calmly, her tone not entirely unpleasant.

I was suddenly overwhelmed with a horrible premonition of my mom laying her—and my—whole sordid past out for everyone to hear. *How could you sleep with my sister's husband? How could you sleep with the father of my child?*

By the grace of God, the question my mom asked out loud was a different one. "What happened to you, Ani?"

The nickname seemed to penetrate the other woman's shields in a way that nothing else had. She wavered, then stepped closer to my mom.

"You have no idea what I've been through. *None.*"

I was so absorbed in their interplay that I didn't notice until it was too late that Lily had pulled her arm away from mine. She walked like a sleepwalker into the fray.

"What *you* have been through?" Lily asked.

"Lily." Uncle J.D. tried to cut in, but Lily shut him up when she swiveled her dark brown eyes to him.

"Hello, Daddy."

The next second seemed to stretch into an eternity, and then a man appeared at Uncle J.D.'s side. I recognized him as Boone's father—one of the four men I'd once thought might be mine.

"J.D.," Thomas Mason said lowly. "You should go."

Lily's father looked past his old friend to where Aunt Olivia was standing, Julia Ames beside her, and Charlotte in front.

"So this is how it's going to be?" J.D. asked.

The only answer he—or those of us watching—got were the same words, repeated. "You should go."

LABOR DAY, 3:28 AM

"*T*his is me crouching. This is me standing. This is me realizing how deep this hole is."

"Do you have to narrate *everything* you're doing?"

"This is me trying to give myself a boost . . . *Oof!*"

"Sadie-Grace."

"I'm sorry! It's just really hard to give yourself a boost."

SIX WEEKS
(AND TWO DAYS) EARLIER

CHAPTER 38

"*Y*ou haven't talked about Ana in a while. Or her baby."
Nick trailed his thumb across my jawline. "Or the Lady
of the Lake."

We were at his place—an aging, single-bedroom houseboat he'd
acquired alongside The Big Bang. This was my third time here in
two and a half weeks.

I was starting to get comfortable.

"I didn't think we were the kind of friends who talked." To drive
home the point—to myself as much as to him—I brought my lips
to his. Kissing Nick wasn't *comfortable*. It wasn't *nice* or *easy*.

Each moment of contact was rough and raw and real in a way
that should have sent me running. It hurt in all the right ways—
more, even, when his touch was light and gentle.

"Right," Nick said, pulling back from the kiss just far enough to
speak, his lips still brushing featherlight over my own. "We don't
talk. You escort me where I need to go, and we . . ."

"Count to seven?" I suggested.

Thinking, flirting, getting physical—as long as I could sound
as sardonic as he did every time he opened his mouth, I knew I'd
manage to stay on the right side of the line.

He bared his teeth in a shark's smile, then brushed his lips against my neck, right where he could have placed his fingers to feel my pulse. "You could," he murmured. "Talk to me, the way you did on Fourth of July." His teeth nipped lightly at my skin.

I thought back to Fourth of July. The way he'd stayed with Lily and me after that ugly business with Ana and J.D. The way he and I had snuck back to the dock that night. The fireworks.

One in particular, courtesy of Campbell's challenge, had exploded in the twin shapes of a snake and a rose, just as Nick had buried his hands in my hair, tightened his grip.

And counted to seven.

I'd spent my birthday this past week much the same way—minus the literal fireworks and plus a few figurative ones.

"Since when do you want to hear about the lives of the rich and scandalous?" I asked him. I forced myself to roll onto my back and sat up. After a moment, I stood. It was better this way. Safer, even if my body objected every time I pulled back. "Besides," I said, unable to keep my eyes from drinking in the sight of his bare chest, my fingers from itching to touch him, "there's not much to tell."

Lily and I hadn't heard anything from Uncle J.D. or Ana. There'd been no more impromptu visits from my mom. No blowups between her and Aunt Olivia. Nothing from Campbell's "friend" at the sheriff's department.

Not a word from Victoria and the White Gloves.

Even Greer seemed to be just biding her time as her "due date" approached.

"Am I allowed to ask how Lily is doing?" Nick asked me, getting out of bed himself. I knew him well enough to know that his tone when he said *allowed* was meant to needle me, but I also knew that he had a soft spot—an inexplicable one—for Lily.

Don't stare at him. Don't get back in that bed. Knowing he'd follow, I walked up the stairs from the cabin out onto the boat's deck. "Lily is . . ." I was debating the answer to his question when I saw someone sunbathing on the front of Nick's boat. "Here."

Since the Fourth of July, Lily's behavior hadn't raised any red flags. She hadn't punched any walls. She hadn't complained of any more headaches. But I had been unable to shake the feeling that she was a time bomb, ready to explode.

"Everything okay?" I asked her, deciding that the *What are you doing here?* was probably implied.

Lily flipped onto her stomach. "Everything's fine," she said. "I just wanted to catch some sun." She turned her face to the side and closed her eyes. "And," she added, as if it was of no particular import, "I just broke up with Walker."

When it became clear that I wasn't going to get anything else out of Lily—and that she had no intention of leaving Nick's boat and didn't need me hovering, *thank you very much*—I called Campbell. Trying to have a conversation with her was made somewhat more complicated by the voices I could hear in the background.

One was Walker's.

One sounded like Boone's.

It took me almost a minute to realize that the third was female. I asked Campbell who was there, and she didn't lie to me.

"Don't overreact, but Walker invited a friend over."

He and Lily had *just* broken up. "What friend?"

CHAPTER 39

I showed up on the front porch of the Ames family's lake house, because some things needed to be said in person. "I didn't realize that Walker and Victoria were friends" was one of those things.

"Join the club." Campbell stepped out onto the front porch and closed the door behind her. "Apparently, they've been talking."

I thought of Lily. I'd left her in good hands—Nick's—but I didn't trust the lack of emotion she'd displayed. I could buy Lily deciding that she didn't want to be in a relationship right now, or reaching the conclusion that she and Walker had grown apart, or even that a large part of their relationship had always been based on other people's expectations.

But I couldn't buy any of those conclusions not hurting.

"How long has Walker been *talking* to Victoria?" I asked Campbell. "And what do they have to be talking about?"

"Right now?" Campbell arched an eyebrow at me. "They're talking about Ana's baby."

• • •

"I want to meet with Ana." Victoria's voice was audible as Campbell and I rounded the side of the house to the back deck. "But she won't see me unless my father sees her."

I didn't wait for them to see me to chime in. "And your father won't see her?"

Walker, Victoria, and Boone turned toward me, their conversation grinding to a halt.

"You're looking lovely, devious, and/or vengeful today," Boone commented. "Whichever you're most likely to perceive as a compliment."

Walker recovered his voice before Victoria did. "Don't take this the wrong way, Sawyer . . ." He softened the words with a trademark smile. "But this really doesn't concern you."

I got the feeling that he wasn't just talking about this conversation. He was talking about his relationship with Lily.

"Irritated in an aesthetically pleasing manner!" Boone tried another compliment on for size.

"To be fair," Campbell said, "Sawyer's been ineffectually trying to locate Ana's baby for weeks."

Considering that Campbell hadn't been any more effective than I was, I could have replied to that in any number of ways, but instead, I decided to reply to Walker's assertion that I had no place here.

"I may be the only person on this deck who's not related to Ana's baby," I said, "but that baby and I have an awful lot in common."

I thought back to my conversation in the cemetery with Lillian— and everything I hadn't been able to put into words. I wasn't sure how many of my secrets Campbell had let slip to Walker, let alone Victoria, but at the moment, I wasn't sure I cared.

"Right now, the 'I Owe My Entire Existence to a Stupid Teen-age Pregnancy Pact' Club has a membership of one," I continued, like I was ripping off a bandage. "If any of you know what it's like to be the result of a planned, adulterous, underage pregnancy that's done a total number on your sense of self, parental relationships, and understanding of the universe, I'd be happy to chat. But otherwise . . ." I crossed the deck and took a seat at the table. "I think I have at least as much reason to be here as someone looking for their great-niece or long-lost cousin."

Victoria didn't say anything about the *great-niece* comment, but Boone did try for another compliment, which didn't bear repeating.

I ignored him in favor of Victoria. "You were saying that Ana wants to see your father?"

"My father has . . ." Victoria considered her words. ". . . favorites. Favorite sons, favorite grandchildren. Back in the day, I've gathered that was Ana. Her mother's a Swedish socialite who's very good at playing to my father's ego. I guess Ana was, too."

"And then she got pregnant," I said flatly.

"She didn't come to him for help." Victoria gave a little shrug. "And she didn't ask for his forgiveness."

Why would she? Delving into Gutierrez family dynamics wasn't my top priority at the moment, but still, the question lingered.

"I might be able to get my father to talk to her," Victoria said. "But we can't count on it. It might be easier to find someone else Ana would talk to."

"Like who?" Campbell asked, coming to sit on top of the wrought-iron table, right between Victoria and her brother.

Walker was the one who replied. "Lily," he said softly.

I stared at him. "Are you kidding me? You're actually sitting there considering asking Lily to talk to her father's mistress?" That was the single worst plan I'd ever heard. "What the hell is wrong with you, Walker?"

Do you not care about her at all?

"She's the one who broke up with me," Walker told me quietly. "I'm not the bad guy here."

Victoria laid her hand on the table, close enough to his that they almost touched. "Neither is she." She allowed her eyes to meet mine. "Asking Lily to talk to Ana is out. What does that leave us with?"

Not much. That was where we'd been—where *I* had been—for months. There were questions I wanted answers to—more than I should have, probably—but there was no straight line to answers. This wasn't the kind of problem that could be solved with determination, elbow grease, and sheer force of will.

We couldn't *make* Ana tell us the truth.

"What about," Boone interjected, "and I'm just throwing this out there: *a party.*"

"How is a party going to help us find Ana's baby?" Campbell asked him.

"I don't know," Boone replied. "That's just how things work around here. Fancy shindig, scandalous happenings, *murmur murmur,* and voilà."

Walker turned to Victoria. "You did say your mother wanted to host something. Do you think you could talk her into inviting Ana?"

"If my mother gets irritated enough with my father and brothers," Victoria said, "anything is possible. I can work on a party—that'll be White Glove convenient anyway—but Ana's attendance is about as far from guaranteed as something can get."

The mention of the White Gloves had me flashing back to that night on King's Island. *You're here because we believe that there's more to you than meets the eye,* we'd been told. *You're here because you have secrets.*

I turned that over in my head. "How do the White Gloves identify Candidates?" I asked Victoria.

She clearly wasn't expecting the question.

"I imagine it involves a lot of research." Campbell caught my drift with impressive speed. "How exactly does one go about putting together in-depth dossiers on Debutante types in three states?"

I remembered Hope rattling off my bio. *Do I want to know how you know that I used to be a mechanic?* I'd asked her.

"Do you do your own research?" I asked Victoria. "Or do you hire it out?"

"Does it matter?" Victoria asked pointedly.

"Ana's baby would be our age. *My* age, within a couple of months. And if Ana thought that the people who adopted her baby could give her child every advantage . . ."

"Then the baby probably went to a certain kind of family," Campbell finished.

The kind of family that the White Gloves tended to recruit from.

"I can't show you those files," Victoria said, "even if I could get ahold of them without the others noticing. That information is private."

Walker leaned toward her. "Vee."

Vee? I was glad Lily wasn't here. No matter how okay she claimed to be, no matter whose idea breaking up had been—hearing that nickname on Walker's lips wouldn't have felt good.

And I wasn't sure how much more *bad* Lily could take.

"I'll look through the dossiers we had our investigator put together when we were looking for Candidates," Victoria told Walker, "*if* you and Campbell will double back and ask your grandfather what else he knows."

The fact that Victoria had brought Davis Ames into this triggered a faint alarm in the back of my head, but I didn't have time to probe that feeling further, because an instant later, Boone jumped to his feet.

"Sawyer!" he said. "We've been summoned. To the Batmobile!"

I stared at him.

"Sadie-Grace just texted me," he clarified. "She's parked out front. She needs us."

"Why?" I asked.

Boone didn't answer. He started trotting for the side of the house, and then glanced back at me. "Your reluctance to follow my lead is a dagger in my heart! But sadly, we don't have time to stand around here talking about your obvious cruel streak. Time is of the essence."

"Why?" I asked again. He didn't answer. I followed him. "What's going on?"

He waited until we were out of earshot to reply. "Sadie-Grace's stepmother just went into labor."

CHAPTER 40

"*G*reer can't be in labor." I stated the obvious as Boone and I climbed into Sadie-Grace's car. "She's not pregnant."

"Her water broke an hour ago," Sadie-Grace said from the driver's seat. "She asked me to clean it up."

That was some next-level deception—and possibly self-deception, given that Greer knew that Sadie-Grace knew the pregnancy was fake.

"I activated the GPS app on her phone a few days ago," Sadie-Grace confessed in a hushed tone, like that was the real scandal here. "You know, Find Your Friend? She's not exactly my *friend* . . . but I found her."

She handed the phone to Boone. "Shockingly," he said, "she's not at a hospital."

Sadie-Grace frowned. "She told my dad she wanted a midwife. She told him everything was arranged. He's in Buenos Aires on business, but as soon as she told him the baby was coming, he chartered a plane to fly him back."

"You have to tell him," I said.

Sadie-Grace couldn't argue with that statement, so she ignored it. "Can you read me off the directions?" she asked Boone. "To find my friend?"

Boone did as she asked.

"Where are we going?" I said as Sadie-Grace put her car in drive.

Boone held out Sadie-Grace's phone, with the Find Your Friend app open for me to see. "A town called Two Arrows."

Based on its size, Two Arrows should have reminded me of the town I'd grown up in, but it didn't. I'd grown up in a part of the state where half the people I'd known had family farms. Things here were dustier. Less green. There were stray dogs in the streets. I didn't have to look too closely at the red dirt beneath our feet to suspect that it was at least a third clay.

"There," Sadie-Grace said, pointing. We'd parked the car a block or so back. The Find Your Friend app, apparently, wasn't *that* accurate. But we'd chosen the right direction to walk in, because there, parked in front of a metal garage that appeared to be full to the brim with lawn chairs and boxes and clothes, was Greer's car.

"Very stealthy," I commented. "A Porsche doesn't stick out around here at all."

Any reply the others might have made was cut off by a bloodcurdling, heartrending scream.

Summertime meant open windows—which almost certainly meant these houses didn't have air-conditioning. Either way, there was nothing to block the sound of the scream, which just kept coming.

"It's okay," I heard a familiar voice say. "I'm here."

Greer.

"Am I the only person thinking that Greer isn't the one whose water broke?" Boone asked.

He wasn't. I thought back to Aunt Olivia shutting me down

when I'd tried to tell her the truth about Greer. She'd insisted that no woman would fake a pregnancy. I wondered what her stance would be if I told her that Greer had somehow secretly—and, given that her husband didn't know and hadn't signed any papers, almost certainly illegally—found herself a baby.

"You have to talk to your dad," I told Sadie-Grace as another round of gritty, voice-breaking screams started up.

"I know," Sadie Grace said, rising up to the tips of her toes in a *relevé*. "It's just—*eep!*"

I was about to ask her what that was supposed to mean when I felt something hard and round press into the small of my back.

As a child, I'd been obsessed with many things—lock-picking and medieval torture and mixing the perfect martini. But one thing I'd never educated myself on was guns.

CHAPTER 41

*O*ur new friends weren't exactly chatty. So far, all we'd gotten out of them was a single word.

"Move."

Apparently, we stuck out here about as much as Greer's Porsche.

"She'll want to talk to you."

That was six more words, said as we were herded around the back of the house. Sitting on the porch was an old woman. She had her back to us, so I couldn't see anything other than her bun—wiry, brown hair, streaked at least three-quarters gray. As we drew closer to the front of the chair, I took in her outfit: an oversize T-shirt, knee-length shorts that revealed legs with a farmer's tan. She was barefoot now, but based on the tan lines, I assumed that was out of the norm.

Her skin was wrinkled and cracked, but it didn't have that paper-thin look I'd seen on other people later in life. I hadn't even seen her face yet, and I was already pretty sure that nothing about this woman was fragile.

There was a dog lying at her feet, a mix, by the look of it—part pit bull, part Lab. The dog lifted his head as we were shoved forward.

"He likes me," Boone declared beside me. "The dog," he clarified, in case that was unclear to anyone. "Dogs always like me. They're very good judges of character."

"We found these three sniffing around up front," the person behind me said, lowering her shotgun. I hadn't processed until this moment, listening to her voice for a second time, that she was female.

"Beth don't need this," the other one commented—also female, also not particularly fond of the lot of us. "She's having a hard enough time already."

"Is that her name?" Sadie-Grace asked. "The girl having the baby? Beth?"

The woman in the chair stood. Given that I was in possession of every ounce of street smarts that the three of us had to share, I prepared myself to handle this and shot Sadie-Grace and Boone looks that I hoped they would interpret to mean that they should cease talking, full stop.

Then the woman in charge turned around, and I realized that I was completely unprepared to handle anything at all.

"You have the look of our family about you," she said, assessing me.

I barely heard a single word, because all I could think was *She has Lillian's face.*

LABOR DAY, 3:35 A.M.

"You're sitting up, Sawyer! That's good."

"You propped me up."

"And you didn't fall over this time. Glass, full!"

"Did you hear that?"

"I would like to say that I didn't, but . . ."

"You did."

SIX WEEKS
(AND *TWO DAYS*) EARLIER

CHAPTER 42

*T*he woman with my grandmother's face gestured for us to sit. Dumbly, I did, and Sadie-Grace and Boone followed suit.

All three of us stared at her.

"I take it my beloved sister never mentioned that she had a twin?"

Lillian and Davis Ames had both referenced the town they grew up in. I knew that Lillian had met my grandfather at a party at the Arcadia hotel, but I hadn't connected the dots that the town where she'd grown up was probably close to Regal Lake.

I hadn't spent much time, if any, thinking about my grandmother's family.

"Lillian never shared that little tidbit," I confirmed. *She never mentioned any siblings at all.*

"You didn't grow up in the city," came the reply. "Accent gives you away. You have to work to lose it, and you haven't."

Neither had she.

"I don't mean to be forward," Boone said politely, "but holy shizz-balls, this was not how I pictured this conversation going."

The doppelgänger across from us stared at him. Hard. Hard

enough that the dog at her feet jumped up, ears back, and gave a token growl.

"Boone's socially awkward," Sadie-Grace said helpfully. "It's part of his charm."

The old woman snorted, and the dog's ears came back up. With one glance back at his mistress, he took a few steps forward and flopped down at Boone's feet, exposing his belly. Boone gave it a scratch.

"Don't go getting a big head," one of the gun-toting women told Boone. "He's a softy. Loves everyone."

"And very especially me," Boone added.

"Last name," the woman in charge barked. It took me a minute to realize that she was talking about Boone—asking about him.

"His last name is Mason," I answered, but then I got a suspicion about what she was really asking. "His grandfather is Davis Ames."

"Thought so," came the reply. "Davey was always the same way—skinny as hell, always tripping over his tongue or his feet."

"Are we talking about the same man?" Boone asked, suddenly serious. "The single scariest, most demanding individual to ever walk this planet?"

The woman let out a cackle of laughter. "I guess we all change." She paused. "Davey changed more than most, after my sister left him high and dry to chase after that rich grandfather of yours."

That part, clearly, was addressed to me.

"He wasn't the only one she left high and dry," Sadie-Grace said suddenly, her voice earnest and sympathetic. "Was he?"

It was hard, once you knew Sadie-Grace, to hold anything she said against her. Her intentions were always good, and she was the kind of empathetic that had her crying at coffee commercials.

But this woman didn't know that, and despite the fact that she had Lillian's face—give or take some wear and tear—the sound of another round of earsplitting screams reminded me that Boone, Sadie-Grace, and I were in a precarious position.

"Don't you go feeling sorry for me, girlie," my great-aunt ordered Sadie-Grace. "I'm the one who told my sister to stop coming around here. I'm nobody's charity case, least of all hers."

Another scream.

"We should go," I said.

"You shouldn't have come here in the first place," the woman countered. "Now I have to deal with *this*."

"*This* as in a trio of promising young people with an impeccable sense of discretion?" Boone asked hopefully.

"This as in *us*," I corrected. I didn't have time to consider my next move as carefully as I would have liked. "Sadie-Grace's step-mother is the one in there with your Beth." That, at the very least, complicated the calculation on their end. "We already knew that Greer wasn't actually pregnant, and we're not the only ones who know that."

"And *she* insisted on secrecy from *us*," one of the gun women muttered.

"Hush." The doppelgänger's tone was mild, but the way that one word sucked the oxygen out of the air told me that she was the kind of dangerous I'd once attributed to Davis Ames.

"What do you propose we do about all of this?" That question, just as mild, was addressed to me.

"Nothing," I told her. "This is Greer's problem, not yours. Let her deal with it."

"It's not that I don't want a little brother," Sadie-Grace blurted out, one of her feet starting to beat back and forth around her other ankle. "I do. I really, *really* do. I just want Greer to tell Daddy that the baby's adopted, because if she doesn't, I might have to, and if I'm the one who tells him, he might not ever forgive me, and he might not ever forgive her, and, worse, he might not go through with the adoption at all."

It's not an adoption, I thought. Adoptions—legal ones—went through the state. Adoptions didn't inspire the parties peripherally involved to press a shotgun into the small of a potential witness's back.

"It's illegal for Greer to pay Beth for her baby," I said, knowing the risk as I said it. "Paying you on a purportedly unrelated matter is more of a gray area." I let that sink in. "Does Beth even *want* to give up her baby?"

I counted the silence that followed that question with the beats of my heart. *One. Two. Three.* I made it to six before I got my answer, in equal parts because my heart was racing and because the woman across from me knew how to use silence as a weapon.

"Of course she does. You think living in a place like Two Arrows makes us monsters? Hell, girlie, I birthed six babies of my own and would give my life for every one. Beth's one of my grandbabies. I'd put all three of you and that hoity-toity bitch inside in shallow graves before I'd let anyone force a decision like this on one of mine."

The woman was, in her own way, as good at guilt-tripping as Lillian was.

"I'm sorry," I said. Two Arrows felt different than the town I'd grown up in, but I was betting the unspoken code of honor was the same. If you insulted someone, you apologized, unless you wanted them to *make* you apologize.

"Seems to me," I continued, "that all of us can get what we want here. You can get your money—Beth's money," I corrected myself, "from Greer. Beth can give her baby to people—including a big sister with not a lot of common sense but an absolutely oversize heart—who will love the tar out of him, and we can all make Greer tell Sadie-Grace's dad the truth."

"What kind of man could find out his wife had faked an entire pregnancy and just proceed on with an adoption?" one of the women asked.

"The thing about my daddy," Sadie-Grace said, "is that he really loves beetles."

Everyone stared at her, expressions ranging from puzzled to concerned.

"And," Sadie-Grace continued emphatically, "he *hates* dating."

"You can do it, honey." Greer's voice floated out to us. "I'm here with you. I'm right here."

"Greer isn't all bad," Sadie-Grace went on optimistically. "She just needs help being good."

My grandmother's twin shifted her attention back to me. "She take after her daddy?" she asked, jerking her head toward Sadie-Grace.

A little bit clueless, a lot anxious, with a heart the size of Texas? I thought.

Out loud, I said, "Yes."

That was the absolutely batty thing about this—there *was* a chance that if Greer told Charles Waters the truth, he would just stare at her for a minute and scratch his head and then start talking about insects.

"Fine, then," the woman across from me said. "The girl calls her daddy—or has that piece of work inside do it—to tell him the full story, and we do this all legal-like, so long as you three can agree not to say a word about any money that might change hands on the side."

What did it say about me that I didn't hesitate to agree with something like that?

In the end, I only had one question for this gray-haired, sun-worn, life-hardened mirror of my grandmother.

"What's your name?" I asked her right before we left.

"Ellen," she replied, and then the set of her features softened, just for a second. "Lil used to call me Ellie."

LABOR DAY, 3:36 AM

"She has to know the drugs are wearing off, Sadie-Grace. You keep saying that she wouldn't really hurt us, but you don't know that. This whole situation is *insane*. You have to get out of this hole. Step on me if you have to. Just get out—and run."

FOUR WEEKS
(AND *TWO DAYS*) EARLIER

CHAPTER 43

"I t's not just that Audie's the *cutest* baby to ever baby," Sadie-Grace said on the other end of the phone line. "It's that he's objectively a better person than other two-week-olds."

This was my fourth phone call today detailing the virtues of Audubon Charles Richard Waters, whose legal adoption was currently in process—with Sadie-Grace's very *forgiving* father's full consent.

"Also," Sadie-Grace continued rapturously, "he's getting really good at pooping."

That was where I drew the line. "I'll see you tonight." I hung up and turned my attention to a bigger problem. As much as I would have preferred being at Nick's—*with* Nick—I had other things on my plate.

Things I found myself wanting to talk to him about. *We'll talk tonight,* I promised myself. *I'll see him tonight. But for now . . .*

Lily was lying on one of the twin beds in the turret room, dressed in lake-formal clothing and listening to music on her phone. With her blond hair spread out on the pillow and her dark eyes focused on the ceiling, she looked like a doll, perfectly styled and perfectly still.

She's not okay, Nick had told me when we'd spoken hours earlier and the topic of Lily had come up. *But she will be someday. Lily's tougher than anyone gives her credit for.*

I wanted to believe that, believe him.

"Are you sure you want to go to this party tonight?" I asked Lily.

In the interest of full disclosure, I'd told her everything—about Two Arrows *and* the plans under way to find Ana's baby. Her only, muted response had been to tell me that Lillian had never mentioned a sister, let alone a twin—no emotion, no real reaction. The fact that neither *Our grandmother has a secret twin* nor *The boy you just broke up with is hatching plans with another girl* had penetrated the fog of her emotions was, in a word, concerning.

Nick's right, I told myself. *Lily will be okay. She has to be.*

Maybe I'd believe it when he told me in person.

"Ana might be there tonight," I reminded Lily, since she hadn't replied to my question about the party. "Are you sure you want to go?" When she didn't respond, I came closer. "Lily?"

Still no response, so I pulled one of her earbuds out of her ear. "Will you just talk to me?"

For months, I'd been afraid of losing Lily. I'd imagined her shutting me out. I hadn't imagined her shutting out the world.

Lily forced her eyes from the ceiling to me. "Tonight isn't just a party, Sawyer. The White Glove text was very specific." She closed her eyes again in a slow-motion blink, like opening them was harder than it should have been. "This is the last event before they decide who makes it and who's out."

Of everything Lily could have chosen to care about, why the White Gloves?

Everyone needs a place to belong, something inside me whispered. I wanted to tell Lily that she didn't need a secret society. I was right here.

But instead, all I said was: "Okay."

I sat down beside her. She went to put her earbuds back in, and as she did, I heard the music she'd been listening to.

Only, it wasn't music.

It was the conversation where Aunt Olivia and Uncle J.D. had argued about the body, on a loop.

CHAPTER 44

*L*ily's instructions from the White Gloves had indicated that she should arrive at the Gutierrez lake estate an hour early. Mine had specified two hours. If I'd thought it would have done any good to stay home with her and go later, I would have.

But nothing I said or did seemed to affect Lily at all, so I ended up driving through the gates of Rustic Mesa by myself, two hours before the social event of the lake season was set to begin. The fact that Victoria's family didn't just have a lake house, but an estate—and the fact that the estate had a name—should have merited some sarcastic mental commentary on my part, but all I could think as I approached the main house was that this night had the potential to go badly on so many levels.

Ana could show up. She could not show up. The White Gloves could cut Lily. She could—

Someone answered the front door before I could finish that thought. I'd been expecting Victoria, or possibly a housekeeper.

I hadn't expected her father.

"A young lady such as yourself should never be made to wait." Victor Gutierrez had salt-and-pepper hair, features that had aged well, and the type of charisma that didn't age at all. "Especially in this heat," he continued. "My apologies. Please, come in."

I stepped over the threshold into a foyer with soaring ceilings. "Is Victoria . . ."

"My daughter will be down shortly."

Before I knew what was happening, I was being escorted to what Lillian would have referred to as a Baptist bar—one that normally hid behind pocket doors. Today, in preparation for the party, they were open.

"Could I get you something cool to drink?" Victor Gutierrez made a study of my expression. "No? Ah, well. You won't mind if I have a little something myself."

He let go of my arm to walk back around the bar.

"I can wait in the foyer for Victoria," I said.

"Keep an old man company," he told me, filling a glass with ice. "Perhaps I might convince you to reconsider some of the ideas you have been putting in my daughter's head."

He was still smiling, so it took me a second to process what he'd just said. "Excuse me?"

He took a sip of his drink and closed his eyes. "I am well aware of why this party is happening and who you are hoping will be in attendance. I suspect the Ames girl has something to do with it, but she is not here, and you are. You will forgive me for asking you to pass the message along."

What message? I thought.

"You may pass it along to the Ames boy as well." Mr. Gutierrez made that sound like an act of generosity on his part. "I know that he and my daughter have been spending time together."

He hadn't referred to Victoria by her name once. She was always *my daughter*.

"If you're concerned about the amount of time Victoria and

Walker are spending together—or the *ideas* in her head—maybe you should discuss it with her," I suggested.

Victor Gutierrez gave a wry shake of his head, with an expression that suggested that I was quite amusing. "Who do you think asked her to dance with Walker Ames at that silly fund-raiser in the first place? She is my eyes and ears."

He told Victoria to dance with Walker? "What is your game here?" I asked. Why aim his daughter at Walker, then ask me to warn Walker away?

"I am an old man, Miss Taft," Victor Gutierrez said contemplatively. "But not too old to remember the wounds of the past."

He could beat around the bush all he wanted. I wasn't obliged to do the same. "Sterling Ames knocked up your granddaughter. You weren't happy about it."

"She was a child!" He pounded his fist on the bar, then recovered his composure in the blink of an eye. "And do not tell me eighteen is not a child. You, Victoria—you're all children to me. My Ana . . ."

He trailed off, and I thought about what Victoria had said about the rift between her father and his formerly favorite granddaughter. "You wanted her to come to you for help."

He'd wanted her to beg forgiveness.

"I wanted to *protect* her," Victor said emphatically. "From her own judgment most of all."

"And now you won't even talk to her."

"She gave away our blood." Victor set his drink down on the bar, his voice softening. "I would have taken her in—her and the child, both. We are family. That is what family does."

But she didn't come to you, I thought. And then I realized why he would have found that so insulting. "Ana went to Davis Ames."

"But for the money he gave her, she could have been made to

see reason," he told me, his dark eyes fixed on mine. "I implore you to see it now."

"Imploring would be more effective if I had any idea what you actually wanted from me," I said.

"Stay away from my Ana," he requested. "You and that family of yours." He smiled then and put a hand on my shoulder as he raised his eyes to the stairs. "Ah," he said when Victoria descended. "There's my girl."

CHAPTER 45

"*Y*our father asked you to dance with Walker Ames."

"I never said that he didn't." Victoria barely spared me a glance as she led me up the staircase and away from her father and the party preparations below. "I did tell you that Campbell's invitation to the first White Glove event had nothing to do with the business between our families' companies, and that was the truth. Now," she continued, leading me into what I presumed to be her bedroom, "do you want to spend the next hour cross-examining me about Walker and my father's grudge toward his family . . ." She nodded to her bed. ". . . or do you want to look at those?"

There were dozens of file folders, possibly hundreds, in neat little stacks.

"Dossiers," Victoria informed me. "Our man is very . . . thorough." She spoke like it was completely normal to have "a man" and refer to him as such, then gestured to the different piles of folders. "Those are the girls the White Gloves considered as Candidates but decided against. Next, we have the ones who made our initial pool, and finally, those"—she gestured to the last pile—"are the ones who've made it to the final round of selection."

I reached for the folder on top of the last pile and flipped it open. Lily's smiling picture stared back at me. Behind the picture, there was a report—a biographical sketch, notes on her parents, a summary of her dating history, which only included Walker. Behind the written summary, there were pictures—of *Secrets on My Skin*.

Once upon a time, that had been the biggest secret—and vulnerability—in Lily's life.

"Your PI didn't say anything about her father's affair," I commented, skimming the file.

Victoria shrugged. "Perhaps he's not as thorough as we believed."

I looked from Lily's folder to the others. "You have this information on all of us?" I asked. "And everyone you considered?"

"Date of birth, family history, known social ties, past and current relationships, and potential . . . *points of interest*?" Victoria inclined her head. "Yes."

Without another word to her, I sorted the folders in all three piles by date of birth. My mom had said that it took Ana a little longer than her to get pregnant, but by December, when my mom had told Lillian she was pregnant with me, Ana was expecting, too. Casting a wide net, that put the date of birth for her child at some point in time between late July and the first week in September.

Once I had pulled the dossiers for all the Candidates and Potentials who had been born in that window, I started reading. I wasn't sure what I was looking for. Three of the dossiers noted that the subject had been adopted, but all three also included copies of the adoption paperwork.

"Has it occurred to you," Victoria said as I scrutinized the three folders in question, "that Ana's child might not know they were adopted? That there might not *be* paperwork?"

Given the situation with Sadie-Grace's baby brother, that thought had crossed my mind.

"Has it occurred to you," Victoria continued quietly, "that the baby might be Campbell?"

"What?" I said. But as I turned the question over in my head, it made sense. Davis Ames had given Ana money. According to his own recounting of events, he'd promised her more when she had the baby but had never heard from her again.

What if he was lying? What if he had a family all picked out? I turned back to the folders I'd set aside as being within the window and shuffled through the Candidates' to find Campbell's. *What if that family was his own?*

I tried to wrap my mind around the way that might have played out. Would Campbell's father have told his wife the baby was his? Would Charlotte really have agreed to pass the baby off as her own?

It might explain some things about Campbell's relationship with her mama.

I flipped open Campbell's file. My birthday was in July. Lily's was the last week in August. Campbell's was September 1.

"When was Walker born?" I asked. He'd been a year ahead of Lily and Campbell in school.

"October," Victoria answered. "Walker and Campbell are only eleven months apart."

"So either their mother got pregnant when Walker was just a couple of months old or . . ."

"*Or*," Victoria echoed. She let that sit with me for a minute and then executed an elegant shrug. "It's a theory, but not the only one I'm working on. There's one more folder you should read through before we join the rest of the White Gloves and Candidates in the guesthouse." She nodded to her dresser. A single folder lay there.

"Why wasn't this in with the others?" I asked.

"Because," Victoria replied, "it's not from a White Glove in your year. Ana's baby would be getting ready to turn nineteen—they're just as likely to be a sophomore as a freshman." I opened the folder and saw a girl with dark blond hair and light brown eyes staring back at me. Then I saw the last name.

"Hope's little sister," Victoria told me. "Also Nessa's girlfriend. Her name was Summer."

"Was?" I asked.

Victoria got quiet for a moment, and I thought of the secret Hope had buried during her initiation process years before. *The cancer came back.*

"Summer joined the White Gloves last August," Victoria told me. "She and Nessa started dating in December." Victoria looked down at Summer's picture—*blond hair, brown eyes, just like Ana.* "She died in March."

CHARLOTTE, LIV, JULIA, THE INTERLOPER, AND THE BOYS SUMMER BEFORE SENIOR YEAR TWENTY-FIVE YEARS EARLIER

"*H*ere are the rules." Liv smiled, leaning into J.D. "First one to jump makes them. Last one down pays the price."

Before anyone could process that statement, Liv was running, full blast, for the cliff's edge. Charlotte watched her in the air. There was something beautiful about this version of Liv. Something wild.

Something that made Charlotte think Liv might have considered jumping, even if there hadn't been water down below.

In the time it took that thought to register, J.D. and Julia had followed Liv's lead. Thomas Mason went after Julia, and that left just three of them on the ledge.

Sterling and Charlotte—and between them, Trina.

"This is a stupid game," Trina said.

"Do I need to throw you over?" Sterling asked her.

Last one down pays the price. Charlotte was wary enough of Liv's ever-changing moods to fear she'd make good on that threat, but the alternative was leaving Sterling up here alone with the girl he'd picked up.

He knew I'd be here. He knew I'd be here, and he brought her anyway.

That thought buzzing through her brain—and her bones and her blood—Charlotte grabbed the whiskey bottle off the ground and took a swig. Then she walked to the edge.

Instead of jumping, she dove.

CHAPTER 46

*F*orty-five minutes before the party was scheduled to start, Victoria pried me away from the dossiers and escorted me down to the guesthouse. Because, of course, the Gutierrez lake *estate* had a guesthouse. When we opened the front, we were greeted by utter silence.

Then I heard an *eep* that was almost certainly Sadie-Grace.

Victoria was undaunted. "They must have brought out the scissors."

That was not the most comforting thing I'd ever heard.

"Scissors," I repeated. "Why would we need scissors?"

In answer, Victoria led me to a small—or at least, smaller, relative to the main house—living room. White Gloves and Candidates sat scattered around the room wearing nothing but their bras and panties.

As promised, one of the White Gloves held a pair of gleaming metal scissors.

"I may be off base here," I said, "but I was under the impression that *getting ready* involved clothing."

Victoria shrugged and shed her own dress. "This way, none of us will get hair on our clothes."

• • •

Popular culture had led me to believe that "trust exercises" generally involved falling backward and allowing another person to catch you. But for the White Gloves, *trust* seemed to involve two key things: underwear and scissors.

"I'll go first." Campbell was awfully blasé for someone whose auburn tresses were practically trademarked. She shook out her hair. "It's getting a little unruly anyway."

Campbell's hair was many things, but unruly wasn't one of them. She was wearing it wavy, not straight—this was the lake, after all—but the waves were salon-perfect, unlike my own hair, which had a habit of waving itself right into knots.

"Who wants to do the honors?" Campbell asked. Hope raised her hand and gave a wiggle of her fingertips. The scissors were passed to her.

"Any requests?" she asked Campbell, giving a snip or two of the blades.

Campbell smiled, undaunted. "Surprise me."

The room held its collective breath as Hope began finger-combing Campbell's hair, and then—*snip*.

A lock of auburn hair, an inch or so long, fell to the floor. More followed. The result brought the hair next to Campbell's face up in a subtle frame.

"Not bad," Hope commented before passing the scissors on to Nessa.

Nessa stared at them for a moment, running a finger along the edge.

"Do me next!" Sadie-Grace said, with the cheer of someone who had clearly never had a bad haircut in her life.

I wondered if it was *possible* to give Sadie-Grace a bad haircut. That question remained unanswered, because Nessa seemed unable to talk herself into doing more than cutting off a fraction.

My turn rolled around, and the topic turned to what should be done with my bangs, which had grown out just enough that they no longer quite merited the term.

"It's not that your bangs are horrible per se," Victoria told me. "It's that whoever cut them did it too bluntly."

Five minutes later, I was the proud (read: somewhat apathetic) possessor of a new side bang.

One by one, the Candidates let the White Gloves take their scissors to our hair, though two refused and a third burst into tears the second the scissors bit into her hair. None of the changes were major. Most weren't even readily visible.

This wasn't about hair or having the right look. This was about *trust*.

Lily went last. Victoria ended up with the scissors. I shot her a warning look. I had no idea what Victoria's deal was with Walker—if she liked him, or if her father had ordered her to get close to him, or what—but regardless, she wasn't exactly a person I trusted with Lily, especially in Lily's current fragile state.

Victoria circled Lily, examining her. "Your hair is long," she commented.

"It always has been," Lily replied.

There was a pause, and then Victoria tilted her head to the side. "Is that what you want?"

I don't know what I want anymore, I could hear Lily confessing. *Or who.*

Victoria stopped her pacing, standing directly in front of Lily. The two of them stared at each other, caught up in some kind of silent standoff.

Lily held out her hand, palm up, and after a second's delay, Victoria handed over the scissors.

"It's just hair," Lily said, bringing the scissors up.

Before I could say a word, she'd grabbed a chunk of her blond hair and sheared it off at the chin.

LABOR DAY, 3:38

"I'm out! Are you okay? I didn't step on you too hard, did I? I tried not to step on you too hard."

"I'm fine, Sadie-Grace. Now go."

"I'm not leaving you."

"You have to. I have no idea where we are, but you need to be somewhere else when she gets back."

"I could try to find help?"

"Yes. Just *go*."

FOUR WEEKS
(AND TWO DAYS) EARLIER

CHAPTER 47

I looked slowly from the long chunk of hair on the floor to Lily, who was still staring Victoria down.

"Hope," Victoria said. "A little help here?"

Hope stepped forward and took the scissors from Lily's hands.

"She's good with hair," I heard a White Glove whisper beside me. "Really good."

As I watched Hope, with her *appreciation for chaos*, assessing the damage Lily had wreaked, I thought back to the picture in the dossier Campbell had shown me. To Summer.

I tried to imagine what it would feel like to be Hope, to have lost a sister.

Ten minutes later, Lily was sporting a chin-length bob.

"My work here is done," Hope declared. She snipped the scissors in the air to accentuate the point.

I let myself look at Lily. The bob didn't look bad at all. Mostly, it looked *different*, which I deeply suspected, for Lily, was the point.

As the lot of us got dressed again and headed for the main house—and the party—I thought back to the night at Arcadia, when Campbell and I had found three keys waiting for us at the valet stand. The White Gloves had already cut Lily once.

But that was before we'd caught her father with Ana in the woods. Before her family had fallen apart. Before she'd broken up with Walker and fearlessly taken a chunk out of her own hair.

Pick her, I thought. *She needs this more than I do, more than Sadie-Grace, maybe even more than Campbell. Pick her.*

Stepping into the foyer, I found myself looking automatically for Nick. Per our plan, he was supposed to meet me here. I would play the role of his escort. His date. We'd mingle. We'd chitchat.

We'd make sarcastic comments about the evils of mingling and chitchat.

But Nick was nowhere to be seen. *Where is he?* I tried and failed to push down the urge to get out my phone. The screen informed me that I had a missed call and a text: three words, which was practically a novel, considering Nick's views on texting.

Something came up.

He didn't say what that something was. *It doesn't matter,* I told myself. I didn't need him here to hold my hand.

To hold me.

The whole point of this party was creating an opportunity for Ana to show up and taking advantage of the opportunity to talk to her if she did. That would be easier without Nick along.

I'm glad something came up. I'd halfway convinced myself of that when my grandmother saw me from across the room. She must not have spotted Lily yet, because she eyed my side bang and crossed the open floor plan to talk to me.

"Sawyer, might I have a word?"

"Do I have a choice?" I asked.

Lillian smiled. "I'm not going to ask you about those bangs," she said, taking my arm and leading me to a nearby alcove in a way that would have suggested to any onlookers that she was interested in doing nothing more than showing me the art hanging on the wall there. "And I'm certainly not going to ask you what your cousin did to her hair."

So Lillian *had* seen Lily. Then why corner me?

"She's not just my cousin," I muttered under my breath. "And I think her hair looks good."

My grandmother studied me for a moment. "Have I done something to upset you, Sawyer?"

"No."

"You've been avoiding me." The fact that Lillian hadn't communicated that information through the use of a pleasant rhetorical question told me how much she was bothered by the observation.

She wasn't wrong. I had been avoiding her—for the past two weeks.

"If this is about your mama . . ." Lillian started to say, but the look on my face seemed to bring her up short. "Or your aunt . . ." she modified. Then, taking in my expression, she paused. "Well, for heaven's sakes, Sawyer, what is this about?"

I made a show of studying the painting in front of me. It was a landscape, and though it didn't strike me as anything special, I had few doubts that the signature in the bottom right corner would have meant something to someone who knew art.

"I went to Two Arrows."

I heard Lillian suck in a breath beside me. In public, that was the most that any revelation could cause her to do.

"Two Arrows is not a safe place for you to go."

I wasn't sure what I'd expected from Lillian, but that sentiment wasn't it—though given the vibe I'd gotten from her sister and her gun-toting associates, maybe it should have been.

"You grew up there," I pointed out. "And you turned out fine."

"That, I believe, is a matter of some debate."

I turned to look at Lillian. She hadn't asked me if I'd met her sister. I knew her well enough to deeply suspect that she wasn't going to.

"You named my mom after her," I said. "Ellen, Eleanor—but both called Ellie."

Lillian was quiet for a moment, and I flashed back to the two of us standing beside her husband's grave, weeks before.

"She was the strong one, growing up," Lillian said. To the outside observer, her expression wouldn't have looked like it changed at all, but I felt a shift in her. I heard it in her voice. "There were days when she didn't eat so I could."

Lillian hadn't said her sister's name—not Ellen, not Ellie. She hadn't commented on the fact that she'd named my mother after someone from whom she was estranged.

"Your sister went hungry for you," I said, finding it hard to believe that there had ever been a time in my grandmother's life when she hadn't considered herself strong. "And you left town and never looked back."

That got me another almost inaudible intake of air, subtler this time, more controlled.

"I would have brought her with me," my grandmother said. "I tried. Did she tell you that?"

Ellen hadn't, but she had said that she didn't want anyone's charity—least of all her twin's. "She didn't want to come with you," I surmised.

"She didn't want to want to, Sawyer. She always hated when I talked about leaving that town, and she hated it when I left. She hated your grandfather. *Edward Alcott Taft*. Even the sound of his name set her to gnashing her teeth. She hated who I was when I was with him. There are days I'm not sure what she resented more—that I left, or that I offered to pull her out."

"She doesn't hate Two Arrows," I said.

Lillian hesitated. "She should."

My grandmother had told me, more than once, that I didn't know what it was really like to be poor. Having been to the town where she'd grown up, I wondered if poverty was the only reason that Lillian had wanted to leave.

I thought about Beth, the woman whose screams we'd heard. Audie's birth mother. She was my second cousin. Given that our grandmothers were identical twins, genetically, she might as well have been a first cousin.

"Your sister had six kids," I told Lillian. "She *has* six kids. Did you know that?"

Did any of them go hungry so that their siblings could eat?

"I did what I could for Ellen's family, Sawyer. I wish to God she'd let me do more."

"There must have been a way," I argued.

"My sister found a way." Lillian's voice was flat now. Her face had lost its perfunctory, performative smile. "There was some violence in Two Arrows, years back. It left some gaps in the local . . . ecosystem."

Because that wasn't vague or anything.

"Ellie—*Ellen*, she filled the gaps. Anything bought or sold in that town, she has a hand in it, and she gets a piece of it."

Anything, I thought. *Like drugs. Or sex.* I thought of Beth again. *Or babies . . .*

"Believe me when I say you do not want to get mixed up in my sister's business," Lillian told me. "Now, this is neither the time nor the place . . ." She trailed off. I was getting ready to remind her that she was the one who'd cornered me when I realized why she'd trailed off.

Ana Sofía Gutierrez had arrived.

Victoria's father had told me that he knew why tonight's party

was being thrown. Did that mean that he knew Victoria was looking for the baby, or that he knew Ana was going to be here?

More importantly, how did he intend to respond?

Beside me, it took my grandmother a moment to recover her
poise but not more than that. "At least she doesn't have *that man*
with her."

There was little question in my mind that *that man* was meant
to be translated to *that bastard*. All things considered, it was a good
thing that, this time, J.D. had decided to stay away.

Across the open floor plan, Victoria began weaving her way
through the crowd to greet Ana. A petite woman with dark hair
and a figure only partially camouflaged by her A-line dress joined
them at the bottom of the stairs. I recognized her from the Arcadia
fund-raiser.

*That's Victoria's mother. And that's Ana, talking to Victoria and
Victoria's mother.*

I didn't realize I was walking toward them until I felt Lillian's
fingers digging into my arms.

"Don't you dare, Sawyer Ann," she said, her for-show smile back
in place. "I put in an appearance tonight because your aunt asked
me to. Public appearances matter. The situation needed smoothing
over. You going over there?"

"Not smooth?" I suggested. "Or discreet?"

I restrained myself from pointing out that Lillian attending a
Gutierrez party hardly seemed like enough of a statement to quell
gossip about the affair.

"I was told that certain parties would not be in attendance," my
grandmother continued. She refused to give a single outward sign
that she'd taken any note of Ana or the way that Victoria and her
mother were leading her through the crowd.

If Victoria can get her father to talk to Ana, Ana might talk to us.

I watched Victoria's mother place a kiss on her husband's cheek and pull him from someone who might have been a business contact, an acquaintance, or a friend.

"Far be it from me to suggest that you're staring," Lillian told me. "But . . ."

But Victor Gutierrez just saw Ana. She said something to him. He's staring at her now. He's taking a step forward. He's smiling.

This was going surprisingly well—right up until the moment when Victoria's eighty-something-year-old father placed a loving hand on Ana's cheek and keeled over.

Dead.

LABOR DAY, 3:45

"Sawyer? Sadie-Grace? Are you guys out there? Can anyone hear me?"

"Oh my God . . . Campbell, *over here!*"

"Sawyer?"

"Watch out for the hole."

"What . . . why are you in a hole? And where's Sadie-Grace?"

"I told her to run. She ran."

"From what?"

"Not from what, Campbell. From *whom.*"

THREE DAYS EARLIER

CHAPTER 48

"*S*till no word from the almighty Victoria?" Campbell readjusted her position on our dock, stretching out in the sun. "Or the White Gloves?"

Campbell had invited herself over and brought Sadie-Grace along. Lily still had enough hostess in her that she hadn't turned either of them away. She wasn't saying much, though. Her birthday had passed the week before with only minimal—by Taft family standards, at least—fanfare. Lily hadn't wanted a party. Now she sat at the end of the dock, facing the lake, silent. Despite the heat, she wore a long-sleeved shirt.

"Victoria's daddy *died*, Campbell," Sadie-Grace said emphatically.

"Not entirely unreasonable that some things would be put on hold," I added. *Like White Glove initiations—or our search for Ana's baby.*

Campbell caught my gaze—and my drift. Sadie-Grace, who was standing between the two of us and Lily, gave a little twirl.

"You're going to pirouette right off this dock," Campbell told her.

"No, she's not," Lily said, without even looking back.

Campbell glanced at Lily. "Will Lily freak out if I ask if y'all have heard the news about Ana?" she asked me.

"Lily doesn't freak out," Sadie-Grace said loyally.

"The bob says otherwise," Campbell replied.

Sadie-Grace put her hands on her hips. "If the bob could speak, it would speak French."

"What about Ana?" Lily interjected, still facing the water.

"She was in Mr. Gutierrez's will," Campbell reported. "In a big way. There's a trust for the other grandchildren, but he left Ana half of her father's share of the inheritance. Directly."

I thought back to the night on King's Island when we'd buried and burned and shared our secrets. "Victoria said she wasn't in her father's will."

"From what I've heard," Campbell replied lightly, "she wasn't. And neither was her mother. Mr. Gutierrez's sons are supposedly charged with taking care of them both, but . . ."

But we'll see how that goes.

"So Ana is set for life now." Lily stood, her hands disappearing inside the long sleeves. She had to be burning up out here but didn't show it. "Maybe she can pay back all of that money my father gave to her."

I searched for some hint of emotion in her tone and came up blank.

"I talked to my grandfather," Campbell said suddenly. "About Ana's baby."

"We don't have to talk about this," I told Lily, unsure if she was in a place to handle any more talk about Ana.

Lily turned back to look at me. "I don't mind."

Part of me was glad that she had gotten to the point where the mention of Ana's name didn't hurt her. The other part couldn't help thinking that pain was the body's warning system. Things hurt because they were supposed to.

That's how you know you're too involved.

"What did your grandfather say?" I asked Campbell, keeping an eye on Lily and my mind in the moment—and not on Nick, who'd never told me why he'd stood me up at the Gutierrez party that night.

"The great Davis Ames told me the same story he told you," Campbell replied. "He paid Ana. She disappeared. He has no idea what happened to the baby."

"Maybe he or she was adopted by a very nice family," Sadie-Grace suggested, stretching one leg up until it nearly touched her ear. "With a very flexible older sister!"

She was obviously thinking of herself and baby Audie, but my mind went to a different place—and to a different older sister. *Hope.*

"Funny you should mention that," I told Sadie-Grace. "My perusal of the White Gloves dossiers did yield a possibility. . . ."

I told them about Summer—about her blond hair and brown eyes, the cancer, her date of birth.

"Was that the only possibility that jumped out at you?" Campbell asked me in a tone that suggested that she was probably going to make me pay for not mentioning any of this until now.

"No," I said, but I couldn't bring myself to elaborate on Victoria's other theory.

As luck would have it, I didn't have to.

"It could be me," Campbell stated, finally earning Lily's complete and undiluted attention. "It's not like my grandfather would admit it if it was."

"You?" Sadie-Grace was almost comically wide-eyed.

"Walker was always Daddy's favorite," Campbell said, looking at Lily, even though it was Sadie-Grace she was responding to. "I was supposed to be Mama's."

"His and hers," I said, because she'd told me that once. "Like towels."

"And yet . . ." Campbell dragged out the words. "Mama and I have always been like oil and water, gotten along like a house on fire, insert conflict-laden cliché of your choice here. She adores Walker. She's never adored me. My birthday's almost here, and she hasn't said a word."

"Do you think your mama forgot your birthday?" Sadie-Grace asked, wide-eyed.

"I'm not really wondering about Mama and *my birthday*," Campbell said, her voice flat.

"You're wondering if you're really hers." I cut straight to the thick of it.

"Maybe I'm not," Campbell tossed out. "Maybe I'm just my father's daughter. It would explain some things, not least among them why Walker and I are so close in age."

"And why your mama . . ." Sadie-Grace started that sentence but didn't finish it.

"Doesn't find me to her taste?" Campbell suggested. "I always just figured she fell head over heels in love with Walker the day he was born, and I came so soon afterward there just wasn't any more oxytocin bonding hormone left over for me."

"What about Boone?" Sadie-Grace asked suddenly. "He's the right age, too. Your dad and his mom are twins. And he's so much more injury-prone than the rest of you."

I so did not want to know how Sadie-Grace had injured Boone now.

"I'm going to change the subject," Campbell told Sadie-Grace, "before you take a shortcut to TMI." She pivoted. "In case any of you were wondering, I'm planning an epic birthday party, but it is *so* epic that it will require months of planning and will thus be held on my half birthday, once this summer and all of its drama is just a blip in the mirror." Campbell didn't give any of us the chance to reply before she changed the subject a second time. "Now, who wants to hear my update on the Lady of the Lake?"

I saw Lily shiver, even though she couldn't have possibly been cold. It was a hundred degrees out, and the rest of us were sweltering in swimsuits.

"What update?" Lily said quietly.

"My 'friend' at the deputy's office says they're bringing in a forensic sculptor." Campbell awaited our response.

Sadie-Grace raised her hand. "Do I want to know what a forensic sculptor is?"

"That depends," Campbell replied coyly. "Do you want a play-by-play on how someone can reconstruct a face from a skull?"

CHARLOTTE, LIV, JULIA, THE INTERLOPER, AND THE BOYS SUMMER BEFORE SENIOR YEAR TWENTY-FIVE YEARS EARLIER

"*L*ast one in pays the price." Liv shot a playful look at Sterling. "That would be you. Or . . ." She stretched the word. "Would it be her?"

All of them were in the water now. Sterling and the local girl had come down together.

I can't be the one who says it, Charlotte thought.

For once, she was glad that Julia seemed able to sense exactly what she was thinking. "My brother hit the water a second before she did." She glanced at the new girl. "That makes you last, sweetie." Julia flipped onto her back to float. "You were the first off the ledge, Liv. What are the rules—and what's the price?"

"The rest of us head back up," Liv decided, pushing off J.D. and swimming for the shore. "And, new girl, let's see you tread water."

CHAPTER 49

"I'm worried about Lily."

Nick and I were lying on the front of his boat, our limbs entangled, my hair damp from the lake. I could see beads of sweat on his chest and feel them running down my own.

He traced his fingers lightly down my stomach. "More worried than usual?"

"After Campbell and Sadie-Grace left this morning, Lily put in her earbuds."

He moved his hand to the small of my back, which was the only thing that allowed me to continue.

"She's just listening to the recordings of her parents, over and over again."

"And you're here," Nick commented. "With me."

I'd been spending more time here. With him. The reminder was less welcome than his touch. I rolled over on top of him, both hands on his chest. "I'll stop talking."

He caught his thumb under the strap of my swimsuit. "I didn't ask you to."

He never did. He just let me talk. At this point, I was fairly certain I could tell him that I'd discovered that several key members of high society were actually tigers wearing people suits, and he would have just muttered, "It figures."

"What if Lily's parents knew the Lady of the Lake?" I asked Nick. "What if they had something to do with her death?"

It was easier, somehow, to ask him than it would have been to think it myself.

Nick considered my questions, then came back with one of his own. "And if they did?"

I let out a long breath. "I don't know."

He stared at me, in that way that made me feel like he was memorizing something about my face.

I tried to focus on the conversation, not on the way he looked, looking at me. "Lily . . . it's like she's barely inhabiting her own body anymore. She just shut down. But I can't shake the feeling that something's going to happen, and she's going to snap."

"Okay," Nick replied evenly. "Say Lily snaps. She loses it. She lashes out. What does that look like? Is it really the end of the world?"

I don't know.

"I'm done talking now," I told him.

Nick didn't argue. He never did. Instead, he pulled me nine-tenths of the way into a kiss and waited for me to close the distance. I probably should have pulled back. I probably should have left.

Instead, I lost myself in the kiss and in him.

At some point, we fell asleep. We woke up to a girl standing over us.

"Is this what you meant when you said you had to work?" she asked Nick.

Who the hell is that? My brain was already supplying answers—horrible ones about why another girl might come looking for Nick—when I scrambled to my feet. I flashed back to the text he'd sent me the night of the Gutierrez party.

Something came up.

If it had just been physical, if I hadn't just been talking to him, confiding in him, this wouldn't have been a problem.

You knew better, Sawyer. You damn well knew better.

"What the hell?" Nick jumped to his feet.

I am so stupid, I thought, looking at the girl. *It was just supposed to be me, repaying what I owed. It was just supposed to be for show.*

It was just supposed to be physical.

It was just supposed to be talking.

It wasn't supposed to hurt.

"Jessi!" Nick's aggrieved tone barely managed to penetrate the cacophony of reprimands my brain was launching in my direction.

People can only hurt you if you let them.

I grabbed my keys and shoes and was already halfway past him when I processed the name he'd said and the particular shade of annoyance in his tone when he'd said it.

I recognized them both.

"Jessi," I repeated, turning back to face him. "Your little sister?"

"And you must be the girlfriend." Jessi grinned. Now that she was no longer backlit by the sun, I could see a resemblance—and just how young she looked.

"She's not my girlfriend," Nick told her.

That shouldn't have hit me hard. It shouldn't have hit me at all. *He's right. I'm not his girlfriend. I'm really, really not.*

"Sawyer . . ." Nick started, then backtracked. "Wait for me at my car, Jess."

Nick's sister looked at the two of us, then shrugged and issued a parting shot. "Whatever you say, big brother. I've always admired your 'work' ethic."

"Smart-ass," he grumbled as she turned and flitted away.

"I should go," I said once she was gone. I didn't give him a chance to reply. I was halfway to the edge of the boat when his voice stopped me.

"You never asked me why I stood you up at that party."

I quelled the impulse to turn around and face him again. "I don't care," I said.

"That's strange," he replied. I could practically hear the smirk in his voice. "Because you definitely cared when Jessi showed up, before you realized she was my sister."

He sounded just satisfied enough about that, I had to turn around. "Asshole."

Nick took that as a compliment. "That night, I canceled on you because there was a problem with Colt."

His brother. "Is he—" I started to ask.

"He's fine," Nick told me. "Still comatose. Still not here when he should be, and I still think of that sometimes when I look at you."

I hadn't had anything to do with putting Colt in that coma. I hadn't helped cover it up. But I was who I was, and the Ames family and mine were intertwined, going back generations.

"And then," Nick said, "I think that if Colt were here, he'd tell me I was an idiot."

I swallowed. "For being with a girl like me?"

"There are no girls like you," Nick said. "You're not like other people, *Miss Taft.*"

He only called me that when he wanted to piss me off, so why did I feel like this time was different? Why couldn't I shake a single thing he'd said?

"I should go."

"Should you?" Nick countered, stepping closer to me. "Tell me one thing first, Sawyer. Why is it that you feel everything else so deeply, that you love everyone else in your life—from your grandmother and Lily to godforsaken Campbell Ames—so loyally and so fiercely, but you can't even admit to a moment of jealousy when it comes to me?"

My mouth felt dry all of a sudden. My skin was humming. "It wasn't jealousy," I said.

It was a warning of all the ways this thing between us could go south.

I made myself turn back to the shore, take one step away from him and then another.

"You told me once," Nick said quietly, "that after your grandfather died, your mother started wearing all black, and your aunt ran away."

That was just random enough that I found myself able to stop and reply. "For almost a year."

Nick strode toward me. I could hear him walking, but I didn't turn back around until he stopped, right behind me.

"You think you're like your mother," he told me. "And that Lily's like hers, but you've got that backward. She's the one who turns things in on herself. You're the one who runs."

The tone in his voice was mild, but the intent in those words was not. *You're the one who runs.*

"No, I'm not," I said sharply. "I'm here, aren't I?"

I was still living with my mother's family, even though things had pretty much gone to hell. I was here—with him—now.

I'm not running. I'm not scared.

As if in response to the words I'd just thought, he brought his hands to my face, then ran them through my hair. He kissed me, rough this time, in a way that banished every other thought from my mind. *Count to seven.* His touch turned gentle. His lips pulled away from mine and, moments later, brushed lightly against them again.

And then he spoke. "You're so afraid of being left, you live life with one foot out the door. That's why you won't call Lily on the way she's been acting, even though you're worried about her. Hell, that's why you wanted to find Ana's baby in the first place. Pregnancy Pact Baby Number Two is your backup plan. Backup family."

"That's not true," I said.

"Really?" Nick brushed his lips lightly over mine again. "Then why won't you tell Lily how worried you are?" He looked at me in a way that left me no choice about looking back. "Why were you so quick to believe that Jessi was something other than my sister just now?"

"I'm not having this conversation with you." I pressed my lips to his. He kissed me back but only for a moment.

"What if I told you that I don't want you to run?" he asked.

You know better than to let him matter, something inside me whispered. *You damn well know better.*

"What if," Nick continued, "I told you that I don't need your help to get Jessi into the Symphony Ball anymore? What if I told you your debt was paid?"

I went very still, and the muscles in my stomach tightened. "What are you talking about?"

"I haven't needed to play nice with high society for weeks," Nick told me, his voice as soft as his touch and both like fire to my nerve endings. "Your grandmother told me to consider it taken care of. Turns out she has a soft spot for girls from the wrong side of the tracks with lofty aspirations."

There was nothing chilling in those words. No reason I should have felt dread pooling in my stomach. "When?" I said.

He knew what I was asking. "The fund-raiser at the Arcadia hotel. While you were outside."

That was the first time we went out. Weeks ago. I couldn't make my mind slow down. *Before Fourth of July. Before we were ever . . .*

I stepped back, away from his touch. Away from him.

"See?" Nick told me, his voice low enough that it was almost lost to a sudden, punishing wind. "When things get real, you run."

"You lied to me," I said.

He just looked at me. "That's not why you're pulling away."

I shook my head, feeling cornered and caught and like something horrible might happen—or already had. "I have to go. I told Aunt Olivia I'd be home for dinner. And Lily . . ."

"Lily is dealing with a crap hand life dealt her," Nick told me. "But we both know people who've dealt with worse. She'll come out of this okay. Don't make her your reason for walking out of here and away from me."

I wanted to say something else. I wanted him to be wrong. But he wasn't.

"I have to go," I said again.

"I'm not going to chase you," he told me. "If you're too damned scared to let this be real, if I don't get to matter to you, if I have to let this be *nothing* for you to stay—then go."

Go.

He called after me as I fled. "I'm done playing, Sawyer. If you're too much of a coward to stay? Don't come back."

CHAPTER 50

I have to go. I played the words I'd said to Nick over and over again in my mind. I made it halfway through dinner before thinking about what he'd said in return.

Don't come back.

"Lily, sweetheart, you've barely eaten." Aunt Olivia's attention was blessedly focused on her daughter. Lillian's, too. Neither one of them had clued in to the fact that there was a damned thing wrong with me. "Can I get you something else?"

Beside me at the table, Lily picked up a steak knife and began meticulously slicing her meat. *Slice. Slice. Slice.* She used her fork to spear a delicate piece. "I hear the local authorities are bringing in a forensic sculptor," she said primly, sounding almost like her former self. She dabbed a napkin against her lips. "To identify the body we found."

Focus on that, I told myself. *Think about that.*

Aunt Olivia's reaction to the term *forensic sculptor* was completely predictable. "Lily," she said, aghast, "we do not discuss forensics at the dinner table."

"That's right," John David chimed in. "If I can't politely entertain the idea of zombies who eat their own flesh, you can't talk about dead people."

And that was that. Aunt Olivia didn't seem alarmed. She didn't seem to find the idea of the Lady of the Lake being given a face particularly worrisome. She exhibited no behavior out of the ordinary whatsoever.

Until she invited Uncle J.D. over that night.

He wasn't allowed inside the house—Lillian's orders. So he sat on the back deck, talking to John David and waiting for Lily.

I wondered, when I couldn't keep myself from it, if my response to Nick would have been different if J.D. had responded differently to me. How much of who I was came from years of watching my mom—and how much of it was something, the only thing, he'd given me?

Three hours later, Lily was still in her room, and her father was still out on the back deck. I'd stopped wondering, stopped replaying the conversation with Nick.

Mostly.

But I couldn't keep from thinking about the way Nick had said that the reason I hadn't pushed Lily to say something, do something, *feel* something, was that I was terrified of losing her.

Hell, that's why you wanted to find Ana's baby in the first place.

Eventually, John David went to bed. Eventually, Aunt Olivia stopped coming by to nudge Lily to go out and talk with her daddy.

I found myself standing outside Lily's door. Somehow, she knew that I was there.

"I don't want to talk to him," she said.

"I know," I replied. "But I do."

The last time I'd talked to J.D. Easterling had been in the hospital, the night Lily and I had discovered his affair. He'd told me that it was neither the time nor the place to discuss our relationship. He hadn't made any attempt to contact me since.

"Hello, Daddy." Lily had woven her hand through mine, and she squeezed it a little tighter as she said the words.

I'd pushed. She'd let me. She'd *stayed*.

"Lily." J.D. smiled. "Sweetheart, I've missed you so much. Thank you for . . ."

"Talking to you?" Lily's voice was a little wobbly. She let go of my hand and rested both of hers on the deck railing. "I'm not here to talk to you. Maybe I'll be ready for that someday. Maybe I won't. But right now, Sawyer is."

"Sawyer is what, honey?"

"Ready to talk to you," I elucidated.

He was an affable person. He'd treated me fondly—as his niece. But now?

"I really don't think . . ." he started to say.

"If you want me," Lily said, her eyes fixed on the water down below, without any feeling in her tone, "then Sawyer is part of the package. You can talk to both of your daughters—or neither."

Lily's father straightened slightly in his chair, the only tell I could see that until that moment, he'd been holding out hope that I hadn't told Lily the truth about my parentage.

"This situation is . . . complicated," J.D. said, casting a meaning-ful look at the house. Through the window, I could see Aunt Olivia in the kitchen, watching us.

"I'm not looking for a father," I told him. "Evidence suggests you're not a particularly good one anyway."

"He was," Lily said quietly. "Once."

That, more than anything else, seemed to pierce his armor. "Sweetheart, you don't understand. . . ."

She understood enough. Lily had agreed to come out here with me so that I could get something resembling closure, but standing this close to the man who'd fathered me, I found that I didn't have any real desire to ask him how he'd ever been able to pretend I was just his niece.

I couldn't ask him to fix whatever it was that was wrong with me.

So I asked a different question—for Lily. "What do you know about the Lady of the Lake?"

Lily hadn't been able to stop listening to that recording. She needed to know, and I needed to push her, to trust that I could.

"Who?" J.D.'s confusion was genuine, if momentary.

"The Lady of the Lake," I repeated. At the railing, Lily's hands tightened over the wood. "The body we found." I took a stab in the dark. "The reason Aunt Olivia called you when Lily mentioned a forensic sculptor." No visible response. "The one," I continued, "that Aunt Olivia is holding over your head."

I could see the gears in his mind turning, could see the exact moment when he decided to smile and shake his head and treat me like I was speaking nonsense. "Sawyer, I—"

"Lie to her," Lily said softly. She turned back but looked down at the deck, at the water-marked wood beneath our feet. "You're good at that."

That shot proved true. It hit its target and stopped him in his tracks.

"I know you don't love Mama." Lily couldn't stop now that she'd started. "Maybe you never did. But did you ever even love me?"

I could see the shell she'd retreated into these past weeks starting to crack.

"More than anything on the face of this earth," her father said. "Everything I've done, I have done for you, Lily. There's nothing I wouldn't do for you and your brother. You and John David are my world."

"Ouch," I muttered, under the mistaken impression that treating his words cavalierly might make them hurt less.

"Then tell us about the body," Lily whispered. "Or tell us about the blackmail. Tell me *something* that's true."

"I love you." He looked at her like she was the most precious thing on this planet, then turned to me. "And, Sawyer, I care for you, too. I do. That's why I'm asking you to just leave well enough alone. This family has been through enough. I've put this family through enough."

"It's never enough," Lily said, and the emotion in that abbreviated sentence took me aback. This was the Lily who'd hit the wall. This was the kind of angry that didn't know how to be anything else.

This was what she'd been keeping under lock and key.

"Ask me something else," J.D. begged her. "Lily—if there's something else you want to know, anything else—just ask me."

I expected her to turn around and walk back inside. She'd come out here for me, and it was clear by this point that I wasn't going to get anything resembling closure—or answers.

Instead, Lily asked, "How long have you and Ana been having an affair?"

This was exactly the conversation she hadn't wanted to have. I wished that I could protect her from this. I almost wished I hadn't pushed.

"We got to know each other when you were twelve." J.D.'s answer was immediate and without frills. I knew instinctively that it was true. "It wasn't physical for a few years."

"How long have you been paying her?"

"You don't need to know that."

She stared at him, impassive, until he answered.

"Since you were twelve."

It took me a second to register the fact that J.D. Easterling had just claimed that he'd been giving Ana money before he'd had a physical relationship with her at all.

As far as I knew, he'd never given my mother a dime.

"Why were you paying her?" I asked. "If you weren't sleeping with her, if you were just getting to know her—why give her money?"

J.D. didn't answer. Lily shook her head, disgusted, because he couldn't even give us this.

"I'm not paying Ana anymore." J.D. tried to make it sound like he'd taken a stand, but taking into account what Campbell had said about the late Victor Gutierrez's will, I saw straight through that.

Lily did, too.

"Is there anything else you want to know?" she asked me.

I was on the verge of saying no, of telling J.D. Easterling that I didn't need or want anything else from him, when I realized that was a lie.

There was one thing. Even if he wouldn't say a word about bodies or blackmail, even if he wouldn't acknowledge me, there was one answer he could give me.

"You said that you got to know Ana when Lily was twelve. Where was she before that? Did she tell you anything? Where did she disappear to when she left town, back in the day?"

J.D. didn't shrug off the question. He didn't shrug *me* off this time. "I don't know exactly, Sawyer. She mentioned something about spending some time in a small town near the lake when she was pregnant, and after that, she traveled. Sweden—her mother was Swedish. New York. California. Paris. Everywhere that wasn't here."

Inside the house, Aunt Olivia was washing dishes—by hand, even though we had a dishwasher. That had her positioned near the window, where she could see.

Where, with the window cracked open, she could hear every word.

Beside me, J.D. was talking to Lily again. I didn't really hear what he was saying to her, because the sound of my own thoughts was suddenly deafening. *Open window. Hear every word.* I flashed back to the trip Sadie-Grace, Boone, and I had taken. I saw Ellen in my mind's eye.

I heard Beth, Ellen's granddaughter, screaming through the open window with each contraction.

Anything bought or sold in that town, Lillian had said of her sister, *she has a hand in it.*

The simple, ugly truth of the matter was that Ellen had been perfectly willing to sell Beth's baby to Greer. It hadn't occurred to me at the time to wonder if Sadie-Grace's new little brother was the first baby Ellen had sold.

She mentioned something about spending some time in a small town near the lake when she was pregnant. J.D.'s answer to my question replaced everything else in my mind.

"A small town near the lake," I said. I didn't realize how loudly I'd said it until I realized that both Lily and her father were staring at me. I gathered myself. "What was the name of the town?"

J.D. claimed he didn't know the answer.

But I did. Or, at least, I thought that I might. *Two Arrows.*

"*S*awyer, you do realize you sound both paranoid and delusional, right?"

"Bite me, Campbell."

"That's a pretty way to talk to the person who got you out of that hole."

"I'm not paranoid. Or delusional."

"Okay, well . . . I'm just saying. I've known your so-called kidnapper my entire life. She doesn't have it in her to use the wrong fork at the dinner table, let alone drug a couple of Debutantes and throw them in a hole."

"I'm not going to argue with you about this, Cam. She threw us in that hole, and I got the distinct feeling that after she got whatever she wanted from us, she was going to bury us alive. We have to get out of here."

"Do you even know where *here* is?"

"Enlighten me."

"We're on King's Island, and we really don't want to be here when it starts to storm."

TWELVE HOURS EARLIER

CHAPTER 51

*L*ily didn't say a word to anyone for two days after her father's visit. I came close—more than once—to telling her what I suspected about Ana, Two Arrows, and our grandmother's twin, but I didn't.

I'd seen a crack in the barrier she'd put up between the rest of the world and her emotions, but I wasn't sure what would happen when it shattered. I didn't want to be the one to break her.

Damn Nick. Damn him for being right—and for being the one person I wanted to call. But he'd told me not to come back.

I assumed that meant he wouldn't pick up the phone.

I'm done playing.

"Have you seen your cousin?" Aunt Olivia asked me. Since J.D.'s visit, she'd been, in Lillian's words, *in a bit of a tizzy.* Also known as: full-blown togetherness mode. She'd filled our itineraries with lakeside bonding activities: water sports, mini golf at the yacht club, cookouts, s'mores, ghost stories, midnight movie marathons— pretending the whole time that Lily wasn't silent and in danger of heatstroke with the way she was dressed.

"I'll go look for her," I said.

"I thought we could all go tubing," Aunt Olivia called after me.

"In that cove you like. What's it called?" In true Taft woman style, my aunt answered her own question: "King's Cove."

I found Lily in our closet, hiding from her mother.

"Where's a pantry when you need one?" I asked her.

I saw then that she was holding something in her hands. *A phone.* I stepped closer, and realized that it was mine. "Lily?"

She turned toward me. Her dark brown eyes met mine. "You got a text." She held out the phone. "Three of them."

Nick. My first thought was a nonsensical one, and I knew it. My second didn't come in words. My stomach twisting, I took the phone from Lily.

After more than a month of radio silence from the White Gloves, they'd gotten in touch. *Three texts.* The rose, the snake, a message: *The Candidates are many. The Chosen are few. You have been chosen. Tonight, King's Island, midnight.*

A fourth text came through while I was standing there, one word: *Initiation.*

"Each White Glove chooses her own replacement," Lily said. "I'm betting Victoria chose you—or maybe Hope did. One of them probably chose Campbell, and I think Nessa's halfway in love with Sadie-Grace."

I didn't ask whether Lily had gotten a text. I didn't have to.

"It's stupid," Lily said softly. "That I wanted this so badly." She swallowed. "Even when I stopped wanting anything else."

"It doesn't matter," I told her. "I won't go tonight."

"It does," she replied as she began taking clothes off the hangers. "And you will."

Over the course of the summer, I'd never once unpacked my lake bag. I just swapped in clean clothes for the dirty ones and kept everything else—swimsuits, flip-flops, toiletries—packed. Lily, on the other hand, unpacked her bag every weekend.

And now she was packing. "Stop that," I told her.

"My mama ran away when she was a year younger than we are now." Lily addressed the words as much toward her paisley bag as to me. "Did you know that, Sawyer? I didn't, until your mama let that slip to me over Fourth of July. When my mama was seventeen, she left home, society, all of it, for more than half a year. And when she came back, it was like she was a different person."

"So?" I asked.

Lily zipped her bag. "I'm ready to be a different person, Sawyer."

I reached for my own, already-packed lake bag. "I'll go with you. Forget the White Gloves. We can have a secret society of two."

Lily was quiet for a long time, then managed five words. "That's not what I want."

I felt like she'd hit me, the way she'd punched her fist into the wall of what remained of the King's Island house.

"Don't do this," I told her.

"If I stay," Lily replied, her voice low, "I'm going to do something I'll regret."

To say that Aunt Olivia wasn't pleased when she discovered Lily's absence would have been an understatement. She demanded that I tell her where Lily went, but I didn't know. Lillian got involved.

I still didn't know.

"Do you know when she'll be back?" Aunt Olivia pressed. "You must. Lily tells you everything."

That hurt. *Clearly, she doesn't. Not anymore.* "She took a bag with her," I said. "That's all I know."

Aunt Olivia glared at me. "Don't be ridiculous, Sawyer. That can't possibly be—"

"Ease up, Olivia," my grandmother cut in.

"Excuse me?" Aunt Olivia whipped around to face Lillian. If

they hadn't been wearing lake attire, I would have termed it the Battle of the Twin Sets.

"Leave Sawyer be," Lillian ordered my aunt. "I've been expecting this. Lily needs—"

"Tell me what my daughter needs, Mama." Aunt Olivia wasn't smiling. Aunt Olivia *always* smiled, but she wasn't now.

"Lily needs what she needs," Lillian said evenly. "And I think we both know that she's old enough to decide what that is for herself. Think of yourself at her age. You knew exactly who you wanted to be, *Olivia*."

I heard the emphasis on Aunt Olivia's name but didn't know quite what to read into it, other than the fact that Lillian meant business. And when Lillian Taft meant business, the rest of this family listened.

Myself excluded. That was what I found myself thinking half an hour later, after Aunt Olivia had reluctantly—and temporarily, I was sure—stopped badgering me about Lily. Weeks earlier, my grandmother had as good as told me to stay away from Two Arrows. She had strongly implied that it could be dangerous for me to go there, to get mixed up with Ellen and whatever her *business* was.

Now that Aunt Olivia was occupied with Lily's disappearing act, she wasn't so focused on keeping me within eyesight, and that meant I finally had a chance to do the thing I'd been thinking about for the past two days.

Ever since Uncle J.D. had mentioned the small town where Ana had gone while she was pregnant—right before she gave the baby away and started traveling the world.

Moving quickly and silently, I went back upstairs to get my cell phone. The texts from the White Gloves were still pulled up. I dismissed them. For a moment, I thought about calling Nick. I remembered the way he'd jumped over the bar when that drunken frat boy had gotten physical. I hadn't *needed* his help, but he'd been there, beside me, in a flash.

Once someone starts a bar fight in my establishment and *offers pointers on my tossing-out-dirtbags technique,* I could hear him saying, *we're pretty much on a first-name basis by default.*

If he knew where I was going and what I was doing, if he knew about the gun I'd found pressed to my back the last time I'd gone to Two Arrows . . . would he come?

Would he even pick up the phone?

I could have called. I could have found out. But when Nick had accused me of being a runner, he'd gotten at least one thing right. I was better at leaving than being left.

Don't come back.

I began composing a text. Not to Nick. To Campbell and Sadie-Grace. "Lily's gone," I said under my breath, talking as I typed in the words. "Not sure for how long. I need to go to Two Arrows."

Campbell didn't reply, but Sadie-Grace did. All her message said was *I'll drive!*

CHARLOTTE, LIV, JULIA, TRINA, AND THE BOYS SUMMER BEFORE SENIOR YEAR TWENTY-FIVE YEARS EARLIER

As it turned out, Trina was a good sport. The kind of good sport who had six brothers and could tread water all day long. Charlotte could see the instant Liv decided the new girl was *interesting*.

I don't care if she's interesting, Charlotte thought as the minutes turned to hours. *I'm your best friend.* She glanced at Julia. *Second-best.*

"Don't look so glum." Sterling wrapped a towel around Charlotte's shoulders.

They'd all jumped multiple times. When Trina was finally allowed back onshore, there was drinking.

A campfire.

Another trip over the ledge, in the dark.

And now this. Charlotte let her body lean against his. He knew how she felt about him. He had to. But this was the first hint she'd gotten that he could see it, too.

What the two of them could be, together.

"Want to know a secret?" Sterling asked her, nodding toward the ledge, where Liv sat side by side with the townie girl. "I brought her here to make you jealous."

"Want to know a secret?" Charlotte murmured back. "It didn't work."

Shortly thereafter, Liv volunteered to drive the local girl home.

CHAPTER 52

*T*here were days when I thought Sadie-Grace was the living, breathing embodiment of an exclamation mark. Today was not one of them.

"I'm tired," she told me, practically wilting in the driver's seat as we made our way back to the belly of the beast. "Audie is *adorable*, but he stopped sleeping. At night. Did you know babies can do that? They can stop sleeping. At night."

All I could think in response was that Audubon Charles Richard Waters might not be the first baby that Lillian's twin sister had given someone, in exchange for money.

Don't get ahead of yourself. All you know is that Ana spent some time in a small town near the lake, after which she was baby-free and able to travel the world. You know that Ana says she gave the baby up.

You don't know anything other than that.

That wasn't quite accurate, I realized as Sadie-Grace pulled the car off onto the main road in Two Arrows. *I also know that Ana has a history of asking people for money.* My mom had adapted to life on a budget, more or less. I wasn't sure that Ana had.

And if she did come to Two Arrows, if she left with no baby and money to travel . . .

I didn't let myself finish the thought.

"Am I allowed to ask where Lily went?" Sadie-Grace asked me.

I was getting ready to tell her that I didn't know, and then I saw Lily's car. I wondered if she'd planned, when she left, to come here, to meet Ellen.

I wondered if Lily had even realized this was where she was coming.

This time, there was no welcoming committee. No guns. Sadie-Grace and I stood on the front porch of the house where we'd met Ellen—the house where Ellen's granddaughter Beth had given birth to baby Audie.

The bell was cracked and broken, so I lifted my hand to knock.

The girl who answered the door couldn't have been older than eleven or so. Her hair was tangled, her ponytail lopsided. The dirt on her knees made me think that she'd worked for every tangle and knocked the ponytail off center on purpose.

"We're looking for . . ." I was going to say that we were looking for Ellen, but before I could get that out, I caught sight of Lily. She was standing just outside what I assumed was the kitchen. After a second or two, she turned toward us.

If she was surprised to see me there, she didn't show it.

"You followed me?" There was a flicker of discernible emotion in her eyes, like I'd told her she didn't get to leave me, and she'd responded, *As of right now, I get to do whatever the hell I want.*

"I had no idea you'd be here," I said.

Lily didn't enlighten me as to why she'd come. Instead, she turned back toward the kitchen. "You have guests," she called.

I heard a harrumph. The sound of a chair scraping against linoleum floor came next, and a few seconds later, my grandmother's twin stepped into the hallway behind Lily.

"Funny," she said, in a tone that suggested it really wasn't. "I don't remember inviting you." She swiveled her head pointedly toward Lily. "Any of you."

"Thank you," Lily told her, sounding more like herself than she had in an age. "For the conversation."

What conversation?

Ellen didn't reply—but she didn't harrumph again, either.

Lily turned back to us. Wordlessly, she walked down to the doorway to stand beside the little girl. "This is Makayla," she told us. "She's our second cousin."

"That means our mamas are cousins," Makayla informed me.

Ellen has six children, I thought. *Who knows how many children* they *have.*

"It was nice to meet you," Lily told Makayla, with all the pomp and circumstance of someone thanking the queen for her hospitality. "But I think it's time for me to go."

Lily flicked her gaze from me to Sadie-Grace. "Did you hear from the White Gloves?"

As tired as she was, Sadie-Grace still managed a smile as she nodded. "You too?" she asked. "This is going to be so much fun!"

Sadie-Grace was delighted. Lily was not. *Not delighted,* I thought. *But not hurt. Not anymore.* I wasn't sure what exactly to read into that.

"I want you to promise you'll go to initiation tonight," Lily told Sadie-Grace, before shifting her gaze to me. "Both of you."

If you're leaving, why do you care? I bit back the question, and after Sadie-Grace promised, I offered Lily the barest nod.

"You should try the lemonade," Lily told Sadie-Grace, falling back on idle chitchat. "It's not too sweet." There was a beat of silence, and then Lily turned back to me. "See you around, Sawyer."

I watched her go. It took me until she made it to the bottom of the drive to remember where I was—and why I'd come here.

"What did Lily want?" I asked Ellen.

"A little family history." Ellen let her arms dangle loose at her side. "What do *you* want?"

That wasn't my great-aunt making conversation. That was a challenge.

"We have some questions."

"We?" Ellen looked from me to Sadie-Grace, then back again. "I do something on your last trip to make you think I'm the type of person who likes questions?"

Sadie-Grace—even a tired Sadie-Grace—didn't know when *not* to be optimistic.

"You gave us Audie," she pointed out cheerfully. "We named the baby Audubon. Daddy is almost as fond of bird-watching as he is of bugs, and Greer told him no bug names. Would you like to see a pic—"

"No." Ellen cut her off. "That's not how this works, girl. You're not meant to come back here."

"We're not here about the baby," I said. I let that sink in. "Or at least, we're not here about *that* baby."

CHAPTER 53

*I*t became quickly apparent that little Makayla was damn near expert at knowing when to make herself scarce. I had the distinct sense that Ellen wanted nothing more than to send us trotting after Lily, but instead, she disappeared back into the kitchen.

"Are you coming, or ain't ya?"

I came. In other circumstances, I might have wondered at the fact that her accent had thickened halfway through that sentence, but right now, I had to focus.

"Almost twenty years ago, a girl named Ana Gutierrez got pregnant." I cut straight to it.

Ellen displayed no reaction whatsoever to Ana's name. "Sit," she ordered.

Sadie-Grace, cowed by Ellen's tone, went to plop down where she was standing, but I grabbed her elbow and steered her toward the kitchen table. It was made of a light-colored wood, and stained with years of use, rings burned and etched into its surface.

To me, it almost felt like home.

I sat down in a chair that put my back to the wall. Sadie-Grace

sat down with her back to the door. Behind her, I could see a fraction of the hallway. To my left, I could see the rest of the kitchen,
where Ellen was pouring lemonade out of a white plastic pitcher.
The appliances looked old and none of the colors matched, but
everything in that kitchen was spotless.

Ellen plunked a mason jar down in front of each of us. "Drink."

I drank the lemonade. So did Sadie-Grace. And then I circled
back to what I'd said before. "Twenty years ago, Ana Gutierrez got
pregnant. The baby was a summer baby—or very early fall. Ana
came here to give birth."

I wasn't sure if I meant *here* as in Two Arrows or *here* as in
Ellen's house. I was fishing, and the old woman who sat down in the
chair between Sadie-Grace and me was smart enough to know it.

"You tell my sister you met me?" she asked after a moment.

When I'd first moved in with Lillian, I'd viewed my exchanges
with her as a form of bartering: I'd answer one of her questions
in hopes of her answering mine. We'd progressed past that, these
last few months, but Ellen seemed like the type to respect an even
trade.

Or better yet, a trade that favored Ellen. *Answer the question.
Answer any question she asks you.*

"I told Lillian about my last visit," I confirmed. "I told her that
I met you." Then I volunteered the answer to her next question
before she could weigh the costs and benefits of asking it. "She said
that I shouldn't come back."

"Smart girl." Ellen took a long drink from a mason glass that
very clearly did not contain lemonade. "Lil," she clarified. "Not you."

I probably should have heard some kind of threat or warning
in those words—the implication that not coming back would have
been smart—but I couldn't get past the idea of someone, *anyone*,

referring to the great Lillian Taft, grande dame of society, as a *girl*.

"You're going to catch flies with that mouth if you keep gaping at me," Ellen said mildly.

Nothing about this woman is mild. I had to remind myself of that, and then I circled back around to the point.

"Lillian doesn't know that I came here today. She doesn't know that Ana gave birth in Two Arrows." I waited a fraction of a second to see if that would get me a reaction. It didn't. "Lillian doesn't know that you're the one who arranged for Ana's baby's adoption."

Adoption, a voice in my mind whispered, *or sale.*

Ellen took her time taking my measure, then allowed herself another healthy drink of the concoction in her jar. "Around here, we'd say that a girl like you, making assumptions like those and talking that kind of talk, was getting a little big for her britches."

Her accent was still coming in and out. I wasn't sure what to read into that, but I did have the general sense that this could go badly.

A smarter person would have backed off. "I just want to know what happened to Ana's baby," I said.

"That baby is our friend Campbell's half-sister," Sadie-Grace chimed in. "Or maybe her half-brother? And there's this girl Victoria, and she's the baby's—"

"Ellen doesn't care about Victoria," I told Sadie-Grace.

"There's a lot of things I don't care about," Ellen commented. That, too, was a warning—that I shouldn't get too comfortable here, just because we were related by blood. "And," Ellen continued, "there's a lot of things I do care about. My family. This town."

Your business, my brain filled in. People asking questions was bad for business. And rich people coming around probably wasn't great.

"Just tell us about the baby," I said. "There's no reason not to.

Ana isn't ever coming back here, and it's not like whoever ended up with the baby is ever going to be in the market for another one. It's been nineteen years."

That earned me a heavy stare. My phrasing—talking about *the market* for babies—was tiptoeing its way closer and closer to the word *sold*. It was bad enough, from Ellen's perspective, that Sadie-Grace and I knew her father had shown his gratitude toward Beth with a healthy check. The woman who ran this town couldn't be happy about the idea that we knew—or at least suspected—that Audie wasn't the first child she'd exchanged for a big wad of cash.

"Please," I said. It would have sounded more earnest coming from Sadie-Grace, but I knew in my bones that she'd take the word better coming from me. There was a long silence—tenser for me than for Sadie-Grace, who didn't realize that our situation was precarious in the least.

"If I tell you what you want to know, you'll git?" Ellen asked me finally.

"Immediately and without any further questions," I confirmed.

Another few seconds ticked by. Each one felt intentional. And then Ellen placed her forearms on the table and leaned toward me.

"Before you go getting high-and-mighty, you should know that with Ana, with that baby? I didn't take a dime from anyone. That wasn't business. That was me taking pity on a girl that *your* world had spit out like she was nothing."

I wasn't sure I bought the idea that Ellen had helped Ana out of the goodness of her heart, but I knew better than to say that out loud.

Not when we were *this* close to answers.

"You helped Ana find a home for the baby." My heart was beating in my chest like there was actually a person in there with a gun, firing it over and over into my rib cage. *Thump. Thump. Thump.*

"A good home," Sadie-Grace added.

A certain kind of home, I thought, but what came out of my mouth was: "Did Lillian help you?"

My brain didn't really latch onto the question until after I'd asked it. But it made sense. I had no idea how Greer had found Two Arrows—or Ellen or the pregnant Beth. But when it came to imagining the reverse—Ellen looking for a *certain kind* of home for a newborn—it wasn't all that hard to picture her asking the one person she knew who ran in those circles.

Two, I thought suddenly. *Davis Ames grew up hereabouts. She knows two people who run in those circles.*

"Lillian don't know a thing," Ellen spat, like she meant that, all the way down to the marrow in her bones. "And she certainly didn't *help.*"

"But you found a family," I pressed. "For Ana's baby."

And that family paid Ana, even if they didn't pay you. She left here with enough money to travel. She never had to ask her family for money. All these years later, she still has expensive tastes.

"Just tell me who took the baby," I said. "That's all I want to know, and you'll never have to see either one of us again."

"You don't know what you're asking." For the first time, Ellen sounded like Lillian.

She sounded the way my grandmother had when I'd realized the truth about my father.

What is going on here?

Ellen took another drink. Looked me over. Looked me down. Opened her mouth—and then, before she could say a word, there was a knock at the door. I wasn't sure at first that she was going to answer, but she downed the rest of the drink, then stood.

"Don't take it in your mind to wander," she warned me. "You hear?"

"I hear."

"I also hear!" Sadie-Grace added cheerfully. "No wandering for me."

Ellen snorted and disappeared into the hallway. I heard the front door open, heard a muted, murmured conversation of some kind.

My *eyes* wandered. Ellen had told me to stay put. She hadn't said I couldn't look. The kitchen was small, small enough that I could have reached out and touched the refrigerator from where I sat. There were pictures—dozens of them, if not hundreds—stuck to the side. The latest additions were hung up with magnets: photographs of Makayla and a dozen other kids within five years of her age. Some of them were school pictures, but more had been printed out on plain white paper.

The side and front of the fridge was papered with them, and when I lifted my hand to flip one of the pictures up, I realized there were more underneath.

Years' worth.

The ones on the bottom were faded and taped to the fridge. I looked through them, half expecting to see my grandmother, before I realized that none of these photographs were that old. The oldest one I could spot featured Ellen, looking more like Lillian than she did now, like life hadn't yet carved their fortunes into the wear and tear on the skin. The picture in question was a family photo—Ellen and six kids.

The youngest couldn't have been more than four or five, and the oldest, the teenager was . . .

What the hell . . . I leaned closer, nearly falling out of my chair. The picture hadn't aged well. I couldn't make out the details of the faces as precisely as I would have liked, but Ellen's oldest child bore a striking resemblance to her mother, to my grandmother . . .

And to Aunt Olivia. She looks a lot like Aunt Olivia.

"Anyone ever tell you to keep your hands to yourself?" Ellen reappeared in the hallway outside the kitchen. "I told you not to wander."

"I didn't," I said, letting my hand drop to the side and the years of photographs fall back into place, obscuring the one I'd been looking at.

"I have some business to tend to," Ellen said, giving me a hard look that said my snooping had not gone unnoticed. "I'll give you girls one more glass of lemonade, and then I need you gone."

She walked over to the kitchen counter. Her back was to us as she added ice to the pitcher. My mind went briefly to the *business* she'd referred to—and the person she'd talked to at the door—but I forced myself to focus on the reason I'd come here.

All I needed was a name.

"One more glass of lemonade," I countered as she poured. "And the name of the family that adopted Ana's baby."

Ellen sat down and took a long gulp of her own drink. "Girl."

At first, I thought she was addressing me—or possibly Sadie-Grace—but her next words made her meaning clear.

"The baby was a girl," Ellen said. "Arrived at daybreak. If I'd been naming her, I would have called her Dawn."

Get to the point, I thought. But somehow, in my head, the words came out muddy. Slow. I felt suddenly like I was seeing double. I tried to say Sadie-Grace's name. I might have succeeded, but I wasn't sure.

I was sure that, across the table, Sadie-Grace was now slumped over.

I tried to stand, grabbing at the table in an attempt to find purchase. But all I ended up doing was knocking over the lemonade.

The lemonade.

I could see Ellen in the kitchen, her back to us. I could hear her putting what I'd thought was ice into the drinks.

"What . . ." I couldn't keep standing. I was going to fall. Things were already fuzzy around the edges, and those fuzzy edges were going black. "Why would you . . ."

"Because," another voice said from the hallway, "I asked her to." Heels clicked against the linoleum as their owner strode toward me.

I went down. Ellen caught me under the armpits. I couldn't even feel her grasp as she lowered me to the floor.

I could barely see the person standing over me. I blinked, forcing things to come briefly into focus.

"You brought this on yourself, young lady," Aunt Olivia told me. Then she turned to Ellen. "Thank you for your assistance, Mama."

CHARLOTTE, LIV, JULIA, AND THE BOYS
SUMMER BEFORE SENIOR YEAR
TWENTY–FIVE YEARS EARLIER

*L*iv made it back from delivering Trina to wherever it was she'd come from and greeted Charlotte with a smile—and an order. "Help me unload the car, Char."

It soon became apparent that what Charlotte was supposed to unload was camping equipment—several thousand dollars' worth, at least.

"I tried to talk her out of it," J.D. said as he hauled the tents and sleeping bags down from the car. He'd gone along with Liv to drop Trina off.

Charlotte wondered what else Liv might have come back with if he hadn't.

"You drove?" Charlotte asked him quietly as she helped him unload the supplies.

"Of course I did," J.D. replied. "The last thing she needs is a DUI. Liv's not herself right now, Charlotte."

Charlotte wanted to agree, but she thought back to the way Liv had gone hurtling off the edge of the cliff, the way she'd lorded her power over Trina, then turned on a dime and decided they could be friends.

That was *classic* Liv Taft.

J.D. was just too smitten to see it.

Charlotte woke in the middle of the night to find that Sterling wasn't beside her. He had been, when they'd fallen asleep.

He'd kissed her.

Charlotte could feel her heart beating, just thinking about it. She sat up and realized that Sterling wasn't the only one missing. Julia was asleep on top of her sleeping bag. Thomas was passed out beside her.

But J.D., Sterling, and Liv were gone.

Charlotte stood up. It was dark, but the moon overhead was bright. She heard something in the distance.

In the direction of the cliff.

Wishing she had a flashlight, Charlotte followed the noise. There was a giggle, and another, unmistakable sound.

Cheeks burning, Charlotte quickly turned on her heels. What J.D. and Liv were doing out there was *none* of her business.

And then, on the way back to her sleeping bag, she ran smack-dab into J.D.

CHAPTER 54

I woke up in darkness. At first, I thought there was something wrong with my vision, but as my eyes adjusted, I realized that it was the dead of night. It took me a second to focus visually and longer than that for my brain to catch up. Scant moonlight overhead made it possible for me to just barely see—and eventually, *realize*—where I was.

A *hole*.

I could smell the dirt all around me, but I couldn't feel it against my skin. I was lying on my back, my eyes skyward. I couldn't feel anything except for my face.

I couldn't move.

"Sawyer, are you there?"

Turning my head felt like swimming through cement. I only managed a slight movement, not enough to even brush my cheek against the dirt below me. "I'm here."

"I can't feel my feet," Sadie-Grace told me, her voice high, the words bursting out at rapid speed. "Or my hands. Or my elbows . . ."

To say that Sadie-Grace was not the optimal person to wake up drugged and halfway buried alive next to would have been an understatement. She was 50 percent uncontrollable babbling and 50 percent utterly misplaced optimism.

When Aunt Olivia came to check on us, I fully expected Sadie-Grace to start chatting away and blow our cover, but she stayed quiet. I heard the sound of Aunt Olivia moving up above—and then the sound of a shovel hitting dirt.

I waited for her to toss it in the hole, waited for my proper, prim, perfectionist aunt to properly, primly, perfectly bury us alive.

But she didn't.

After a minute or two, she dropped the shovel and left, and I resumed my job of managing the situation—and Sadie-Grace. The entire time, I silently reminded myself, over and over again, *Aunt Olivia called Ellen "Mama."*

I had no idea what to make of that, and as I listened to Sadie-Grace insisting that the glass was half full and that she could somehow give herself a boost out of this godforsaken hole, I tried to make any of this make sense.

We'd gone to my grandmother's twin to ask her about Ana's baby. Lily had been there when we'd arrived, and by the time we'd gotten midway through our conversation with Ellen, Aunt Olivia had interrupted.

Not my aunt. If she's Ellen's daughter, she's not my aunt.

I thought back to the picture I'd seen on the fridge in the Two Arrows house: Ellen, with her six children. The oldest was a girl, one who closely resembled Ellen—and Lillian.

And Aunt Olivia. The picture was old enough and the resolution crappy enough that I hadn't been able to tell *how* close the resemblance between Ellen's daughter and Aunt Olivia was.

What were the chances that they looked identical?

"I'm not leaving you." Sadie-Grace was stubborn. She'd made her way out of the hole, but didn't want to leave me. Unfortunately, whatever drug we'd been given was wearing off more slowly for me. The feeling was just now starting to return to my body. Even if Sadie-Grace could somehow get me out of what amounted to an open grave, until I could shake the numbness, until I could really move—I'd just slow her down.

"You have to." I willed her to listen to me. "I have no idea where we are, but you need to be somewhere else when she gets back."

The hole was significantly lonelier without Sadie-Grace. I had too much time to think about the fact that I might not get out of here.

About all the things I might never get to say.

I forced my arms to move. The movement hurt. I'd never been so grateful for pain in my entire life. *It only hurts if you can feel it. I can feel my arms. The legs are getting there.*

Sadie-Grace had left me propped up. Trying to shift my weight sent me facedown into the dirt. I managed to roll, all too aware that if I'd ended up facedown when Aunt Olivia—*or whoever the hell she was*—had tossed us down here, I probably would have suffocated.

Who knew what could happen still?

Sadie-Grace will get help. I struggled to my knees, trying not to really think about the fact that I was pinning my future survival on Sadie-Grace Waters, who had once told me, in all seriousness, that she thought that fish probably went to a separate heaven, because in regular heaven, people ate fish.

"Sawyer?" In the distance, I heard someone call my name. "Sadie-Grace? Are you guys out there?"

Campbell, I thought. *Thank God.*

CHAPTER 55

My rescuer quickly proved to enjoy playing hero almost as much as she relished telling me how paranoid and deluded I seemed. And, yes, the story I'd just told Campbell sounded far-fetched, but what about our lives for the past year hadn't? Regardless, persuading Campbell Ames that I hadn't lost my mind currently ranked a distant third priority, behind finding Sadie-Grace and getting the hell off of King's Island before our kidnapper came back.

"Please tell me you have a way off this island." I leaned my weight into Campbell and allowed her to help me hobble toward the edge of the tree line. I might have been able to walk on my own, but for now, as the last of the drugs wore off, I'd take all the help I could get.

"Of course I have a way off the island," Campbell retorted. "Do you think I swam here? My Jet Ski's beached on the east shore."

I wondered if Sadie-Grace had found it yet. The island wasn't that big. I'd taken Campbell in the direction my fellow captive had gone, but so far, there was no sign of her. For someone with an utter lack of stealth, Sadie-Grace was surprisingly good at hiding her tracks.

"How did you find us?" I asked Campbell as we stepped into a clearing. The added moonlight now visible overhead cast just enough light that I was finally able to take in her appearance. "Also: nice robe."

Beneath the scarlet robe, Campbell wore nothing but a thin white shift and long white gloves.

"When I was the only one of the four of us to show up for initiation," Campbell said, "I was suspicious. When Victoria told me that Lily didn't make the final cut, I assumed that you and Sadie-Grace had bowed out in solidarity, but then Victoria said that she'd heard from Lily—that Lily had said the White Gloves should expect both of you in attendance tonight."

"She made us promise," I remembered out loud. At the time, I'd been annoyed.

"How did you know we were on the island?" I asked Campbell again, wondering what strange alignment of the stars had caused Aunt Olivia to bring us *here*.

"We knew you were here because once initiation wrapped up," a new voice said behind me, "we asked Sadie-Grace's little boyfriend to use the Find Your Friend app on his phone, and it told us your location was awfully close to ours."

I turned toward the voice, nearly throwing Campbell off-balance. A moment later, two figures emerged from the woods—Victoria Gutierrez and a beaming Sadie-Grace Waters.

"I found help," Sadie-Grace told me cheerfully. "And you found Campbell!" She paused for maybe half a second and then babbled happily on. "I'm wearing a smartwatch. Miss Olivia took our phones while we were unconscious, but she must have forgotten about my watch, so Boone was able to track it. You know, in a way, this means Boone found us. Very heroic."

Even on the tail end of having been drugged, kidnapped, and

thrown in a hole, Sadie-Grace glowed when she talked about Boone. I couldn't help thinking that it would never occur to her to keep anyone at arm's length. She didn't protect her heart. She wouldn't even have known how.

If I'd been the only one in that hole, there wouldn't have been anyone to track me, I thought, the realization gumming up my brain like tar. *Nick didn't even know that I was gone.*

"Yes, Sadie-Grace," Campbell said with an elaborate roll of her eyes. "Boone is the real hero in all of this. Now, might I suggest we find Hope and get the hell out of here before the storm hits?"

"Hope's here?" I asked.

"Everyone else cleared out after initiation," Campbell replied. "But since Hope's the one with good enough taste to have chosen me as her replacement, she hung back when I did."

"She didn't stay for you," Victoria informed Campbell. "Hope lives on the edge. She *likes* trouble."

"And she's on this island," I said. "Somewhere."

I had no idea what, exactly, the person calling herself *Olivia Taft* had planned to do with us, or why she'd chosen this island as the place to do it, but given that we'd kept all things White Glove a secret from her, I had to believe that she'd expected this island to be as vacant and abandoned as advertised.

Thunder boomed in the distance. Victoria raised the hood of her scarlet robe and turned toward Campbell. "What do you think the chances are that Hope doubled back to the boats?"

"Only one way to find out," Campbell replied. As we limped our way toward the east side of the island, I processed the fact that Victoria hadn't asked a single question about why Sadie-Grace and I had missed initiation or why we were covered in dirt and still unsteady on our feet.

I wondered how much Sadie-Grace had told her.

I wondered how much of what Sadie-Grace *had* told her she'd believed.

The last twenty yards to the shore, I spent every step expecting "Aunt Olivia" to pop out of the shadows. Was she still on the island? Or had she left us, assuming that Sadie-Grace and I were well and truly contained? *Or did she leave when she realized that we weren't the only ones on the island?*

"What the hell?" Campbell's voice went up an octave as we arrived at our destination. "Where's my Jet Ski?"

Even through the dark, I could tell that the gravelly beach on the east shore was bare. *No boats. No Hope.*

"My ride's gone, too," Victoria stated calmly. All four of us stared out at the water.

"Maybe they just floated away on their own," Sadie-Grace said hopefully. "They couldn't have floated far. We could wade out to find them?"

"We could," Victoria allowed. "Or we could wait for daybreak. They'll be easier to spot then, and worse comes to worst, we could just swim to shore."

"I vote we swim for it now," I said. "I know it's dark, but Campbell's cove isn't far." That idea was not met with any level of enthusiasm. "Night swimming," I cajoled. "Gliding our way through pitch-black water with only the scantest moonlight to guide us. Seems like a White Glove kind of thing to do. Hell, we can do it naked, if that helps."

"Or," Victoria countered evenly, "we could find Hope and wait for daybreak."

"Hanging around here is *not* a good idea," I replied. "And for all we know, Hope left." Something in my stomach twisted. "Did Sadie-Grace tell you . . ."

"I told her everything!" Sadie-Grace chirped. "Especially about the part where I got the feeling in my body back."

"Your aunt's gone off the deep end," Victoria summarized. "I have no idea why she would stick you guys in a hole on an abandoned island, but I suppose everyone has a breaking point. I can relate."

I thought back to Ellen's house, to the moment when Aunt Olivia had told me that I'd brought this on myself. *What breaking point did I hit?*

"Relax, Sawyer," Campbell told me. "There's four of us and one of her. I seriously doubt Olivia Taft—or her mystery lookalike—is secretly some kind of suburban brawler."

"Heaven forbid," a pleasant voice said. Aunt Olivia—or whoever she was—walked slowly out of the shadows. She held a flashlight in her left hand. "I've never been much for brawling," Aunt Olivia commented. She looked down to her free hand, and my eyes followed. "I am, however, the best shot in this family. Isn't that right, Sawyer?"

Who's the best shot in this family? That was something I'd heard Aunt Olivia say to John David, my first day at Lillian's house.

Ellen's daughter has been playing the role of Olivia Taft for at least a year, I realized. I didn't say that out loud. I didn't say anything.

I was too busy looking at her gun.

CHAPTER 56

*T*he best shot in the Taft family forced us back across the island. Not to the hole—to the charred remains of what had once been a house.

"Miss Olivia." Campbell was the first to speak up once we were all shut inside. "You simply cannot think . . ."

"Campbell, dear, I can and do think—frequently. And let's drop the pretense of manners on your part, shall we? I've had your number since you and Lily were seven. Given the circumstances, I don't feel particularly obligated to continue pretending that you aren't a real piece of work."

The mention of Lily's name set my teeth on edge and freed my voice. "Since Lily was seven? You've been pretending to be Olivia Taft since Lily was *seven*?"

On some level, I'd thought that this woman—Ellen's daughter—was a recent replacement, but from the moment she'd referenced being the best shot in the family, it had been clear to me that I'd never known the real Olivia Taft.

How long has this been going on?

Aunt Olivia—I couldn't think of her as anything else—burst into a peal of laughter. "Oh, Sawyer, honey, you are just too much.

You went to Two Arrows. You met Ellen. You were snooping around and asking questions left and right. And don't think I didn't overhear every word you said to J.D. about—what is it you girls call her?—the Lady of the Lake."

The Lady of the Lake? I tried to make sense of the direction Aunt Olivia's statement had gone. *The body. The one she was blackmailing Uncle J.D. about.*

"And still," Aunt Olivia continued, tickled pink, "you ask me how long I've been Olivia Taft?" She shook her head, lifting the gun and assessing it the way I'd seen her appraising a piece of family jewelry, just before putting it on. "Sweetheart, I'm the only *Olivia* Taft there's ever been."

KACI
SUMMER BEFORE SENIOR YEAR
TWENTY-FIVE YEARS EARLIER

*K*aci was going to catch hell for staying out so late, but what else was new? These days, catching hell was all the world would let her do. *No college. No real opportunities.*

Nothing.

Kaci had always wanted more, and nothing her mama said or did could change that.

She was twelve when she'd started promising that, one day, she'd leave Two Arrows and never come back.

Thirteen when her mother had snapped that she was *just like her.*

Fourteen when she'd discovered that the *her* in question was her mother's sister. A twin sister that the rest of town knew better than to even mention.

Kaci was fifteen the first time she'd hitched a ride into the city to spy on Lillian Taft. She'd had a plan to introduce herself. She'd daydreamed that Lillian would take one look at her and bring her into the Taft family fold.

And then Kaci had seen *her*. Not Lillian. Lillian's daughter—*Liv.*

Her hair was longer than Kaci's then, and she wore it blown out straight. Her skin was tan in the way that people who occasionally tanned were, not in the way that Kaci's was, from living in the sun.

But otherwise? *They were identical.*

At least, it had looked that way from a distance. In the three years since, Kaci had found ways to get closer. She'd found pictures of Liv. Kaci had grown out her hair and taken to blowing it straight. She carefully measured her time in the sun.

It still wasn't enough. No matter how much she looked like Liv, no matter how often she watched her—Kaci wasn't Liv.

Kaci would never be Liv.

And she couldn't shake the feeling that Lillian wouldn't want her, not when she had a daughter like that of her own. Liv was popular—and fearless. She had pretty manners, but she decided when to use them—and when to break the rules.

Liv had a perfect boyfriend. Liv had perfect friends. Liv was just starting her Debutante year.

And Kaci had nothing.

Don't think about that. Just watch. Kaci had gotten good at watching. It was easy. Liv wasn't the type to worry or look over her shoulder. She took it for granted that the world was as it should be.

As she wanted it to be.

Just watch. Kaci pressed closer. It was dark enough that she could take some chances, late enough that there was no point in going home now.

Hours earlier, Kaci had watched as Liv and her friends—*Julia and Charlotte, Sterling and J.D. and a boy called Thomas*—had set up camp. Kaci had pushed back a snort of laughter when they'd been unable to set up the fancy tents Liv had bought and decided to just make use of the sleeping bags.

She'd watched them pair off.

She'd watched Liv with her boyfriend. The boy Kaci had recently found herself dreaming about, more and more.

J.D. Easterling.

As Kaci watched from the shadows, Liv disentangled her limbs from his. Kaci was torn. Now that Liv was awake, she should leave.

She should go before she got caught.

Then again, what harm was there in lingering a bit longer? In staying close and hidden and imagining herself lying down next to Liv's boyfriend?

Don't. The warning came from the snake part of her brain, the place where her fight-or-flight instincts lay in wait. Kaci hadn't gotten away with watching Liv for this long by being sloppy. *Stay very still.*

Oblivious to her presence, Liv crouched next to one of the other boys. *Sterling Ames.* Kaci cataloged what she knew about him: *wealthy, handsome, too charming for his own good—or anyone else's.* Liv's friend Charlotte had been pining for him.

They'd kissed, just hours ago.

And now, as Kaci watched, Sterling Ames was getting up with Liv. Liv was pulling him toward the cliffs. It was dark, but Kaci could imagine the smile on Liv's face almost exactly.

Kaci knew what was happening. She knew what Liv was doing. *Why? Her life is perfect. Why does she keep trying her damndest to mess it up?*

Kaci might have left then. She might have gone home and taken her lumps as they came. But then J.D. got up. He went to the bathroom.

Had he noticed Liv was gone? Would he look for her?

The next minute went by in a blur. Charlotte woke up. She saw J.D. The two of them heard Sterling and Liv.

J.D. and Charlotte went toward the noise.

And, keeping to the shadows, so did Kaci.

"What the hell?" J.D. had the kind of voice that carried. "Get off of her!"

J.D. was on Sterling Ames in a heartbeat. For a moment, Kaci's heart pounded in her throat as the two of them exchanged shoves. *The cliff. Watch the cliff, J.D.*

And then Charlotte took a hesitant step toward Liv. "How could you?" At first, Charlotte couldn't manage more than a whisper; then she escalated. "How could you?" she shrieked. "How could you . . . you . . . you . . . *bitch*."

"Oh, don't be a baby, Char."

One second, Charlotte Bancroft was frozen, and the next, she'd hurled herself at Liv.

Neither one of them, Kaci thought as the two grabbed for each other's hair, *can fight worth a damn.*

J.D. came between them. He pulled Liv back and held her when she struggled against his grasp, trying to get at Charlotte again, screaming like she was the one who'd been betrayed, like all of this was something that had happened to *her.*

"Let me go," Liv demanded. She was crying. Or laughing. Or both.

"You were supposed to be my friend." Charlotte wasn't crying. She was irate.

"Go back," J.D. told her.

"Why should I?" Charlotte asked. "So you can forgive her? So you can tell yourself it's not *her* fault? Because her poor daddy just died?"

"You know what?" Liv was still spitting mad. "We're done, Char. This friendship, or whatever you call it? Consider it over."

"You're drunk," J.D. told her. "And you're hurting."

"*You* are hurting me," she countered, straining weakly against his grip.

He let go.

The cliff. Watch the cliff.

Charlotte leaned forward. "You're right, Livvy. We're not friends, because I'm not friends with *sluts*."

Liv lunged for Charlotte. Charlotte hit back. J.D. got between them. Liv walloped him, and he pushed her back. Charlotte leaped for her again, and Sterling edged forward.

Watch his foot, Liv. Don't trip.

The silent warning went unheeded, and Liv—popular, fearless, privileged Liv—went over the ledge.

CHAPTER 57

I'm the only Olivia Taft there's ever been.

I remembered everything my mom had ever told me about her sister, including the way Aunt Olivia had run away during her own Debutante year, right after their father had died.

Twenty-five years ago. Liv Taft ran away twenty-five years ago, and when she came back . . .

She'd told everyone to call her Olivia. My mom had several go-to descriptors for the woman her sister had become. *Ice queen* had been one of them.

Another was *fake*.

"The Lady of the Lake is Liv Taft." I said the words out loud, still trying to wrap my mind around them. "She never ran away. My mom said her sister was gone almost nine months, but really . . ."

"I was preparing," Olivia said. "Learning. I'd been watching Liv for years, but that wasn't enough. If I was going to take her place, people's memories needed time to fade. They needed to be able to tell themselves that *she'd* changed, and I had to make myself into something new. I had to be perfect."

Perfect. I thought about the way Lily had described her mama to me, back at the beginning of our Debutante year. *Mama just likes things to be perfect.*

"You took her place," I said, swallowing hard. "You killed the real Liv, and nine months later—"

"I didn't kill her!" That was the first flash of real emotion I'd seen out of "Olivia." There was a depth of feeling in her voice—wild, unconstrained grief. "I *never* would have hurt Liv. I just watched her, that's all. I wanted to find a way to introduce myself. We were supposed to be like sisters! But . . ."

"But you killed her." I pressed again. Since Olivia had started ranting, she hadn't looked at the gun even once.

She seemed to have forgotten she held one.

What was it I'd said to Sadie-Grace in the hole? *The name of the game is stall.*

"I did *not* kill Liv." Olivia stepped toward me. "J.D. did." She turned to Campbell. "And so did your mother. And your father. I was there. I saw them. They pushed her. She went over the edge. I *heard* her body hit the side of the cliff on the way down. J.D. dove in. Sterling, too. And all useless, vapid Charlotte could do was stand on the edge and scream. Eventually, Julia woke up. Thomas, too. And I watched." She shook her head, closed her eyes. "I watched her friends drag her out of the water. I watched J.D. try to revive her. I heard them all agree, when he couldn't, that it was an accident."

It was an accident. I could hear Lily's father saying those words on John David's recording. I could hear him telling Aunt Olivia to *say her name.*

And then he had said it. *Liv.* I'd thought he was using a nickname.

"They were all just going to leave her there," Aunt Olivia continued, eyelids flying open, "but then they saw the marks the fight had left on her arms. It didn't look good—for any of them. Sterling's DNA was all over her. J.D. had a motive. Charlotte, too."

"So they sank her." Campbell seemed to be taking this better than I was.

"It was Julia's idea," Aunt Olivia said. "She cared about her brother more than she ever cared about Liv. Even Thomas, who was new to the group—he went along with it. They promised him the moon, and he promised to keep his mouth shut."

I forced myself to connect the flurry of names to the people I knew. Julia and Thomas were Boone's parents. Charlotte and Sterling were Campbell's. "They weighed her body down," I said, trying to imagine how they could have made a decision like that. "And then they told everyone she'd run away."

"I kept expecting the body to be discovered," Aunt Olivia said. "I thought about calling the police, but for all I knew, Liv's rich friends and their rich families would try to find a way to turn it all around on me."

"So you didn't say anything." I stared at her. "You didn't call the police. You bided your time, and then you took over her life."

There was a moment of elongated silence, and then Victoria burst into a speed of rapid-fire and very emphatic Spanish. She ended in English. "Who *are* you people?"

She meant the question as an indictment of just how twisted this situation was, but I repeated her question with a different framing—and intent.

"Who," I said, taking a step toward Aunt Olivia, "are you?"

"I'm Olivia Taft."

"You're Ellen's daughter, not Lillian's."

"I'm Olivia Taft," she repeated, chin held high. "I'm Lily's mama—and John David's. I am the *perfect* daughter to Lillian. I have been a *wonderful* wife. I knew you were my husband's child, and I welcomed you with open arms, Sawyer, because you were like me. You grew up with nothing, and you deserved everything, and I helped give it to you. Doesn't that mean anything to you?"

There was truth to those words. I hadn't expected the woman my mom had referred to as an ice queen to welcome my presence in Lillian's house, but Aunt Olivia had. She'd hugged me and loved me and taken care of me.

Drugged me. Tossed me in a hole. Pointed a gun at me.

"You just couldn't leave well enough alone." Aunt Olivia stepped toward us, her grip visibly tightening over the firearm in her hand. "I didn't kill Liv. I loved her. I think, if she'd had the chance, she would have loved me. She would have *wanted* me to . . ."

"Become her?" I thought back to what Lily and I had heard on the tape. "You blackmailed her boyfriend into marrying you."

That's all I ever was to you? A charade? I flashed back to the recordings, to the questions Aunt Olivia had tossed at her husband. *When are you going to understand that I'm better for you than she ever was?*

"J.D. wanted to marry me," Aunt Olivia insisted. "He wanted to forget what had happened. He wanted me to *be* her." She paused. "The others just wanted him to keep me happy, because I knew."

At the Fourth of July picnic, when Uncle J.D. had brought Ana, Boone's father had been the one to tell him to leave. Charlotte and Julia Ames had closed ranks around Aunt Olivia.

"You blackmailed *all* of them," I realized, thinking back to the message that Campbell's mother had drunkenly instructed me to deliver to my aunt, back before she'd had reason to worry that J.D.'s infidelity might push Olivia over the edge.

It doesn't matter how they dress you up, Charlotte had said, *or what little tricks you learn, or how well you think you can blend. You are what you are, sweetheart, and you'll never be anything else.*

"You should have *seen* their faces when I showed up," Aunt Olivia reminisced, "days before our debutante ball. I looked like Liv. I sounded like her. I spun the right story, and Lillian was so glad to have me back." She smiled. "They couldn't tell anyone the truth. Who would have believed them? They had no idea who I was or where I'd come from, and it wasn't like they could go to the police and tell them they knew I was an impostor, because they'd killed the real Liv."

She looked at me for a moment. "Did you know that, genetically, I *am* Lillian Taft's daughter? Genetically, there's no difference between her and Ellen. I thought Lillian might do a DNA test when I showed up, but I knew that mine would come back as a match for hers. As long as she didn't try to test me against Liv's little sister's DNA, I knew I would be fine."

Liv's little sister. "My mom knew," I said. "She might not have *known* known, but she sure as hell knew you didn't feel like her sister anymore."

"That wasn't my fault. I wanted to be a good sister to Ellie, but she just made that so impossible! I had to keep her at a distance, and she never forgave me for that. J.D. could never quite forgive me, either. And that, sweetheart, is how this family ended up with *you*."

Aunt Olivia raised the gun. She held it on us but didn't fire. Instead, she walked over toward the door and picked something up.

It took me a moment to realize that it was a can of lighter fluid.

One secret to bury, I thought, hysterical laughter bubbling up inside of me. *One to burn.* The White Gloves couldn't have equipped Aunt Olivia better for this insanity if they'd tried.

Campbell lunged forward, but Aunt Olivia whipped the gun toward her and shot. "Consider that your only warning, young lady," she said as the bullet buried itself behind Campbell in the wood. "I won't deign to miss again."

"You were always nice to me," Sadie-Grace said quietly. "When my mama died, you were the one who held me, not my daddy. I stayed at your house for weeks."

"I know, sugar," Aunt Olivia replied gently. "This isn't what I wanted. Believe me."

"What did you think was going to happen when you drugged Sawyer and Sadie-Grace and tossed them in a *hole*?" Campbell asked.

Aunt Olivia didn't answer the question. "This wasn't what I wanted," she repeated.

"You wanted things to be perfect," I said. I still wasn't sure what had led Aunt Olivia to thinking *this* was the solution to her problems, but I did know there was power in telling people what they wanted to hear. "Maybe they still can be."

"Don't be silly." Aunt Olivia dismissed that notion out of hand. "If we'd been the only ones on this island, this could have been contained. But now? Campbell is trouble. She always has been, and don't even get me started on—"

"Sawyer's right," Victoria interjected. "This can still be contained. As the only outsider to this whole situation, allow me to assure you that literally no one would believe any of this if we tried to tell them a word of it."

"Besides," Campbell added, "do you really think my mama is going to let anything about what happened to the real Liv come out? Aunt Julia? My grandfather?" Campbell seemed to have recovered from her near miss with the bullet. She tossed her auburn hair over one shoulder. "My father is already in prison. There is no way on this planet that my grandfather would allow a scandal like this one to touch my only remaining parent and both of Boone's."

There was a moment's silence, which Sadie-Grace obligingly filled. "I don't mind about the hole," she promised sweetly. "Accidents happen. Lily and I once accidentally kidnapped Campbell and tied her to a chair for three days, and that turned out fine."

"You *what*?" Aunt Olivia said.

"You can still walk away from this," I reiterated, putting everything I had into those words. "Things don't have to be perfect. They can just *be*."

For a moment, I thought she was considering that. And then she finished dousing the wood in lighter fluid and pulled out a lighter.

CHAPTER 58

"This isn't just about Liv." Aunt Olivia toyed with the lighter for a moment, morose. "I could have dealt with the body washing up. That forensic sculptor nonsense—well, like Campbell said, I imagine someone in her family will be motivated to take care of it."

"If this isn't about the body," Sadie-Grace said quietly, "what *is* it about?"

What in the world had possessed Aunt Olivia to give up the game, ask Ellen to drug us, and haul us out to this island? Why dig the hole? Why throw us in?

"I thought I could talk to you," Aunt Olivia told me. "Make you understand."

"Because drugging people really puts them in an understanding frame of mind," I said.

"Also," Sadie-Grace added seriously, "holes."

"I wanted you sedated and contained," Aunt Olivia explained. "I wanted time to make this right, to do damage control. I never said anything about a hole."

"Ellen," I said out loud. "You asked *Ellen* to sedate us, and *she* had us tossed in a hole."

"I'm afraid she's never once attacked a situation with a scalpel that she could go at with a hatchet. I thought I could handle this situation, have a little chat with you girls. She was a bit less optimistic. Hence, the hole."

"So, what?" I said. "Ellen or her henchwomen helped you haul us out here, and the plan was just to keep us captive for a bit of chitchat?" Unbidden, my eyes went to the gun in Aunt Olivia's hand. *Was that the backup plan?*

"It pains me to say this," Aunt Olivia sighed, "but Ellen was right. Talking was never an option. There's too much of your mama in you, Sawyer. You can't ever just let things be. You push and you push, and the consequences be damned."

What consequences? She'd already said that this wasn't just about the body. Back at Ellen's, she'd told me that I'd brought this on myself. But I hadn't gone to Ellen's asking about the Lady of the Lake.

"The baby," I said. I hadn't quite pieced this together yet, but that was the only explanation that made any kind of sense. "We went to Ellen to ask about the baby."

Campbell's eyes widened. "Am I missing something here?" she asked.

I glanced at her. "I texted you about going to Two Arrows. You didn't answer."

"You went." Aunt Olivia spoke over me. "And so did Lily. You told her about Ellen, Sawyer. My little girl shouldn't have been there. She shouldn't have ever gone there."

"Why?" Sadie-Grace asked.

Why was it okay for me to go to Two Arrows, but not Lily? Why did my aunt care that I'd *pushed* and *pushed* about the baby?

I remembered something then, a tiny, seemingly meaningless detail that Lillian had told me when I'd confronted her with the truth about my father.

Lily was just two months younger than me.

Years ago, when my mom had gone to tell her mother that she was pregnant, Aunt Olivia had beaten her there. She'd already told Lillian that *she* was pregnant.

With Lily.

"Lily is two months younger than me," I said out loud. *And so is Ana's baby. Lily has blond hair and dark brown eyes. Ana came to the hospital when Lily was injured.*

There was a reason that Aunt Olivia hadn't wanted Lily to go to Two Arrows, why she hadn't taken kindly to me asking Ellen questions about Ana.

"Ellen said she didn't take a dime from the people who adopted Ana's baby," I told Aunt Olivia. "Ana got paid, but Ellen didn't." I paused. "Ellen wouldn't take *your* money."

"Wait a second," Campbell interjected. "Are you implying . . ."

That Lily is Ana's baby.

"I went to Ellen." Olivia spoke before I could. "To my mama. Do you know how hard that was, Sawyer? How humbling? When I left Two Arrows, she said *Good riddance.* And if she'd known where I was going—what I was planning to do . . ." Aunt Olivia shook her head. "I never wanted to go back there, but I'd told Lillian and my husband that I was pregnant. I'd beaten Ellie to the punch. Back then, J.D. would have left me if I'd given him half an excuse. But if he thought I was pregnant with his child? If Lillian thought her beloved oldest daughter was pregnant, when she heard about the mess Ellie had gotten herself into?"

"You lied," I translated.

"I protected myself," Olivia countered. "You should understand that better than anyone, Sawyer. People like us—we have to protect ourselves. No one else is going to do it for us."

I thought of Lillian, telling me that I was a fighter, telling me that neither of her daughters ever had been.

I thought about Nick and the way I'd always seen both of us as people who could take care of themselves.

"You lied about being pregnant," I repeated. "And then you needed a baby."

"Mama never liked me much," Aunt Olivia said. "I was too much like Lillian, not enough like her. I wanted *more*. God knows what possessed me to go to her for help. But when I did, when I came clean about where I'd been and the life I'd been living, do you know what she said? She said that the things I wanted might have been Lillian things, but the way I'd gone about getting them? The focus and determination and grit? That was all her." Olivia smiled. "She said that blood was blood, and I was hers, and she'd help me pull one over on her holier-than-thou sister."

Help you. As in get you a baby. How had Ellen found Ana? How had she talked Ana into giving up the baby?

"Did Ana even know who she was giving her baby to?" I asked out loud.

Aunt Olivia's response was immediate. "Lily is mine," she said, in a tone I recognized—one that brooked no argument. She'd used the exact same tone when she'd dismissed my assertion that Greer was faking her pregnancy, telling me not to be ridiculous, that no woman would do a thing like that.

Because she'd done it, too.

"I love my daughter more than life," Aunt Olivia said fiercely. "John David, too, and before you ask, yes, I carried him my own self, though quite frankly, I don't see how that matters." She closed her hand over the lighter, just for a moment. "My children are the best thing I've ever done, and I won't let anyone ruin that."

She repositioned her grip and flicked the lighter. The second I saw the flame, my mind dissolved into a mess of overlapping thoughts—*lighter fluid, a house made out of old wood. Ana's baby. Uncle J.D. The way he claimed he'd started paying Ana before they were ever involved.*

What if she'd run out of money? What if she'd known—or figured out—who had been raising her baby?

What if she'd told J.D. *exactly* who she was?

For all their faults, Lily's parents loved her. I'd never doubted that, and as I took a step toward her mother, I didn't doubt that now.

"Lily loves me," I said out loud. I took another step toward Lily's mama. "She would be heartbroken if anything happened to me. You know that."

"I know," Aunt Olivia said. "But accidents do happen—especially at the lake."

I wondered if that was why she—and Ellen and whoever else had helped them—had brought us to King's Island. Did Olivia know we'd spent time here earlier this summer? Or was she just looking for a place where she could stage an accident?

What kind of accident involves a fire and a gun? I took another step.

Aunt Olivia swung the gun toward me, her other hand still holding the flame. She spoke again as she began backing toward the door. "You stay right where you are, Sawyer Ann."

"I think," Sadie-Grace whispered beside me, "that this is bad."

The gun. The lighter. Old wood, soaked in an accelerant.

Before I could say another word, someone else beat me to it. "Olivia, please."

It took me a second to place the voice, whose words hadn't sounded like a plea so much as the kind of chiding John David typically received when he farted loudly—and intentionally—at the dinner table.

Olivia sucked in a breath and turned toward the voice's owner. "Mama."

Not Ellen, I realized as the speaker walked toward us.

"Lillian," I said. I'd never been so glad to see anyone in my life.

There was a split second of indecision on Aunt Olivia's part, and then she turned the gun on my grandmother.

Lillian was not impressed. "For heaven's sakes, put that thing away, Olivia. You're being ridiculous."

"She's pathologically *unhinged,*" Victoria corrected.

Lillian spared her but a single look. "My condolences about your father, dear." Because, of course, Lillian Taft would express condolences in the middle of a hostage situation. Without missing a beat, my grandmother turned back to my aunt. "Are we quite done here?"

She still has a gun pointed at you, Lillian. I don't think that qualifies as "done."

"Get over there," Olivia ordered my grandmother. "With them."

"Am I to believe you're going to kill all of us?" Lillian asked. "You'll do no such thing."

Even with a gun pointed at her, she answered her own questions.

"You have no idea what I'm capable of," Aunt Olivia said. "Now move."

"Kaci," Lillian stated, exasperated, "I will do no such thing."

The name—*Kaci*—froze Aunt Olivia in her spot.

"Kaci?" I repeated.

"You know." Aunt Olivia's voice shook, like Lillian knowing her real name was somehow more unfortunate than the fact that she'd been caught holding us hostage at gunpoint. "Did . . . did Ellen tell you?"

"My sister hasn't spoken to me in forty years," Lillian replied.

"Thankfully, I am plenty capable of putting two and two together myself, though I will admit it took me some time."

"*What?*" I said. "You knew?"

"Not right away," Lillian told me. "Not nearly soon enough. I was grieving. I'd lost my husband. I couldn't stand the idea of losing my daughter, too. When she came back, I thanked God and put it all behind me."

"You couldn't have known," Aunt Olivia insisted. "I practiced. I got everything right."

"You were perfect, sweetheart." Lillian gave a faint shake of her head. "And Lord knows my Liv was never that. Her daddy spoiled her. I did, too, truth be told." My grandmother managed a very small smile. "For years, I told myself that Liv had changed—that whatever she'd done to get over her daddy's death had changed her. I told myself that she'd grown up. But last year, when I brought Sawyer back here, and I watched you treat her like she was your own . . . This summer, when I heard you and J.D. arguing and realized you were aware of her parentage . . ." Lillian closed her eyes. "That was when I finally let myself ask the questions I should have been asking all along. That was when I knew."

"No," Aunt Olivia said again. "You didn't. You would have said something. You would have done something."

"After twenty-five years?" Lillian asked. "To what end? You're Lily's mama and John David's."

I realized that Lillian still didn't know that Aunt Olivia had faked her pregnancy with Lily, but right now, that hardly seemed to matter.

"You were my daughter for twenty-five years," Lillian continued, staring at *Olivia*. "You tried *so hard*, and when I finally got past seeing what I wanted to see, I was able to catch a glimpse of something else. You were hungry, Olivia—not physically, but down in the depths of your soul *hungry*, wanting things in a way that people who grow up with everything never will. Weeks ago, I recognized that, and then I recognized you."

"You didn't know about me."

"It had been years since I had seen you," Lillian countered. "The resemblance was less uncanny then, between you and my Liv. You could have passed for sisters, but not twins. Genetics are funny that way. Ellen and I got less identical as we got older, and you and Liv . . ."

"You knew?" Aunt Olivia—I couldn't bring myself to call her Kaci, the way Lillian had just once—seemed unable to get over that. "You knew about me, back when Liv was still alive? You could have come for me. You could have brought her. You could have . . ."

"Ellen wouldn't let me visit. She certainly wouldn't take my money, but I did what I could to make sure you kids didn't go hungry. I kept eyes on you, for a time."

I did what I could. That was the same thing Lillian had told me at the Gutierrezes' party. At the time, I'd felt like she couldn't have possibly done enough for her sister's family. But now, listening to my grandmother tell Aunt Olivia that she'd known quite well she wasn't her daughter and allowed the charade to continue . . .

"What about the real Liv?" I asked my grandmother. "Don't you care?"

"Of course I care," Lillian said quietly.

"It wasn't me," Aunt Olivia said urgently, before Lillian could finish. "I didn't hurt her, Lillian. I *wouldn't* have. . . ."

"I know that," my grandmother said. "You've been by my side your entire adult life. I know you didn't hurt my Liv. I know you won't shoot me or hurt these girls. You're a fighter, Olivia. Always have been. But you're not a killer. Put the gun down. Now please."

Obediently, the hand with which Olivia held the gun sank to her side. But the lighter—she held on to the lighter.

"I won't snuff that flame out for you," Lillian told her sternly. "You have to do that for yourself. Prove to yourself and these girls that no matter what ideas your mama put in your head, no matter what the stakes, you were never going to hurt them, any more than you would have hurt Liv."

They stared at each other. And since they were staring at each other, neither one of them was looking at me.

I stepped forward, ready and willing to take that lighter by force. But the woman who'd been Olivia Taft for two and a half decades didn't give me a chance.

She killed the flame.

CHAPTER 59

"I'll take care of . . . this." Even in the most trying of circumstances, never let it be said that my grandmother was not discreet. An abandoned house soaked in lighter fluid? An impostor daughter who'd kidnapped us, drugged us, and held us at gunpoint?

All summarized in a single word: *this*.

"You girls head home."

"And how do you suggest we do that?" Victoria was the first one to recover her voice. "Someone *took care of* our Jet Skis."

Lillian was not ruffled in the least. "Lily and Walker are the ones who called me. They brought me here. They're waiting on the east side of the island, and they have a boat."

A hundred questions swirled and collided in my head. What were Lily and Walker—and for that matter *Lillian*—doing here in the first place? And what could my grandmother possibly be planning on doing to contain this situation?

The only question that came out of my mouth was: "If we take the boat, how will you get home?"

Lillian turned toward the woman who'd been her daughter longer than the original Liv Taft had lived. "I suspect Olivia has a way off this island," she said quietly. "But first, I'd like to finally hear, after all these years, what happened to my girl."

Campbell, Sadie-Grace, Victoria, and I spent the first half of the walk back to the east shore of the island trying to figure out what—if anything—we should do. I knew what Lillian's preference was. I could practically hear her ordering me to let her handle it.

Just this once.

"I meant what I said to Lily's psychotic mother," Victoria offered behind me. "I cannot imagine that trying to tell the police any of this would go particularly well."

"For what it's worth," Campbell told Victoria, "more than one person might be willing to pay you to keep your mouth shut."

Campbell had a vested interest in the truth about the Lady of the Lake not coming out. Given Sadie-Grace's relationship with Boone, she did, too. As much as I might want to, I wouldn't say a word to the authorities without Lily's blessing—and Lillian's.

That just left Victoria.

"Generous," Victoria commented. "But I'll pass. If the last month has taught me anything, it's that I don't need my father's money—or anyone else's. I have his brain."

"But you'll keep quiet?" Campbell asked. "For Walker."

I had no idea what, if anything, had passed between Walker and Victoria since Walker and Lily had taken a step back from their relationship.

Oh, God, I thought suddenly. *Walker and Lily.*

If Lily was Ana's baby, then her father was Sterling Ames. And if Lily's father was Sterling Ames, that meant that Campbell was her half-sister.

And Walker was her half-brother.

• • •

The light on the front of the boat was bright enough to illuminate Lily, who sat on the bow, her knees pulled to her chest, her arms around her knees. Her back was straight, her chin held at an angle that made her neck look miles long.

Walker stood behind her. "Everything okay?" he called when he saw us.

Not even a little bit.

"We have to tell them," Campbell said softly beside me. "Don't we?"

Given the way we'd left things, I didn't know why Lily had come back. She probably shouldn't have. *And once we tell her the truth . . .*

There would be no recovering from that.

The water surrounding the island was too shallow for Walker and Lily to bring the boat any closer, so we had to wade out to board. Lightning struck in the distance. I mentally counted as I stepped into the lake and began making my way through the water.

I made it to five before I heard the thunder.

"Storm missed us," Walker commented. "It's headed the other direction now."

On the front of the boat, Lily was silent. I wondered what she was thinking. I wondered what, if anything, she knew about what her mother had done.

But mostly, I wondered how in the world I could tell her that Walker was her brother. He was the only boy she'd ever dated. The only one she'd ever loved. Even if she wasn't sure what she wanted now, even though they'd broken up . . .

This will destroy her.

I was waist-deep in water now. Campbell was on one side of me, Sadie-Grace on the other. I twisted to look for Victoria and discovered that she was still on the shore. As I watched, she bent and retrieved something from behind the brush. It wasn't until we'd all made it onto the boat that I realized what Victoria had gone back for.

"Here," she said, handing a scarlet robe to me and one to Sadie-Grace. The gloves came next. "You're shivering."

I wasn't sure if she was talking to me or Sadie-Grace. The night air was warm, but still, with my clothes soaked through, I could feel goose bumps rising on my flesh.

Lily's eyes flickered over the lot of us, over the robes and gloves in our hands. "Go ahead," she told me. "Put them on."

I did as she said, then met her eyes. "There's something we have to tell you." I glanced toward Walker. "Both of you."

Before I could say more than that, Campbell stepped in front of me, literally coming between us. "How did you know where to find us, anyway?" she asked her brother.

I recognized an attempt to stall when I saw one.

"Victoria texted me," Walker said.

"No, I didn't." Victoria took a few steps toward him, then stopped. She reached into the pocket of her robe. "My phone is gone. It doesn't get reception out here anyway. . . ."

So who sent the text?

"Hope," I said suddenly, answering my own question. "Do you think she got off the island?"

"With my phone?" Victoria said. "Sounds about right." She turned back to Walker. "What exactly did this text say?"

I realized between one breath and the next what she was really asking. *How much does Hope know? What did she see—and hear?*

"The text just said there was an emergency." Walker paused. "That it involved Sawyer and Lily's mama, that you were all trapped on King's Island, and I shouldn't call the police."

That didn't exactly answer the question of how much Hope knew.

"So he called me," Lily said. "And I called Lillian."

"You came," I said, feeling the weight of what I had to tell her a thousand times more.

"Of course I came," Lily told me, sounding offended. She hesitated. "Is my mama okay?" she asked. "Victoria's text—or Hope's, I guess—was a little vague on the details."

Because Hope didn't know them? Or because she was being discreet?

"Details later," I told her. "For now . . . your mama's fine." That was what Lillian would have called *a bit of a stretch.* "More or less."

"I sense that this is a very long story," Walker put in. "And based on how closely Campbell is standing to me right now, I have the general sense that it doesn't have a happy ending."

We have to tell them.

"Remember how you spent most of the summer being mad at me for things that weren't my fault?" Campbell said flippantly. "Pretty sure what I'm about to tell you is going to extend that by a few dozen years."

"Wait." Victoria stopped Campbell. She moved toward Walker. "I need you to tell everyone on this boat what you told me at my father's funeral, Walker."

From what I'd gathered, Victor Gutierrez's funeral had been a private one. Family only. I hadn't realized Walker had attended.

By the looks of things, neither had Lily.

You should have left, I thought, unable to look away from the frozen expression on her face. *Wherever you were going—you should have run away and never looked back.*

"Vee," Walker said lowly. Clearly, whatever he'd told her wasn't something he particularly cared to share with the rest of us.

"Trust me," Victoria told him, "you'll be very glad once this secret is out. *Very. Glad.*"

"Fine." Walker turned his attention to the boat's console and hit a sequence of buttons that had the anchor pulling up. The noise was loud enough to drown out anything that was said, so he waited until the job was completed. "I'm a bastard."

"This again?" Campbell asked. "I thought you got all of that pesky self-loathing out of your system last year."

"He's illegitimate," Victoria clarified. "Your father isn't Walker's father."

There was a moment of stunned silence, and then Lily spoke up. "How long have you known?" she asked Walker. I thought of everything that had passed between them this summer.

"Since Mama started drinking," Walker replied. "She never would have told me if he hadn't gone to prison."

"Back up," Campbell ordered her brother curtly. "Explain."

"They got married because Mama was pregnant," Walker said. "He didn't know I wasn't his."

"No way," Campbell replied.

"She had me tested, right after I was born."

"Daddy didn't know," Campbell said decisively. "You were his favorite. You're *still* Mama's favorite. . . ."

"She told me that she loved me extra—in case he didn't."

Campbell took a moment to recover from that and then shrugged. "In that case," she said, pivoting, "Lily, we have slightly less devastating news for you."

Sadie-Grace took off her scarlet robe and placed it around Lily's shoulders. "Just remember," she cautioned, "what we're about to tell you doesn't change who you are. It's just like musical chairs, but with parents."

CHAPTER 60

"So, to recap," Lily said, sounding calm, but not entirely apathetic, "Campbell isn't your half-sister. She's mine, because my daddy's mistress, who had Campbell's daddy's baby way back when, is actually my biological mother, and that baby was me. Victoria is my great-aunt, and technically, so is Lillian, because my adoptive mama is actually Lillian's identical twin sister's daughter. The real Liv Taft was killed twenty-five years ago in what might—or might not—have been an accident, involving practically every adult I know." Lily paused. "Does that about sum things up?"

It was just the two of us now. Walker had driven the boat across to the Ames family's lake house. Campbell, Sadie-Grace, and Victoria had stayed there, but I'd known without asking that Lily needed to get away.

I'd asked Walker if we could take his car.

He'd told us to keep it.

"You forgot the part with the lighter fluid and the imminent threat of death," I told Lily. "But otherwise, that seems to be a fairly accurate summary."

Lily started giggling. Hysterically.

"This isn't funny," I told her.

"I know," she agreed. "It's not funny at all. I just can't stop laughing, because if I do . . ." The muscles in her throat tightened convulsively.

"I know," I said. Lily had already been pushed past her breaking point before any of this had come out. There wasn't any place left to go.

"I thought I could get away," she said, giggling madly. "Do you know why I went to Two Arrows? Because that's the place that Lillian got away *from*."

I doubted my grandmother had ever imagined, when she'd entered high society, that it was a place that decades later, another member of her family might want to flee.

"This is so messed up," I said, because someone had to say it.

"It is," Lily agreed. She still didn't have the laughter under control. "You know the crazy thing?" she wheezed. "I'm not even mad anymore. It's just all so . . ." She shook her head, unable to put it into words. "And to think, I was so terrified about the *Secrets* blog becoming public knowledge. At this point, I could literally become a porn star, and I still wouldn't be the real scandal in this family!"

"Do you have aspirations toward the adult film industry?" I joked.

"Very funny." And just like that, she was very serious. "I don't even know where to go now. Or what to do." Her voice was hoarse. Her breathing turned jagged. "I spent weeks trying *not* to feel all of this, and then, when I finally let it come, I just wanted to start over. I was supposed to run away and find myself, Sawyer. Even when I said I was done with it all, I was still trying to be like her. I was still emulating my mama."

"If it's any consolation," I told her, "I've spent the summer trying *not* to be like mine. I saw her fall head over heels so many times, to no avail." I closed my eyes. "So I spent this summer *not* falling for

Nick. He accused me of living life with one foot out the door. He said that *I* was the runner, and that you'd be fine."

"Guess we showed him," Lily said, in a laugh-or-cry kind of way. "And besides, Mama never ran away. She didn't find herself. She's been pretending all these years."

I tried to think of something I could say that would make the evening's revelations hurt less. "It wasn't all pretend, Lily."

"That's the kicker, isn't it?" Lily said. "Because she really does love me." Lily paused. "She wouldn't have hurt you or Sadie-Grace or Campbell, even if Lillian hadn't shown up. I believe that, Sawyer."

"She hurt you," I pointed out.

Lily was quiet for just a moment. "They all did."

Her father. Aunt Olivia. Ana, who'd birthed her and taken money in exchange.

I wanted to say the right thing, but I couldn't even begin to imagine what that might be, so instead, I opted for: "There's a club."

Lily arched an eyebrow at me.

I elaborated. "The 'I Owe My Entire Existence to a Stupid Teenage Pregnancy Pact' Club. I'm the founding member."

And Lily was member number two. I'd wanted someone who understood. I'd wanted someone to process this with. And all along, it had been her. Nick was right. I'd never needed a backup family, or an exit plan, or ten layers of protection around my heart.

I was done *knowing better*, when I didn't really know anything at all.

"Does the 'I Owe My Entire Existence to a Stupid Teenage Pregnancy Pact' Club have an initiation?" Lily asked me, after several minutes of silence. "Because you're still wearing that stupid robe."

FOUR MONTHS LATER . . .

CHAPTER 61

*C*atcalling Lily was a mistake that most customers at
The Holler only made once.

"Do I come to your place of employment and make rude noises
in your direction?" she asked the man leering at her over the bar.
"No. No, I do not. And would you appreciate someone talking to
your daughter or sister that way? No. No, you would not."

"Honey," the man drawled. "You're wound awfully tight. How
'bout I loosen you up?"

"Want me to take this one?" I offered.

Lily shook her head. "My parents raised me to be a lady," she
told the man primly. "And now I'm a lady who knows an awful lot
about a whole range of medieval torture techniques. . . ."

The one-bedroom house Lily and I were sharing was smaller than
the one I'd grown up in, but instead of dollar-store shower curtains, a hand-sewn privacy curtain sectioned Lily's bedroom off
from the living room. She'd taken to shopping at flea markets and
thrift shops to furnish our place, and the decorations—even the
faded and chipped ones—showcased what even I could recognize
as impeccable taste.

"Knock, knock!" my mom called as she entered through the front door.

We really needed to start making use of the lock.

"Trick still huffy that I told that gentleman exactly what I could do to him with a sterling silver salad fork?" Lily asked.

Normally, my mom would have grinned in response. She'd been surprised four months earlier when we'd shown up on her doorstep, to say the least.

Coming back to the town where I'd grown up had been Lily's idea. I'd spent a year in her world. She'd wanted to give mine a try. I'd asked her once and only once if she was sure about putting college on hold, and she'd told me that college would still be there when we were ready.

Both of us.

Lily needed a chance to figure out who she was when she wasn't trying to be what other people wanted, and I needed to find my way to putting the past to rest and living *now*, with no backup plans and no feet out the door.

I thought of Nick most days but had only called him once. He hadn't answered.

"Is Trick actually upset with me this time?" Lily asked, startled by my mom's lack of response to her initial question about The Holler's owner.

"Trick couldn't get upset with you if he tried," my mom assured Lily. "And no one would dream of taking umbrage to any threats you may or may not have made involving salad forks and soup spoons."

"What were you going to do with the soup spoon?" I asked. But my gaze stayed on my mom, because something had brought her to our door, and I had the general sense that something wasn't good.

"Lily, sweetheart . . ." My mom's tone confirmed my assumption. "There's someone at the bar looking for you."

My mom almost never referred to The Holler as "the bar."

"Is it Lillian?" I asked. I'd been waiting for this since the night Lily and I had shown up here, both of us wet and me wearing a scarlet robe.

"No," my mom said gingerly. "It's Ana."

It took everything I had to stay in the position I'd taken up near the pool table and not join Ana Gutierrez and Lily at the bar.

"She's going to be okay," my mom told me. "Our Lily's equal parts sugar and steel."

I picked up a pool cue and nodded for my mom to start racking up the balls. I needed to keep busy, if I was going to persevere in giving Lily space.

"Are *you* okay?" I asked my mom once she'd finished racking.

My mom glanced back at Ana. "I just keep thinking that this was how it was supposed to be—Ana and her daughter, me and mine."

Things between us weren't the same as they'd been before my debutante year. Too much had happened since, and my mom was still learning to just let me be. A lifetime of interdependence was a nasty habit to kick.

"Sawyer? I know the pact was stupid." My mom grabbed the cue ball and broke, sending the rest of the balls scattering around the table. "It wasn't just our lives we were playing around with. It was yours, too. I know that it was selfish for me to think that you could solve everything that was wrong with my life, fill every hole."

In the months that Lily and I had been here, this was the first glimmer I'd gotten that my mom had really changed.

That at least some part of her understood.

"You were a kid," I said, lining up my first shot. "You were dealing with a lot. And if you hadn't been . . ." I hit the ball. "You wouldn't have me."

The day after we'd arrived, I'd told my mom the truth about Liv. I'd expected her to explode, to go storming back to the city, demanding to know how Lillian felt about having chosen an impostor over her.

Why she was protecting Olivia still.

But instead, my mom had grieved. She'd told me, a few nights back, crying for her sister, that the truth hadn't been a blow. It was a relief. The sister she'd known *hadn't* iced her out. The disconnect she'd felt with Olivia wasn't in her head. Her teenage anger at being forced to pretend otherwise, the grief that no one had understood . . .

It was real.

"You're stripes," my mom commented when my first shot went in.

"Ellie." Ana cleared her throat behind us.

I turned around first. A few seconds later, my mom followed suit.

"I want you to know," Ana told her, "that I've stopped seeing J.D."

"Good for you?" my mom ventured.

It was on the tip of my tongue to ask if she wanted a prize, but then a horrible thought occurred to me. "He's not back with Aunt Olivia, is he?"

"Not as far as I know," Ana said. "I'm moving to the East Coast. I need a fresh start, and Victoria has talked me into investing in a start-up she's been working on. I'm going to be following up with other potential investors while she finishes her degree."

I had no idea what Victoria was majoring in, but somehow, I wasn't surprised that she seemed to be landing on her feet. I wondered briefly what the chances were that the other potential investors were former White Gloves.

"What did you say to Lily?" my mom asked Ana.

Lily's biological mother glanced back to the bar, which Lily was wiping down maniacally with a damp rag, going back over the same spots again and again.

"That's between my daughter and me."

"She almost lost me."

Lily and I were lying in the field behind our house. It was unseasonably warm for December, but still cold enough that we should have been wearing jackets.

We weren't.

"That's what Ana said," Lily continued. "Late in her second trimester, she almost lost the pregnancy. She couldn't afford the hospital bills, and she said she just kept thinking—what if something happened to me after I was born? What if I got sick? What if I needed medicine she couldn't afford?"

"She could have gone to her family," I said, thinking back to my conversation with Victor Gutierrez.

"She would have," Lily said softly. "And they would have controlled her entire life—and mine." She paused. "She thought about going back to Davis Ames, too, but Ellen found her first."

The rest of the story came pouring out of Lily's mouth—how Ellen had sold Ana on the idea of a loving couple who couldn't have children of their own, a couple who would pay Ana's expenses, who would give the baby everything, who *wanted* to make sure their baby's biological mother had a real shot at life, once she'd given birth.

Ana hadn't found out who that couple was—or that said couple's infertility was a lie—until later. Once she'd discovered that, once she'd realized all the ways she'd been lied to, she'd decided that the price she'd been paid wasn't nearly enough.

"She said that she went to Daddy when I was twelve," Lily continued. "She told him the truth, and he told her that he'd give her whatever she wanted, do anything she wanted, if she'd just leave me where I was."

Beside me, Lily closed her eyes. I kept mine open and skyward.

"He used to bring her pictures," Lily murmured. "That was part of their deal. He gave her money, and he told her all about me."

Neither one of us had heard a word from Uncle J.D. in the past four months.

"I feel like I stole him from you," Lily said suddenly, opening her eyes and turning to face me. "If he'd known I wasn't his from the beginning, he wouldn't have—"

"He raised you," I interrupted her. "You're his, Lily. He clearly feels that way, and I don't need a father." She was on the verge of objecting, so I continued. "With a sister/cousin/pregnancy-pact buddy like you, I'm good."

Lily snorted—quite possibly the most unladylike sound I'd ever heard her make.

Catching sight of movement near the house, I sat up. "What's my mom doing here?" I asked as she started striding across the field toward us. "And why is she carrying formal dresses?"

CHAPTER 62

*T*he previous December, my mom had shown up unannounced on Lillian's front porch, moments before the whole family had left for the annual Christmas party at the club. Why Ana's visit had convinced her to pull a repeat performance, I couldn't say, but there was no talking her out of it, and she was dead set on dragging Lily and me along.

"Hold still," Lily gritted out as she twisted my French braid—which she'd just finished—into some kind of updo and jabbed a half-dozen bobby pins directly into my skull.

"That hurts," I told her.

"Pain is beauty," Lily retorted. She stepped up behind me in the mirror, and her expression shifted. The dresses my mom had bought us matched. Hers was navy, mine a brighter, cerulean blue.

"You know," I said, thinking back on the past year, "I never really understood that phrase—*pain is beauty*—until now."

I expected my mom to drive straight to Lillian's house—or to Northern Ridge Country Club itself. Instead, she took a detour by the cemetery first. Lily and I followed her down a gravel path to a small wrought-iron fence. Inside the fence, there were two tombstones—small cement crosses.

And in front of each tombstone stood a woman wearing heels and diamond earrings and, in Lillian's case, pearls.

"You came." Aunt Olivia sounded surprised. "We've been leaving messages for weeks, Ellie. We didn't think you'd—"

"I had a change of heart," my mom said, but Aunt Olivia wasn't looking at her anymore.

She was looking at Lily and me.

"The last time I was here," I said, making a mental note to kill my mom for bringing us into this unprepared, "there was only one tombstone."

Lillian stepped to the side. "Your hair looks good like that," she told me. "One barely notices the bangs."

I looked past her to the writing on the tombstone she'd just stepped away from. There was no name on the cross, no year, but an inscription had been added.

May her memory be eternal.

"People will think that tombstone is yours," my mom told Lillian. "They'll say you have a big head, writing your own epitaph like that."

My grandmother gave an elegant little shrug. "People will think what they want. I daresay they always do."

My mom swallowed, her gaze locked on to that inscription. "How did you get her body?"

Lily finally caught on to what was happening here. She stared, wide-eyed, at the second tombstone. "That's . . ."

"Liv," I finished quietly.

"The Lady of the Lake was identified," Aunt Olivia told us, sounding just as she ever had, even though her chin quivered slightly as she spoke. "Her name was Kaci. She disappeared years ago, and the body came back as a DNA match for her mama."

Of course it did.

"So that's that," I said after a moment. As promised, Lillian had handled the situation, and Aunt Olivia—and J.D. and Charlotte and the rest—had gotten away scot-free.

"Not quite," Aunt Olivia replied. "Mama and I were talking . . ."

"Which mama?" Lily muttered.

"We were talking," Aunt Olivia reiterated, "and we decided that this family really should have a charitable foundation."

"A sizable one," Lillian continued. "When I die and go to the good Lord, God willing, everything I have—except for what's held in trust for John David and you girls—will go to that foundation."

"Assuming," Aunt Olivia added, "that Ellie is okay with that plan."

"I don't need your money," my mom told Lillian. "I never did."

"I thought perhaps," Lillian replied, "that you might enjoy helping the girls run the foundation."

"Is this some kind of bribe?" Lily asked, finally finding her voice again. "You're letting us give away a fortune, and all we have to do is come back to the fold?"

"I'm entrusting you with your grandfather's legacy," Lillian said. "And mine. No strings attached."

I was fairly certain Lillian Taft had never made a deal with no strings attached in her life. Given everything I knew about what she'd done from her time as a girl in Two Arrows until now, I was also pretty sure that her real "legacy" was a lot more complicated than the assets she'd inherited from her husband.

"We'll give you a moment," Aunt Olivia told my mom. "To say goodbye."

She and Lillian passed through the gate. Lily and I stayed behind, until my mom asked to be alone.

"John David misses you," Lillian told us casually, proving once and for all that she was as expert at guilt-tripping as she was at issuing bribes. "Both of you."

"I was always coming back." Lily beat me to responding. She said it like that was less of a decision than a fate. "I just had some things to figure out first."

"And did you?" my grandmother asked.

Lily stole a glance at Aunt Olivia and then turned back to me. "What do you think, Sawyer? Have we got it all figured out yet?"

I thought of all the changes I'd seen in Lily in the past few months—and all the ways I'd changed in the past year. "Let's just call that a work in progress."

CHAPTER 63

*N*orthern Ridge Country Club had really taken their Christmas tree game up a notch. Last year's tree had been two stories tall; this year's was two stories tall *and* decorated entirely in crystal. There were hundreds of ornaments—maybe thousands—and they all caught the sparkling lights like ice.

"I believe," Lillian said beside me, "that we'll skip the family portrait this year."

"Why?" John David asked. He'd grown what seemed like about a foot since summer, and in the five minutes since we'd left the valets to park the cars, he hadn't mentioned zombies even once. "We're still a family, aren't we?"

It was Lily who answered. "Of course we are."

The Northern Ridge gingerbread was a thing of legend. Personally, I intended to drown myself in it and sneak at least three pieces out in my purse.

"Careful," a voice said beside me. "I have it on good authority that people here *really* don't like thieves."

I turned to the last person I'd expected to see at this shindig. "Nick."

He was wearing a tuxedo—the same one he'd worn to the lake-side fund-raiser. This time, however, he wasn't overdressed, and he didn't look like he was on the verge of ripping off the jacket.

"Don't say a thing about the monkey suit," he told me.

I called you. You didn't answer. I left, and you told me not to come back.

Once upon a time, that would have had my guard up—almost as much as the way my heart was beating in my chest. I remembered what it was like to kiss him, what his body felt like next to mine. The feel of my hands in his hair.

The moment he'd told me that he wasn't "dating" me for any reason other than the fact that he *wanted* to.

It had been four months since I'd walked away from him, and he looked exactly the same.

"I won't say a word about the monkey suit," I offered, "if you don't ask me how many armed men I could disable with the excessive number of bobby pins in my hair."

Nick managed a smile. "Seems like a fair trade."

It took me longer than I wanted to decide what I should say next. "You never mentioned joining Northern Ridge," I said.

"I prefer not to think about the fact that I've sold my soul and joined the dark side."

"Part of Lillian's plan to get Jessi into Symphony Ball?" I asked. Nick nodded.

"I called you," I said. "You didn't answer."

"I know."

A few months ago, that would have thrown me into self-protection mode, if I wasn't there already. Before that night on

King's Island, I wouldn't have let myself want this—want him—want *anything* at all.

"You didn't call me back." I smiled. "Want to call that an oversight?"

Another guy might not have recognized that for what it was. A normal person might have wanted an apology. A heart-to-heart. A promise that I'd changed.

Something.

But Nick just stared at me for a full three seconds, then held out his hand. "I think it's about time you gave me a second dance."

I gave him two before Lily pulled me away, outside to the patio overlooking the winterized pool below. At first, I thought she'd brought me out here to discuss what had happened at the cemetery, but then I saw Campbell.

A split second later, Sadie-Grace literally bowled me over with a hug.

"I love college," she told me, scrambling to her feet and helping me up before resuming her aggressive hug campaign. "I'm majoring in dance and also Russian literature, and combined, Boone and I have only broken two bones!"

"Both Boone's," Campbell clarified.

"His bones are my bones," Sadie-Grace insisted. "And vice versa. Unless that's creepy? I've discovered I have a really hard time telling what's creepy, but on the bright side, I haven't been kidnapped or kidnapped anyone else this semester, so that's good."

"And you?" I asked Campbell, wondering how she'd spent the months Lily and I had been away.

"Same old, same old," Campbell said. "Freshman year at an institution where I'm already a legend, planning world domination and plotting my revenge for the disappearing act the two of you pulled."

She turned her gaze pointedly to Lily. "Not very half-sisterly of you, was it? Not very polite, either."

"Oh, shut up, Campbell."

I wondered if either one of them realized that they'd acted like squabbling siblings for about as long as I'd known them.

"Just for that," Campbell told Lily, "I'm not going to tell you what Walker's doing *or* give you the present I had specially made a few months back. In fact, I won't give any of you your presents."

"Presents?" Sadie-Grace smiled, then turned to Lily. "Walker is going to college—in *Scotland*." Sadie-Grace said Scotland like Walker might as well have been attending university on Mars. "Boone keeps asking him to mail home haggis and a kilt, but either that's illegal or Walker just really doesn't want to." Waiting a beat, Sadie-Grace turned back to Campbell.

"Presents?" she said hopefully.

"I'll give them to you," Campbell promised coyly, "just as soon as Sawyer thanks me for getting her out of that hole."

I had a feeling she'd be lording that over me for an eternity—and then some.

"Campbell?" I said calmly.

"Watch your language," Lily murmured preemptively.

But all I said was: "Thank you."

"You're welcome." Campbell smiled sweetly. "You're not forgiven for ditching me—you either, Lily—but you're welcome. Now close your eyes and hold out your hands."

In normal circumstances, that would not have struck me as a particularly risky proposition, but between the events of our debutante year and the summer that had followed, I couldn't rule out the possibility that, once I closed my eyes, Campbell might calmly place a stolen masterpiece or a still-beating human heart in my palm.

Hell, if history was any indication, I couldn't testify with any level of certainty that I was talking to Campbell and not her evil—or *evil-er*—twin.

Sadie-Grace closed her eyes and held out her hand. Lily did the same.

"Sawyer," Campbell prompted.

"Fine." Eyes closed, hand held out, I waited, and then Campbell placed something in my hand. I opened my eyes and determined the present in question to be a necklace. The chain was simple and delicate, and the tiny charm on the end was . . .

"A shovel?" Lily said. "Really, Campbell?"

Campbell smirked. "They're platinum. Custom-ordered. Honestly," she continued as she affixed her own shovel necklace in place, "the White Gloves are proving a little mild for my taste. I deeply suspect the four of us can do better."

"A shovel!" Sadie-Grace did the math. "Like the kind people use to dig holes!"

I could have done without the insignia Campbell had chosen, but I put the necklace on anyway.

"We're ladies," Campbell said as Lily and Sadie-Grace slipped their necklaces on, too. "And my mama raised me to believe that ladies play to win."

When I'd taken Lillian's deal more than a year earlier, it had been because I wanted to find my father, but deep down, what I'd really been looking for was *family*. I'd been looking for my people, for a place where I belonged. I hadn't imagined finding it among the Debutante set.

With Lily, with Sadie-Grace, even with the devil herself, Campbell Ames.

But here I was, wearing a platinum shovel around my neck and walking back into the party with the three of them, arm in arm.

"Do you know anything about the new class of Debutantes?" Lily asked Campbell as the world around us blurred into a mix of champagne and black ties, fresh flowers and live music.

"Nothing worth repeating," Campbell replied. "You know the girls the year below us. They're boring. Now, if you start to look a couple of years down the line? Two of my little cousins on the Bancroft side will be coming out. I trained them in my own image."

That was terrifying. I thought of Nick's sister, as much an outsider to this world as I'd ever been.

"Is this the part where we say *Bless their hearts*?" Sadie-Grace asked.

I brought my hand to the delicate shovel charm nestled just above my collarbone. "How about"—I thought of every single thing that had happened since I became a Debutante myself—"*Good luck*?"

ACKNOWLEDGMENTS

The longer I'm in this business, the more keenly aware I become of how lucky I am to have a truly one-of-a-kind team in my corner. I wrote the first draft of this book as the sleep-deprived mom of two kids under the age of two. I literally could not have done it without the incredible support and creative work of my editor, Kieran Viola. When I needed more time, she gave me more time; when the book needed *more*, she knew exactly how to get us there. Most of all, her love for these characters and this series got me to where I needed to be to get the story where it needed to be. An editor is a creative collaborator, a sounding board, a champion, and so many more things, all rolled into one, and I could not ask for a better one. Thank you, Kieran.

Another champion who deserves special recognition is my agent, Elizabeth Harding, who has seen me from being a teenager, writing YA from my college dorm room, to a professor/mom/writer attempting to juggle all three. I know very few writers who are still with their first agent; I am lucky to have found an incredible advocate and partner, right out of the gate. Thank you, Elizabeth, not just for this book (number twenty!), but for everything that's come before. Here's to the future!

A third person I'd like to give a very special thanks to for this book is Marci Senders, cover designer extraordinaire, who designed not just one but *two* amazing covers for each book in this series. So much of a book's success relies on the cover, and I cannot communicate what a constant relief and blessing it is to know that I am in Marci's capable hands.

I also owe a huge thanks to the rest of the Freeform Books team—particularly Emily Meehan, Seale Ballenger, Christine Saunders, Cassie McGinty, Dina Sherman, Holly Nagel, Maddie Hughes, Elke Villa, Frank Bumbalo, Mary Mudd, and Vanessa Moody—and to my team at Curtis Brown—particularly Sarah Perillo, Ginger Clark, Jonathan Lyons, Sarah Gerton, Maddie Tavis, and Jazmia Young. I'd also like to give a special thank-you to Holly Frederick, who has been my book-to-film agent for twenty books now and has been a more incredible advocate for all of my books than I could say.

Huge thanks also go out to the writing friends who see me through, book after book, especially Rachel Vincent, Ally Carter, and every last BOB. I'm also incredibly grateful to all of the wonderful authors who lent their support to *Little White Lies*, especially Jennifer L. Armentrout, Brittany Cavallaro, E. Lockhart, Rachel Hawkins, and Katharine McGee for their generous blurbs.

I owe so much to my family. To my mom and dad, who have been known to drive four hours round trip just to lend a helping hand when I am on deadline—THANK YOU. And to my husband, who is a true and incredible partner in every conceivable way: I couldn't have made it through the past couple of years (or books) without you.

Finally, thank you to every reader who followed me from *The Naturals* to *Little White Lies*—and everyone who has discovered me since. I will never get over the awe of knowing that there are people out there reading my words. Thank you, thank you, thank you.

KEEP READING TO DISCOVER THE NEXT THRILLING
MYSTERY FROM JENNIFER LYNN BARNES!

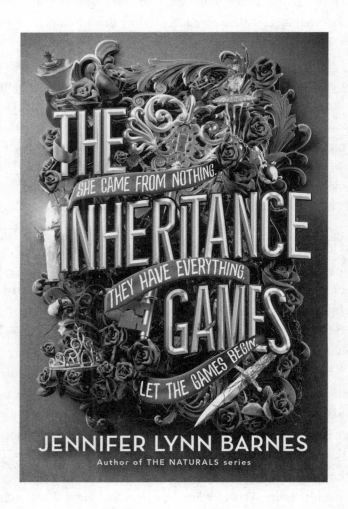

CHAPTER 1

When I was a kid, my mom constantly invented games. The Quiet Game. The Who Can Make Their Cookie Last Longer? Game. A perennial favorite, The Marshmallow Game involved eating marshmallows while wearing puffy Goodwill jackets indoors, to avoid turning on the heat. The Flashlight Game was what we played when the electricity went out. We never walked anywhere—we raced. The floor was nearly always lava. The primary purpose of pillows was building forts.

Our longest-lasting game was called I Have A Secret, because my mom said that everyone should always have at least one. Some days she guessed mine. Some days she didn't. We played every week, right up until I was fifteen and one of her secrets landed her in the hospital.

The next thing I knew, she was gone.

"Your move, princess." A gravelly voice dragged me back to the present. "I don't have all day."

"Not a princess," I retorted, sliding one of my knights into place. "Your move, *old man*."

Harry scowled at me. I didn't know how old he was, really, and I had no idea how he'd come to be homeless and living in the park where we played chess each morning. I did know that he was a formidable opponent.

"You," he grumbled, eyeing the board, "are a horrible person."

Three moves later, I had him. "Checkmate. You know what that means, Harry."

He gave me a dirty look. "I have to let you buy me breakfast." Those were the terms of our long-standing bet. When I won, he couldn't turn down the free meal.

To my credit, I only gloated a little. "It's good to be queen."

I made it to school on time but barely. I had a habit of cutting things close. I walked the same tightrope with my grades: How little effort could I put in and still get an A? I wasn't lazy. I was practical. Picking up an extra shift was worth trading a 98 for a 92.

I was in the middle of drafting an English paper in Spanish class when I was called to the office. Girls like me were supposed to be invisible. We didn't get summoned for sit-downs with the principal. We made exactly as much trouble as we could afford to make, which in my case was none.

"Avery." Principal Altman's greeting was not what one would call warm. "Have a seat."

I sat.

He folded his hands on the desk between us. "I assume you know why you're here."

Unless this was about the weekly poker game I'd been running in the parking lot to finance Harry's breakfasts—and sometimes my own—I had no idea what I'd done to draw the administration's attention. "Sorry," I said, trying to sound sufficiently meek, "but I don't."

Principal Altman let me sit with my response for a moment, then presented me with a stapled packet of paper. "This is the physics test you took yesterday."

"Okay," I said. That wasn't the response he was looking for, but it was all I had. For once, I'd actually studied. I couldn't imagine I'd done badly enough to merit intervention.

"Mr. Yates graded the tests, Avery. Yours was the only perfect score."

"Great," I said, in a deliberate effort to keep myself from saying *okay* again.

"Not great, young lady. Mr. Yates intentionally creates exams that challenge the abilities of his students. In twenty years, he's never given a perfect score. Do you see the problem?"

I couldn't quite bite back my instinctive reply. "A teacher who designs tests most of his students can't pass?"

Mr. Altman narrowed his eyes. "You're a good student, Avery. Quite good, given your circumstances. But you don't exactly have a history of setting the curve."

That was fair, so why did I feel like he'd gut-punched me?

"I am not without sympathy for your situation," Principal Altman continued, "but I need you to be straight with me here." He locked his eyes onto mine. "Were you aware that Mr. Yates keeps copies of all his exams on the cloud?" He thought I'd cheated. He was sitting there, staring me down, and I'd never felt less seen. "I'd like to help you, Avery. You've done extremely well, given the hand life has dealt you. I would hate to see any plans you might have for the future derailed."

"Any plans I *might* have?" I repeated. If I'd had a different last name, if I'd had a dad who was a dentist and a mom who stayed home, he wouldn't have acted like the future was something I *might* have thought about. "I'm a junior," I gritted out. "I'll graduate next year with at least two semesters' worth of college credit. My test scores should put me in scholarship contention at UConn, which has one of the top actuarial science programs in the country."

Mr. Altman frowned. "Actuarial science?"

"Statistical risk assessment." It was the closest I could come to double-majoring in poker and math. Besides, it was one of the most employable majors on the planet.

"Are you a fan of calculated risks, Ms. Grambs?"

Like cheating? I couldn't let myself get any angrier. Instead, I pictured myself playing chess. I marked out the moves in my mind. Girls like me didn't get to explode. "I didn't cheat." I said calmly. "I studied."

I'd scraped together time—in other classes, between shifts, later at night than I should have stayed up. Knowing that Mr. Yates was infamous for giving impossible tests had made me want to redefine *possible*. For once, instead of seeing how close I could cut it, I'd wanted to see how far I could go.

And *this* was what I got for my effort, because girls like me didn't ace impossible exams.

"I'll take the test again," I said, trying not to sound furious, or worse, wounded. "I'll get the same grade again."

"And what would you say if I told you that Mr. Yates had prepared a new exam? All new questions, every bit as difficult as the first."

I didn't even hesitate. "I'll take it."

"That can be arranged tomorrow during third period, but I have to warn you that this will go significantly better for you if—"

"*Now.*"

Mr. Altman stared at me. "Excuse me?"

Forget sounding meek. Forget being invisible. "I want to take the new exam right here, in your office, right now."

CHAPTER 2

R ough day?" Libby asked. My sister was seven years older than me and way too empathetic for her own good—or mine.

"I'm fine," I replied. Recounting my trip to Altman's office would only have worried her, and until Mr. Yates graded my second test there was nothing anyone could do. I changed the subject. "Tips were good tonight."

"How good?" Libby's sense of style resided somewhere between punk and goth, but personality-wise, she was the kind of eternal optimist who believed a hundred-dollar-tip was always just around the corner at a hole-in-the-wall diner where most entrees cost $6.99.

I pressed a wad of crumpled singles into her hand. "Good enough to help make rent."

Libby tried to hand the money back, but I moved out of reach before she could. "I will throw this cash at you," she warned sternly.

I shrugged. "I'd dodge."

"You're impossible." Libby grudgingly put the money away, produced a muffin tin out of nowhere, and fixed me with a look. "You *will* accept this muffin to make it up to me."

"Yes, ma'am." I went to take it from her outstretched hand, but then I looked past her to the counter and realized she'd baked more than muffins. There were also cupcakes. I felt my stomach plummet. "Oh no, Lib."

"It's not what you think," Libby promised. She was an apology cup-cake baker. A guilty cupcake baker. A please-don't-be-mad-at-me cupcake baker.

"Not what I think?" I repeated softly. "So he's not moving back in?"

"It's going to be different this time," Libby promised. "And the cup-cakes are chocolate!"

My favorite.

"It's never going to be different," I said, but if I'd been capable of mak-ing her believe that, she'd have believed it already.

Right on cue, Libby's on-again, off-again boyfriend—who had a fond-ness for punching walls and extolling his own virtues for not punching Libby—strolled in. He snagged a cupcake off the counter and let his gaze rake over me. "Hey, jailbait."

"Drake," Libby said.

"I'm kidding." Drake smiled. "You know I'm kidding, Libby-mine. You and your sister just need to learn how to take a joke."

One minute in, and he was already making us the problem. "This is not healthy," I told Libby. He hadn't wanted her to take me in—and he'd never stopped punishing her for it.

"This is not your apartment," Drake shot back.

"Avery's my sister," Libby insisted.

"Half sister," Drake corrected, and then he smiled again. "Joking."

He wasn't, but he also wasn't wrong. Libby and I shared an absent father, but had different moms. We'd only seen each other once or twice a year growing up. No one had expected her to take custody of me two years earlier. She was young. She was barely scraping by. But she was *Libby*. Loving people was what she did.

"If Drake's staying here," I told her quietly, "then I'm not."

Libby picked up a cupcake and cradled it in her hands. "I'm doing the best I can, Avery."

She was a people pleaser. Drake liked putting her in the middle. He used me to hurt her.

I couldn't just wait around for the day he stopped punching *walls*.

"If you need me," I told Libby, "I'll be living in my car."

CHAPTER 3

My ancient Pontiac was a piece of junk, but at least the heater worked. Mostly. I parked at the diner, around the back, where no one would see me. Libby texted, but I couldn't bring myself to text back, so I ended up just staring at my phone instead. The screen was cracked. My data plan was practically nonexistent, so I couldn't go online, but I did have unlimited texts.

Besides Libby, there was exactly one person in my life worth texting. I kept my message to Max short and sweet: *You-know-who is back.*

There was no immediate response. Max's parents were big on "phone-free" time and confiscated hers frequently. They were also infamous for intermittently monitoring her messages, which was why I hadn't named Drake and wouldn't type a word about where I was spending the night. Neither the Liu family nor my social worker needed to know that I wasn't where I was supposed to be.

Setting my phone down, I glanced at my backpack in the passenger seat, but decided that the rest of my homework could wait for morning. I laid my seat back and closed my eyes but couldn't sleep, so I reached into the glove box and retrieved the only thing of value that my mother had left me: a stack of postcards. Dozens of them. Dozens of places we'd planned to go together.

Hawaii. New Zealand. Machu Picchu. Staring at each of the pictures in turn, I imagined myself anywhere but here. Tokyo. Bali. Greece. I wasn't sure how long I'd been lost in thought when my phone beeped. I picked it up and was greeted by Max's response to my message about Drake.

That mother-faxer. And then, a moment later: *Are you okay?*

Max had moved away the summer after eighth grade. Most of our communication was written, and she refused to write curse words, lest her parents see them.

So she got creative.

I'm fine, I wrote back, and that was all the impetus she needed to unleash her righteous fury on my behalf.

THAT FAXING CHIPHEAD CAN GO STRAIGHT TO ELF AND EAT A BAG OF DUCKS!!!

A second later, my phone rang. "Are you really okay?" Max asked when I answered.

I looked back down at the postcards in my lap, and the muscles in my throat tightened. I would make it through high school. I'd apply for every scholarship I qualified for. I'd get a marketable degree that allowed me to work remotely and paid me well.

I'd travel the world.

I let out a long, jagged breath, and then answered Max's question. "You know me, Maxine. I always land on my feet."

CHAPTER 4

The next day, I paid a price for sleeping in my car. My whole body ached, and I had to shower after gym, because paper towels in the bathroom at the diner could only go so far. I didn't have time to dry my hair, so I arrived at my next class sopping wet. It wasn't my best look, but I'd gone to school with the same kids my whole life. I was wallpaper.

No one was looking.

"*Romeo and Juliet* is littered with proverbs—small, pithy bits of wisdom that make a statement about the way the world and human nature work." My English teacher was young and earnest, and I deeply suspected she'd had too much coffee. "Let's take a step back from Shakespeare. Who can give me an example of an everyday proverb?"

Beggars can't be choosers, I thought, my head pounding and water droplets dripping down my back. *Necessity is the mother of invention. If wishes were horses, beggars would ride.*

The door to the classroom opened. An office aide waited for the teacher to look at her, then announced loudly enough for the whole class to hear, "Avery Grambs is wanted in the office."

I took that to mean that someone had graded my test.

———————⫸————⫷———————

I knew better than to expect an apology, but I also wasn't expecting Mr. Altman to meet me at his secretary's desk, beaming like he'd just had a visit from the Pope. "Avery!"

An alarm went off in the back of my head, because no one was ever that glad to see me.

"Right this way." He opened the door to his office, and I caught sight of a familiar neon-blue ponytail inside.

"Libby?" I said. She was wearing skull-print scrubs and no makeup, both of which suggested she'd come straight from work. In the middle of a shift. Orderlies at assisted living facilities couldn't just walk out in the middle of shifts.

Not unless something was wrong.

"Is Dad..." I couldn't make myself finish the question.

"Your father is fine." The voice that issued that statement didn't belong to Libby or Principal Altman. My head whipped up, and I looked past my sister. The chair behind the principal's desk was occupied—by a guy not much older than me. *What is going on here?*

He was wearing a suit. He looked like the kind of person who should have had an entourage.

"As of yesterday," he continued, his low, rich voice measured and precise, "Ricky Grambs was alive, well, and safely passed out in a motel room in Michigan, an hour outside of Detroit."

I tried not to stare at him—and failed. *Light hair. Pale eyes. Features sharp enough to cut rocks.*

"How could you possibly know that?" I demanded. *I* didn't even know where my deadbeat father was. How could he?

The boy in the suit didn't answer my question. Instead, he arched an eyebrow. "Principal Altman?" he said. "If you could give us a moment?"

The principal opened his mouth, presumably to object to being removed from his own office, but the boy's eyebrow lifted higher.

"I believe we had an agreement."

Altman cleared his throat. "Of course." And just like that, he turned and walked out the door. It closed behind him, and I resumed openly staring at the boy who'd banished him.

"You asked how I know where you father is." His eyes were the same color as his suit—gray, bordering on silver. "It would be best, for the moment, for you to just assume that I know everything."

His voice would have been pleasant to listen to if it weren't for the words. "A guy who thinks he knows everything," I muttered. "That's new."

"A girl with a razor-sharp tongue," he returned, silver eyes focused on mine, the ends of his lips ticking upward.

"Who are you?" I asked. "And what do you want?" *With me*, something inside me added. *What do you want with me?*

"All I want," he said, "is to deliver a message." For reasons I couldn't quite pinpoint, my heart started beating faster. "One that has proven rather difficult to send via traditional means."

"That might be my fault," Libby volunteered sheepishly beside me.

"What might be your fault?" I turned to look at her, grateful for an excuse to look away from Gray Eyes and fighting the urge to glance back.

"The first thing you need to know," Libby said, as earnestly as anyone wearing skull-print scrubs had ever said anything, "is that I had *no* idea the letters were real."

"What letters?" I asked. I was the only person in this room who didn't know what was going on here, and I couldn't shake the feeling that not knowing was a liability, like standing on train tracks but not knowing which direction the train was coming from.

"The letters," the boy in the suit said, his voice wrapping around me, "that my grandfather's attorneys have been sending, certified mail, to your residence for the better part of three weeks."

"I thought they were a scam," Libby told me.

"I assure you," the boy replied silkily, "they are not."

I knew better than to put any confidence in the assurances of good-looking guys.

"Let me start again." He folded his hands on the desk between us, the thumb of his right hand lightly circling the cuff link on his left wrist. "My name is Grayson Hawthorne. I'm here on behalf of McNamara, Ortega, and Jones, a Dallas-based law firm representing my grandfather's estate." Grayson's pale eyes met mine. "My grandfather passed away earlier this month." A weighty pause. "His name was Tobias Hawthorne." Grayson studied my reaction—or, more accurately, the lack thereof. "Does that name mean anything to you?"

The sensation of standing on train tracks was back. "No," I said. "Should it?"

"My grandfather was a very wealthy man, Ms. Grambs. And it appears that, along with our family and people who worked for him for years, you have been named in his will."

I heard the words but couldn't process them. "His *what?*"

"His will," Grayson repeated, a slight smile crossing his lips. "I don't know what he left you, exactly, but your presence is required at the will's reading. We've been postponing it for weeks."

I was an intelligent person, but Grayson Hawthorne might as well have been speaking Swedish.

"Why would your grandfather leave anything to me?" I asked.

Grayson stood. "That's the question of the hour, isn't it?" He stepped out from behind the desk, and suddenly I knew *exactly* what direction the train was coming from.

His.

"I've taken the liberty of making travel arrangements on your behalf."

This wasn't an invitation. It was a *summons.* "What makes you think—" I started to say, but Libby cut me off. "Great!" she said, giving me a healthy side-eye.

Grayson smirked. "I'll give you two a moment." His eyes lingered on mine too long for comfort, and then, without another word, he strode out the door.

Libby and I were silent for a full five seconds after he was gone. "Don't take this the wrong way," she whispered finally, "but I think he might be God."

I snorted. "He certainly thinks so." It was easier to ignore the effect he'd had on me now that he was gone. What kind of person had self-assurance that absolute? It was there in every aspect of his posture and word choice, in every interaction. Power was as much a fact of life for this guy as gravity. The world bent to the will of Grayson Hawthorne. What money couldn't buy him, those eyes probably did.

"Start from the beginning," I told Libby. "And don't leave anything out."

She fidgeted with the inky-black tips of her blue ponytail. "A couple of weeks ago, we started getting these letters—addressed to you, care of me. They said that you'd inherited money, gave us a number to call. I thought they were a scam. Like one of those emails that claims to be from a foreign prince."

"Why would this Tobias Hawthorne—a man I've never met, never even heard of—put me in his will?" I asked.

"I don't know," Libby said, "but *that*"—she gestured in the direction Grayson had gone—"is not a scam. Did you *see* the way he dealt with Principal Altman? What do you think their agreement was? A bribe…or a threat?"

Both. Pushing down that response, I pulled out my phone and connected to the school's Wi-Fi. One internet search for Tobias Hawthorne later, the two of us were reading a news headline: *Noted Philanthropist Dies at 78.*

"Do you know what *philanthropist* means?" Libby asked me seriously. "It means *rich.*"

"It means someone who gives to charity," I corrected her.

"So…*rich.*" Libby gave me a look. "What if *you* are charity? They wouldn't send this guy's grandson to get you if he'd just left you a few hundred dollars. We must be talking thousands. You could travel, Avery, or put it toward college, or buy a better car."

I could feel my heart starting to beat faster again. "Why would a total stranger leave me anything?" I reiterated, resisting the urge to daydream, even for a second, because if I started, I wasn't sure I could stop.

"Maybe he knew your mom?" Libby suggested. "I don't know, but I do know that you need to go to the reading of that will."

"I can't just take off," I told her. "Neither can you." We'd both miss work. I'd miss class. And yet…if nothing else, a trip would get Libby away from Drake, at least temporarily.

And if this is real… It was already getting harder *not* to think about the possibilities.

"My shifts are covered for the next two days," Libby informed me. "I made some calls, and so are yours." She reached for my hand. "Come on, Ave. Wouldn't it be nice to take a trip, just you and me?"

She squeezed my hand. After a moment, I squeezed back. "Where exactly is the reading of the will?"

"Texas!" Libby grinned. "And they didn't just book our tickets. They booked them *first class.*"

JENNIFER LYNN BARNES

has written more than a dozen acclaimed young-adult novels, including *The Inheritance Games*, *Little White Lies*, *The Lovely and the Lost*, and the Naturals series: *The Naturals*, *Killer Instinct*, *All In*, *Bad Blood*, and the e-novella *Twelve*. Jen is also a Fulbright Scholar with advanced degrees in psychology, psychiatry, and cognitive science. She received her PhD from Yale University in 2012 and is currently a professor of psychology and professional writing at the University of Oklahoma. She invites you to visit her online at jenniferlynnbarnes.com or follow her on Twitter @jenlynnbarnes.

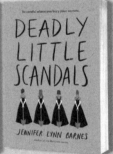